SOULMATES

Soulmates

The Soulmates Series
Book One

Liv Rancourt

Soulmates
© 2020 by Amy Dunn Caldwell

Cover Art: Amy Caldwell
Editor: Linda Ingmanson

ISBN-13: 978-0-9985822-9-0

Dedicated to those who look for ways to help others out. We need each other, because the world is too hard a place to go it alone.

TABLE OF CONTENTS

GLOSSARY

Ádh mór balbh - good luck, dumbass
Affaire du cœur — love affair
Amore mio — my love
An marbhdhraoi — a necromancer
Beurteilung — *assessment* - werewolf term
for resolving conflict with a fight to death
Dia á sábháil — Oh my God
Meascach — halfbreed
Mo bhanríon — my queen
Mo chath — my battle
Mo chontúirt — my perils
Mo leannáin — my lovers
Mo mhuirnin — my dear, my darling
Mo rúndiamhra — my mysteries
Mo rúin — my secrets
Mo shíorghrá — my soulmate
Tá mé ag siúl fear marbh.- Dead man walking

PART ONE: MOONLIT SOUL

CHAPTER ONE

TRAJAN

Aphone call stops me from walking into the sun. I'm poised at the sliding door to my west lanai, one hand on the blackout curtains. It would be so easy to step outside onto the small deck overlooking the ocean. To revel in the momentary torment as my body burns to ash.

Instead, I'm awash with…annoyance.

The phone rings again. For the moment, I'm too caught up in feeling to answer. My skin crawls with irritation; not the same as the fear I'd been chasing, but enough to prove I'm alive.

If there's one thing my long, long life has taught me, it's that living is the only thing. To die is to drop into the void, and while I may play games with the prospect, I'll never go willingly. The possibility, though, scrapes along my nerve endings, sensation fighting the murk surrounding me.

Another chime, and this time I pick up the phone. The screen shows me the name. Jacques Bettencourt, my maker. Our paths first crossed in New Orleans around 1875. He turned me, taught me, and for years I was his right-hand man. Over time he made other children and I took on projects of my own. Still, I owe him a nightclub, some real estate, and this twelfth-floor condominium where walls of glass give me a view of everything.

Our relationship has had 145 years to get complicated, though, and I answer the phone reluctantly. The sound of his voice, the normalcy of his call, will surely drag me down. "What can I do for you?"

"Well, hello, Trajan." Jacques's voice teases, as if he knows I'm standing at the edge of the pit and has deliberately called to draw me back. "How's every little thing?"

Every little thing weighs heavy on my soul. "I'm fine."

"Great. That's just swell." He coughs, a remnant of the consumption that nearly killed him before he left his mortal life.

I give him a moment to get his breath back. "Was there something—"

"Of course there's something," he snaps.

His rapid shifts from lighthearted to angry have long ceased to startle me.

"Be here an hour after sunset."

"Certainly." I keep my tone even. After so many years as his puppet, it's no good to try to cut the strings now. I end the call and stand for a moment longer, fingering the heavy rope holding the drapes together.

Blocking out the sun.

In the end, I obey my maker. My various business interests run with minimal personal attention, but I cannot delegate this task. Jacques lives on Mulholland Drive in the kind of house that's too expensive to ever be put up for sale. A map might say it's fifteen miles from me, but LA traffic can swallow an hour with very little effort. I'll need to leave as soon as I can stand the light.

I run a hand through my hair. Stringy. Greasy. How long has it been since I showered? Long enough that I'll have to hurry.

I leave the temptation of the lanai doors. My living room has high ceilings and a stone fireplace dividing the dining area from the rest of the space. The colors are bland except for the dark wood floor and the rough stone. I like to watch the lights as the neighborhood shifts from day to night. From my bedroom, I can watch the sun rise, teasing myself by standing on the small lanai until the eastern edge of the sky turns from plum to lavender to rose.

I play this game a lot, because when Connor left, all my joy followed.

It's strange how loss works. One moment I'm engulfed in darkness, and the next I'm staring into the mirror, wondering if I've used enough product on my hair. *Shallow fucker.* Black suit, black shirt, black tie, slicked hair, and sunglasses. Yeah, I look every inch the hit man. I grimace, baring my canines. Haven't needed a gun since the turn of the century. The last century.

On a whim, I put on a ring I'd won playing seven-card stud in about 1902. It's a nugget of gold the size of a walnut, mounted on a thick band. I keep it in a small safe hidden in an old printer along with a tidy collection of deeds and stock certificates. The only person who would hide a safe inside a printer is a paranoid vampire who doesn't own a computer.

The weight of the ring on my hand steadies me. *There.* I'm ready to go.

In March, the sun sets at around seven o'clock. At ten minutes after eight, I park my Escalade in front of a secluded Spanish-style compound, made more private by a riot of foliage concealing the house from the street. It satisfies Jacques's perversity to pay gardeners to create something he'll never see in the daylight.

I pause, testing the air. Evil has a scent, though even the worst humans rarely disturb me. They're too easy to take down. I pay attention to weres and shifters because they can be trouble. Some of the lesser magicals, like harpies, revenants, and pixies, are a pain in the ass, but it's the necromancers and demons I really have to watch out for. Necromancers play with the dead, which makes me vulnerable in a way I have trouble counteracting. And demons? Jesus, just keep me away from the spawn of Satan.

All the way up his long driveway, I vow to listen to Jacques's line of bullshit and leave without making promises.

We meet out by the pool, under an overhang growing thick with grapevines and white dragon fruit flowers. Their scent is heavy, cloying, and the moon is the brightest light. Jacques is paler than usual, with dark smudges under his eyes. Vampires don't suffer illness easily. His appearance—along with the sudden summons after so many months—makes me nervous.

Jacques stifles a cough. He once told me he'd had to choose between death and undeath, and while the turn made him stronger and more vigorous than he'd ever been in life, he hadn't been able to shake the lingering effects of the disease that almost killed him.

"Jacques." I pause a few feet away from him.

"Sit." He gestures to the cushioned chair opposite a low table and sits. On the table, there are two champagne flutes half filled with blood. "I took the liberty of pouring us a beverage."

He might be my maker, but I wouldn't have survived all these years without a healthy sense of suspicion. I didn't watch him pour the blood, and if he slipped something-or-other in the glass, I'm done. He may or may not have a reason for wanting me truly dead, so I lift the delicate crystal and pretend to sip. It smells like blood—hell, it smells a lot better than the shit I get in the bag—but I don't trust the situation.

The pool is a mirror, reflecting the flickering torches that line the perimeter.

"You're late." Jacques stops and coughs hard into his fist. The smell of blood strengthens, and it's not from our drinks.

I shrug. "Traffic in Santa Monica…" I let the sentence drift. Anyone who's spent time in LA really doesn't need to hear the details. Traffic sucks. It's a thing.

"Looking good." His smile stays in place, chilling me with his joie de vivre. "It's been too long, my friend." He raises his glass.

I tap his glass with my own. He drinks. I sniff, making it quick and subtle, then fake a sip. "You look well." His suit is midnight blue, perfectly tailored. His shirt and tie are the color of moonlight. I do my best not to get trapped in the cold light of his silver eyes. He owns me, fair and square. I just need to wait it out, to see how he wants me to repay my debt this time.

"I don't think I've seen you since…" He pauses, stabbing me with the memory. He hasn't seen me since Connor, since I lost the one thing that made this endless life worth living.

I force myself back to the present, though the past claws and scratches. "It's been a while."

He relaxes, gently twirling his glass between his fingers. "How's business? Club doing well?"

"It's fine." At least things look okay when I bother to read the monthly statements.

"Drink up, Trajan. I have a situation that needs your attention."

I fake another sip. "Figured."

He shifts sharply, clasping his hands, his knuckles nearly brushing my sleeve. "I figured you'd figure." Again with the chilling smile. "I need to put that big body to work, give you something to do besides feel sorry for yourself."

It takes everything I have not to respond to his jibe. He has no idea what I'd shared with Connor. *None.*

"Look at you. When's the last time you fed? Properly fed?"

I stare into the ruby liquid in my glass, the torchlight flickering across the surface. I have a deal with a blood bank. Yeah, the stuff is old, but I can get it cheap.

"Fine. Be that way." Jacques sets his glass down gently. A young woman walks out of the house. She's pretty and sleek, and small bruises mar her throat. She smiles at Jacques and slips off a soft gray robe, revealing a swimsuit of the same color. It's a one-piece suit that reveals more skin than some bikinis, and the stretch fabric has a pearlescent sheen. There's something off about her, but I can't place it, and in the grand scheme of things, Jacques's sketchy girlfriend is down on my list of concerns.

"Have a good swim, baby doll," Jacques says, the predator replaced by a besotted boy.

She trails a toe in the glassy water. "Always, doll baby." She shoots him a smile and dives neatly, swimming underwater to the opposite end.

Jacques is watching her, a dopey smile on his face, and I'm watching him. He's been a romantic for over two hundred years, and this girl could be any of fifty, maybe more. *Baby doll* and *doll baby* are extreme, though, even by his standards.

A cough takes him, sudden, and he fists his trousers. When he speaks, his voice is raspy. "You've heard of Randolph Collins, right? The American Were Authority Alpha?"

I unclench my jaw enough to say yes. The werewolves have this country organized in an impossibly arcane fashion, with family packs rolling up to regional, then national levels. The only thing I know for sure is there's one guy on top, and I wouldn't want to run across him in a deserted building. Vampires and werewolves coexist, but we aren't friends.

"Well, Mr. Collins called me the other day, and he asked me a favor." Between his frosty smile and his silver eyes, Jacques could freeze my soul. "His son is coming to LA for spring break, and he needs someone to keep an eye on him.

"The kid's name is David." He keeps his voice low. "He'll arrive on Saturday and he's here until the twenty-seventh. You'll just need to hang around and, you know—"

Doll Baby rises from the pool like a modern Aphrodite, and Jacques is distracted by the rivulets of water running down her thighs. Or that's my guess, anyway. Still, he's left me hanging. *What am I supposed to know?*

"Hang around and keep him alive."

Our glasses clink together.

"I mean, if the Alpha's calling me, there must be some kind of trouble."

I relax into the seat, considering Jacques's words. Usually his "situations" mean I have to kill somebody, so this is unexpected. The dark mood I've been wrapped in has a strong opinion. I should refuse him. I should hide. I should go back home and lock the door and go through with the dare from this afternoon.

But…

Jacques has other scions, other vampires who owe him life. Hell, he could hire one of the Securitas, the supernatural version of the FBI and the CIA combined. Yet despite his options, Jacques chose me to deal with a potentially tricky situation. Somewhere in the tortured landscape of my mind, a tiny light flickers to life. Nothing as bold as curiosity or pride or hope, but some nascent forerunner of those emotions. Fighting through the darkness, I meet Jacques's frigid gaze.

"Keep in mind that if anything happens to the Alpha's son, the consequence would be dire," he says. "Do your best not to start a war."

Four nights later, I stand near the baggage claim at LAX holding a small sign with the name David Collins on it. I'm not happy about being here, though this assignment has made stepping into the sun less of a priority.

I've been waiting a couple of hours because David's eight p.m. flight from Seattle was delayed. Now it's after midnight and traffic down the escalator picks up, as if a large flight has landed, so I expect to see him.

Not that I really know who I'm looking for. Jacques emailed me a bio and a picture of Randolph Collins, one I recognize from just about every news story involving werewolves. Collins Senior is short and stocky, with thick dark hair and a face that wouldn't have to shift very far to form a muzzle. Even in a copy of a black-and-while photograph, though, his eyes glare with a fierceness I'd be just as happy avoiding in real life.

The picture of David Collins shows a young man no taller than his father, but maybe sixty pounds lighter. David's hair is shoulder length and he's clean-shaven, at least in the photo. Other than that, he'd masked himself with an artfully wrapped knit scarf and a pair of sunglasses. He won't be all covered up in LA, though judging by his winter apparel, I'm looking for an effete hipster with his father's glare.

And he'll smell like a wolf, which will be a dead giveaway.

There's a gap in the escalator crowd. The next person to glide into sight turns heads with the kind of energy that often draws a pack of paparazzi. He — my best guess is he — is wearing skintight jeans and an open mesh shirt. His hair is blond and starched into a high curving wave rising from his forehead. He's wearing wrap-around shades, plum lipstick, and high-heeled black pumps, and over it all, he's tossed a glossy fur coat.

Near the bottom of the escalator, he gives a little jump, then fishes a phone out of somewhere. I'm not really watching, but he's by far the most interesting person in the area. His fingers fly over the screen and his mouth works like he wants to chew somebody out. Pocketing his phone, he surveys the baggage claim area, then strides across the space in my general direction.

I don't want to make it obvious I'm staring, so I ignore him, checking out the escalator for signs of David Collins.

"You are *so* not serious."

The words catch me off guard, but not as bad as finding the man in the fur coat standing right in front of me. I inhale. Yep. Wolf. "Are you David?"

"Yes dear, and who are you? Al Pacino's grandson?" He cocks one hip and plants his knuckles on his waist. "Got you a pimp ring on and everything."

Maybe I should have left the nugget at home. I look him up and down, meeting his attitude with a little rudeness of my own. "You aren't what I was expecting either."

He has to tilt his head to meet my gaze. Even in his heels, he can't be five feet eight inches, give or take, and I stand a little over six feet.

"So Dad said you'd be driving me around."

"Chauffeur, bodyguard" —I give him another once-over, this time with a smirk— "babysitter."

He snorts. "Well, let's go, sunshine. I need a cigarette."

I don't move. "You can't smoke in my car."

"Listen." He covers the space between us in two long, swinging steps. "Between Alaska Airlines and the Seattle weather, it's taken me well over eight hours to make a three-hour flight." He pokes me in the chest with the tip of his blunt, unmanicured index finger. "I need a cigarette and a shot of scotch and a blow job, not necessarily in that order. I'm putting up with having a chauffeur because I hate driving in traffic and it'll keep my dad off my ass." He taps me once, hard, and I grab his wrist.

"But I don't need a bodyguard." He wrenches his hand free of my grasp. "And I absolutely do not need a babysitter."

With that, he turns and stalks off, the defiant swivel in his hips giving me the first real smile I've had in weeks, maybe longer. I still don't move. If he gets much past the baggage carousel, I'll track him. He isn't leaving the airport without me, because Jacques had one thing right. This kid is going to be trouble.

CHAPTER TWO

It takes all of half an hour to begin debating whether I should kill the bastard myself.

"Here. You can carry these." He drags two oversized suitcases from the baggage carousel. "Maybe you should get a cart, because, you know, we don't want to make it too obvious."

I swallow down a mass of irritation. "What?"

"Um, vampire, right? Although you barely talk, so maybe you're a revenant or something. Here, take this, too." He tosses me his coat and stands with his arms crossed, twisting his full, plum-colored lips into a sneer.

I just stare at him, telegraphing my annoyance by dropping his jacket onto the nearest suitcase.

"Come on, Tony. Get a cart. *On se casse.*" He's still wearing shades. One look at his eyes and I'd know whether he's deliberately trying to annoy me, or if he really is a stupid little fuck.

For my money, the odds are even.

"My name is Trajan." I don't offer to shake his hand.

"Trajan, Tony, whatever."

We glare, locked in some kind of unspoken standoff. I'll keep him alive, but hauling his shit around belongs on some other sucker's to-do list.

With a disgusted "tsk," he scoops up his coat and stalks over to the rack of carts. When he's back, I lift one of his suitcases onto it, and he handles the other one. He doesn't say thank you, and I don't tell him what I think about guys who antagonize me.

The bright fluorescent lights are giving me a headache. "Come on." I take hold of the cart's handle and push it toward the door. David fiddles with his phone until we get to my Escalade, ignoring me — or pretending to. Without prompting, he loads both suitcases into the car.

Winding down the spiral exit from of the parking garage, I figure it's time for us to talk. "I changed your reservation."

He stares out the front window, and his jaw tightens. "You what?"

"That hotel you picked was too open. I found someplace a little less showy." His lack of response puts me on the defensive. "I cleared it through your dad's office."

Another disgusted snort. "Whatever. I want to stop at a club on the way there."

We reach the gate and I slip the parking ticket into the machine, along with my debit card. "Don't you want to get your stuff—"

"No." Moving fast, he snaps off his seat belt, rises up on one knee, and grabs ahold of my wrist. The gate lifts, but I don't put the car in gear. His hand darkens and his touch grows hot. Shaggy fur-covered claws dig into my flesh.

"I don't want to stop at the hotel." His voice drops, almost a growl. "Unless you're planning to suck my dick when we get there."

A car behind us honks their horn. I don't know what he sees in my face, but he lets go of me and falls back into his seat.

"That's what I thought. Come on, Guido." He buckles in, head turned deliberately toward the window. "We can take the stuff to the hotel later."

I manage to roll the car through the gate before it swings down. A succession of thoughts crashes through my mind. Flashes of irritation, fear, and a grudging respect. It's been months since I've been in a night club that I don't own, longer since I've sucked anyone off. I have a type, and flashy femme isn't it, but the amount of power and control it takes to make a partial shift means he's someone I cannot underestimate.

If nothing else, David Collins is one seriously dangerous werewolf.

I let the silence between us settle until we reach a stoplight where I'll have to either take a left toward the freeway or a right to keep to the surface streets. "Did you have a particular club in mind?"

"They said I should go to the Fubar."

I shoot him a quick glance. He sounds…sad. "Whatever. Can you google the directions?"

The light turns green, and Siri directs me to get on the 405. Traffic is almost light, but then it's about one thirty in the morning. I drive, and David touches up his lipstick. Fascinating. Without his sneer, his bottom lip has a sweet little curve. He's taken his sunglasses off, and thick lines of kohl edge his lower lashes.

Yeah, I don't do femmes, but there's a delicacy to David's features that makes me want to see him with all the paint washed off.

There had been nothing delicate about Connor. Tall, strong, and Irish, he'd been exactly my type. His loss slams into me again, catching me off guard, the way it has for almost two years. I never forget him, but sometimes I get distracted. I have moments where the pain doesn't wrap me up quite so tightly. Then his memory lurches in from an unexpected angle and takes me down.

For better or for worse, the search for parking on Santa Monica Boulevard keeps me from wallowing too deeply in my own head. The club is crowded and slutty, men packed tight. David shoves his fur coat into my hand. "Don't drink and drive, Sal."

He doesn't smile, but his eyes flash like he could light me on fire. Then he's gone, diving into the dance floor, which pulses like a single organism. Between his heels and his blond hair I can keep him in sight. The beat takes him and he waves his hands in the air, his grin bright enough to draw the attention of every man on the floor.

Draws my attention, too. I shake my head, my dick giving a half-hearted twitch. Without the fur obscuring my view, his ass and thighs are gorgeous. I blink, shake my head. David might not be my type, but this club is a fucking buffet. And I've been on a starvation diet.

The beat slams against my temples, the flashing lights scorch my eyes, and the bundle of fur draped over my arm is hot and heavy. I head for the bar. Tequila won't do more than take the barest edge off, but it's better than nothing.

The bartender's an elf. Tall, lanky, he's wearing a glamour to cover his more eccentric features. I watch him carefully as he pours. Elves are mean, and I don't trust him not to spit in my drink.

He slams the glass in front of me. I forget to leave a tip.

LA is a big city. It used to freak me out when I ran into someone who wasn't human. Now I figure live and let live, unless they get up in my face — or spit in my tequila. Then I might decide to live and let die.

I slide through the crowd, edging around the dance floor. David's sandwiched between two men, and they've worked their way into the corner. I climb onto a riser to get a better view, staring down a go-go boy who'd like to make me part of his act. All it takes is a quick nudge from my mind for the nearly naked twink to find another dance partner, and I turn my attention to David.

His mesh shirt is missing, and his head rocks back against one guy's shoulder. That guy's got his face pressed against David's neck, hiding behind a drape of long dark hair. The other guy's working David's front, twisting his nipples, a thick thigh jammed between David's legs.

The look on my target's face makes my jaw tight. Utter abandon. He circles his arms up and back, pulling the long-haired guy closer. The one in front isn't much taller than David, but bulky and hairy and covered in ink. He leans in and whispers, and David gives him a slow, dirty smile.

A moment later, the three of them slip off the dance floor.

I can almost hear David's laugh over the noise.

I don't know where they're going and I don't know the layout of the club. Tracking a wolf in a relatively spacious airport is one thing. Tracking him in a club dense with human and nonhuman scents, every one of them loaded with testosterone and lust, will be much harder. I leap off the riser and set my glass on the nearest table. Too bad. It was good tequila. Making my best guess at the direction they're headed, I follow.

The club is small and narrow and claustrophobically packed with men in suits, men in leather, men in satin and sequins. There are very few women. I slide around people, dampening my presence so no one will remember me. I can't see David, but I catch a taste of wolf on the back of my tongue and shift my course.

I end up near the restrooms. They're down a narrow, dimly lit hall. The men are mostly in pairs, sometimes threesomes. They're teasing and talking and groping. I pause, inhaling. Wolf, and maybe another shifter. Something feline that makes my skin crawl. I hate cats. A breeze swirls, carrying jasmine and exhaust, and I notice a third door. Working methodically, I check each bathroom.

No wolf.

The third door, however, leads to a small parking lot behind the building. A single streetlight glares down on the concrete, leaving the perimeter in shadows. There are men out here, too, hiding in the cover of a bougainvillea-covered fence and under the spreading branches of an old bay fig.

I move slowly, every one of my senses on alert. I'd only seen the one elf behind the bar, but fighting with those fuckers will slow me down. And if I manage to cross one of the big cat shifters, things will get ugly fast. *Come on, David Collins*. I beam the message into the night. Didja have to go whoring around right here, right now?

Across the street, there's a gas station. I catch another trace of wolf and jog toward it. There. His laugh, coming from behind the single-story white building. I find a shadow on the side, and, bending from the knees and hips, I thrust, smoothly jumping to the roof. I land on the balls of my feet and stay crouched, scuttling across till I can peer at him over the edge.

David and the dude with long hair are kissing, deep and messy, while the burly guy is on his knees, working on the fly of David's jeans. I still my breathing, listening hard, but the only thing I hear is Burly bitching about too-tight pants.

I don't want to interrupt them, but I can't seem to help watching, hypnotized by David's sensuality, the slow roll of his hips, the playful intensity of his kisses. I don't want him. I want what he's doing, and for a moment, I come close to losing control, leaping off the roof to find someone in the club.

Someone for me.

But if bad things happen to David, Jacques will kill any part of me the werewolves don't destroy, so I stay. The sounds distract me, slick and sticky, low groans and muttered curses. I bite down on my lip, fangs aching. In a way, it's a relief. Even this lukewarm desire is more than I've managed in over a year.

Time passes differently when you know you'll never run out. When I was still human, celibacy was for priests. Now it's a phase, a mood, a circumstance like any other. Though the living porno down below is going to speed me to the end of my abstinence.

A dense crack ends my reverie faster than a bucket of ice water. I drop down on my belly. Figures move around either corner of the building. Dressed in black, with knit caps and fabric wrapped around their lower faces, there are two of them, and they're both armed. *Sonofabitch.*

Burly falls over, curling on his side in a pool of glossy black. The long-haired guy screams. He plasters himself to the wall, dragging David with him so they're standing side by side.

"Shut up," one of the gunmen says. We're less than a block from Santa Monica Boulevard, a few storefronts down from a jam-packed nightclub. Someone has to be hearing this.

"Both of you stand still." The other gunman stops just outside of the puddle Burly is making. The injured man is moaning softly, piteously. I bide my time, waiting for the right moment.

"Which one of you fools is David Collins?"

I don't know who said it, but it's my cue. I'm unarmed, except that no vampire is ever completely weaponless. I drop over the side, landing between David and the gunmen. Their eyes widen, but neither backs down.

"If you see the chance," I say, hoping David hears me, "run. Both of you."

The space between the gas station building and the chain-link fence at the perimeter is about eight feet. To my right is a side street and to my left is a row of garbage cans and recycle bins. The gunman closest to me laughs. He shifts his Glock from one hand to the other and, pulling a smaller pistol from a pouch on his thigh, takes aim.

"Big bad vampire come to save the day, right?"

I stride toward him. He shoots, but it doesn't stop me. I figure a bullet's only going to hurt for a minute. But it's not lead, and it's not a single bullet. It's silver, and it's buckshot, and it sprays across my chest, tearing through the fabric of my suit.

"Tony!"

David's voice is coming from far away. Silver hurts, a grinding, searing pain, and worse than that, it weakens me. I don't have much time. I'm close enough to grab the pistol. I do, and the gunman laughs. There's a flash of light and heat behind me. Not good. Putting as much strength as I can gather into my fist, I smack the laugh off his face.

He falls, and I pivot slowly, dreading what I'll see.

David and his long-haired friend are still pressed against the wall. They can't run. Not anymore. The flash of light was the other gunman shifting form. Now, instead of a puny human, I face a lioness.

"I didn't realize your friends would be so eager," I say to David. My lungs are on fire, but I've got to stay on my feet. I've got to fight off this beast. I've got to get David out safely and get the injured man to a hospital and wipe the other guy's mind before he goes crazy. Which is a tall order, considering I'm not sure I can draw my next breath.

Ironic that just a few days ago, I'd teased death, welcoming the final flames. Now, as the darkness blurs the edges of my vision, I fight it with everything in me.

"Fuck. These are my favorite jeans." David's voice barely registers. There's another flash, and the man from the club cries out as if he's been scalded. With a low growl, David saunters between me and the lion. The blonde wave, pouty lips, and killer ass are gone. In their place is the biggest, darkest wolf I've ever seen.

The two animals scent the air. There's not much space for a fight. David's growl bounces off the cinderblock wall, and the lioness answers with one of her own. I stumble over to where Burly still lays on the concrete. The rich scent of his blood torments me. I bend, almost toppling over, and check his pulse. I can't find one. David's growl turns into a series of barks, short and harsh and deep. The lioness crouches down like she's going to pounce.

I can't help the poor soul at my feet, and I'm tempted to kneel down and lick his blood from the street. It's a lot warmer than the shit I get from the blood bank, and it would help me heal. I stay standing. Must not be desperate enough.

Something happens on a level I'm too foggy to sense, and the two predators launch themselves at each other. I fall back against the wall, drawing the man from the club close. He's whimpering, as if these events have pushed him past his ability to cope, so I stroke his brow, blurring the memories. Just because humans know about supernaturals doesn't mean they like it when their hookup sprouts fur.

David's wolf is bleeding from where the lioness caught him, but he throws himself at her, knocking her off her feet. He gets his front paws planted on her chest, turning his big body sideways to avoid the eviscerating claws on her rear legs. Before she can tear into him, his jaws snap tight on her neck. I have no idea how a fight between a true wolf and a lion should go, but few animals can match the son of the Alpha. With a vicious strike, David rips open her throat and howls his victory.

I worry about the noise, but then figure if no one in WeHo heard the gunshots, we were okay. With the last of my strength, I murmur a charm to the man with long hair, making him forget. The dark wins, and my eyes close.

CHAPTER THREE

A sharp slap brings me around. I lay on the cement between the gas station and a chain-link fence. David kneels next to me, his expression grim. The pain in my chest has dulled from open flame to smoking coals. There's tension, as if my muscle fibers are caught in a fight between the need to expel the silver pellets and my innate ability to heal.

"Wake up, Tony." David raises his hand again, but I turn my head out of his line of fire.

"Name's Trajan."

"Whatever." He sits back on his heels. "I brought your car around. We need to get the hell out of here." He runs a hand through his wrecked hair, telegraphing worry and fear. "Is there someone I can call?"

He glances around, and I realize he's looking at the bodies.

"Stone." I struggle onto one elbow and fish in my pocket for my phone. "In my contacts. Tell him I need a cleanup."

I'd known Stone for about ten years. Half troll and half human, he'd come to LA to get rich playing drums. When that didn't pan out, he traded on his supernatural inheritance and became the go-to guy when the mess won't fit with LAPDs specs.

I try to stay with it, but the blackness rolls in. Before I fade completely, David introduces himself to Stone without using his last name.

When I wake for the second time, I'm in the passenger seat of my SUV. David's shaking my arm hard enough to make me bite my own tongue. "What?"

"Where are we going?"

Nausea's a drone under pain's shrill song. I hate him for dragging me back to consciousness. He had to, but I'd rather stay down. His pants catch my eye. They're black and stained and twice as big as the pretty jeans he'd had on at LAX. I don't ask. "You still got my phone?"

He tears his gaze away from the rearview mirror. "I gave it back."

I reach around, patting. He's stuck it in my left rear pocket, and the idea that he might have fondled my ass in the process sits weirdly in the back of my mind. I manage to pry both eyelids open, but I have to squint to focus. I read off the hotel's name and address and manage to get my phone into the inside pocket of my shredded jacket.

David is still entering the address into the Escalade's GPS when I drift out again.

Third time's the charm, I guess. He's got ahold of my arm like he's trying to pull it off my body. There's a sleepy valet ready to park my car, and David's got the passenger door open. The blue and white neon TRAVELODGE sign hits me like a hot poker. David's standing too close; the combination of wolf and hair product and pain makes me want to puke.

"You need to check us in, Tony, 'cuz we look like a couple of homeless dudes."

To my shame, he has to help me out of the car. Once I'm on my feet, though, I take two or three deep breaths and get a handle on the burning in my chest. When we get up to the room, I'll have to dig out every pellet. The thought preoccupies me while I get us registered and wipe the desk clerk's memory.

Finally, we're in our suite. The place is nowhere near fancy, coming much closer to ugly, but it's one of the only chains with vampire-ready rooms. David's room looks out over the city, and beyond that, the Pacific. Mine is windowless and spartan, and I want to crawl in and lock the door.

He pulls off his borrowed trousers as soon as the bellhop leaves. I avert my gaze, surprised by his lack of modesty. "For tomorrow…" My words fade away because he's bent from the waist, digging into one of his trunks. *That ass.* Embarrassed for ogling, I clear my throat and start again. "My friend Sheena will be here at noon."

"Sheena? Seriously?" He stands, clutching a flimsy piece of fabric that doesn't cover nearly enough. A scattering of hair covers his chest, much darker than the hair on his head. "Why is she going to be here, and why does she have a cartoon name?"

"She's an Amazon, and she's the only person I trust to keep you safe during the daylight hours."

He gapes at me as if he can't grasp my intent.

"I figure you're going to want to go to the beach, right?"

He drops the fabric, and God help me, I can't help but flick a glance down. Which is crazy, because it's all I can do to stay conscious, but for the first time in over a year, my cock stiffens.

So does his.

He stalks across the room as if I'm prey and not as fierce a predator as him. "Guido, Guido, Guido," he mutters. "For a dick, you're not half bad." He's close enough to touch, and I'm having trouble breathing.

He touches my suit jacket, the fabric punctured and blood-stained. "I hope my father's given you an expense account."

No one's paying me for this. I inhale hard. Wolf. Blood. My mouth waters.

"Let's get this off you, then." He grasps the lapels and pulls. My white button-down is in even worse shape. He doesn't bother with buttons, tearing it free. My skin is smooth, healed, a dozen or so faint white scars marking where the silver hit me.

He puts a hand on the center of my chest and pushes. I take a step back. His eyes are sky blue and smudged with kohl. Another push. He backs me up till my legs hit the bed in my room. "What are you—"

"Shush." He shoves, and I sit down. Then he straddles me, tracing circles over the smooth skin of my chest. "Don't scream."

Before I can respond, he forms a single claw from his index finger. He slices into one of the white scars, a look of intense concentration on his face, and then he flicks the silver pellet onto the bedspread.

I don't scream, but it's a very near thing.

He bends close, his expression even more focused. His breath is warm, and he licks, a single smooth stroke, clearing away the blood. My skin heals before he finishes.

"There." His grin is brief, a flash of lightning. Catching his lower lip in his teeth, he finds another scar.

I grab his wrist. "Wait."

"Sorry." He jerks his hand free and digs in. His touch burns. Another silver pellet falls free. This time, he hums as he cleans the wound.

"They told me vampire blood was freaky good."

"This the same 'they' who told you to go to the Fubar?"

"Hm." He nuzzles my neck, a moment of sweetness. "Guess we need to talk about that."

Before I can respond, he finds another scar and pierces it. The pain is sharp and fast and cleansing. We do need to talk about why a pair of gunmen showed up with his name on their lips, armed for vampire. For the moment, however, I'm helpless against his cruel tenderness. He gouges out every bit of the silver, and by the end, his long licks have turned into lingering kisses.

I want to pick him up and throw him out of the room, and I want to drag him closer so I can impale his ass on my dick. I'm still not sure I like him, but

I've been alive for too many years not to appreciate when fate drops a warm, willing werewolf in my lap.

He eases away, giving me time to make him stop. I don't. Standing at the side of the bed, he's nude and fully erect. I try to say something, but the words won't come.

"They say getting fucked by a vampire is intense, too." He strokes himself, his eyelids heavy.

My body is still weak. I need to feed, but I won't. Not from David. I won't repeat the same mistake twice. "Shouldn't believe everything you read on the internet."

"It's almost dawn. You sure there's nothing else I can do for you?"

So many things. "No."

"I'm going to take a shower." He runs his thumb over the head of his cock, still teasing. "How will I recognize your friend when she gets here?"

"Blonde Amazon."

His smile is the closest to honest I've seen from him. "Got it. Guess I'll see you after I get back from the beach." He turns toward the door.

"Wait."

Glancing over his shoulder, he smirks like he can tell my gaze is stuck on his perfect ass. "What?"

"Why did you drag me out of there?" He could have left me to meet either the sun or the LAPD. "I mean, I appreciate it, but…"

His grin softens. "Dad hired you." He shrugs. "That makes you pack adjacent."

"Pack adjacent," I muse. That's a new one. "Well…thanks."

"Don't mention it."

With that, David Collins, alpha werewolf, leaves to jack off in the shower. I come very close to crawling after him.

I rise before sunset. Our rooms are quiet, empty. Everything's done in earth tones with pops of purple. I packed light, maybe too light since my button-down and suit coat went through the shredder. My only choice is a black silk crewneck shirt and jeans. Since I'm dressed like a bodyguard, I slick my hair and pump my biceps to reinforce the image.

I'm leaving my room when I hear voices in the hall. *David.* My dick jumps.

Apparently, I need to get laid, too.

He sashays through the door. Cancan kicks send his flip-flops flying against the wall. His bleached hair is in pigtails and his shoulders are bronzed. David's outfit might have been purchased from a rack of playsuits made for middle school girls. It's pink and white with stripes across the chest, stars across his ass, and sparkly ties at the shoulders.

He blows me a kiss, and all I can do is shake my head.

Sheena's standing in the doorway, shaking her head along with me. Her sandy-blonde hair is pulled into a floppy bun on the top of her head, giving her another couple of inches on me. She's already a good three inches taller and could likely bench press double my weight.

Amazon.

Amazons only give birth once, and Sheen's mother had traveled to Greece to conceive, as was their tradition. She'd moved to LA to raise her child, under the possibly erroneous impression that Sheena would have a broader mind.

Instead of a child who spends her time on spiritual growth, she raised a 6'4" lesbian who makes a comfortable living as a bodyguard to the stars, with a side gig at my club as a leather-wrapped dominatrix.

"All right, sunshine. I guess I'll see you tomorrow." Sheena drawls the words, sliding her aviator sunglasses into place.

"Thanks, Mom," David trills from his room. He slams the door shut, continuing to holler at us. "I'm ordering room service and taking a shower. Do. Not. Disturb."

There's a pause where I wonder if I should laugh or apologize to Sheena. I do neither. "I appreciate the backup."

Sheena crosses her arms, letting the door frame take more of her weight. "First time I've seen you with a man in a while."

"I'm not *with* him. It's a job."

She gives me an easy, one-shouldered shrug, and I can feel the weight of her gaze through her shades.

"Little asshole reminds me of Connor."

I must still be exhausted from the fight, because as far as I can tell, David bears a closer resemblance to a Pekinese than he does to my ex. There's no good answer, so I keep my mouth shut.

"Yeah, I hear you thinking over there." Sheena chuckles. She's not as old as I am, but she's had over 100 years to observe human behavior. "They both have the devil in their eyes."

Her use of present tense, as if Connor's still out there somewhere, cuts me to the quick.

Fortunately, David pops through the bedroom door, a loose towel riding low on his hips. "Did I tell you I have a date tonight?"

Surprise chases away the sadness, at least for the moment. "What?" No time to squander on the past when I've got a flighty werewolf to keep track of.

"Yep. Gotta meet him at eight." David gives me a once-over. "I'll tell him you're from the Mafia branch of the family, okay, Guido?"

He disappears, the door slams, and Sheena starts to laugh. "Oh shit. I think Jacques is going to owe you double when this is all over."

"Get out of here." I crack a grin and drop onto the tan, tailored couch. "When Spunky comes out, we're going to have a little chat about rules."

"Sure you are."

"And then maybe I'll ask him who might have tracked him to a club as soon as he got off the plane." It's muggy, and my sockless feet squeak against my leather loafers. "They knew where we'd be, and they knew to pack silver buckshot."

Sheena gives the barest shake of her head. "Only thing I saw today was him working his way from man to man down the beach." She swipes her tongue across her lower lip. "That's it, but I'll keep an eye out tomorrow."

I shrug. "He's a snazzy dresser anyway."

"Snazzy." She laughs. "What decade are you in?"

We ask each other that question fairly often, and the door closes behind her before I can say thanks. I slide my phone out of my pocket. The subtle hiss of the shower is overridden by a siren's screech from the street below us. I can't check the security of the windows because the sun hasn't set. Fawn-colored drapes shield me from the light, but I can't go any closer. There are no messages on my phone. I'm not sure if that's a good thing or not.

This job is starting to give me a very bad feeling.

Very few people know the son of the Alpha is traveling with a vampire. Jacques. The Alpha himself. And who else? I should call Jacques and ask if he'd told anyone. I slide my phone back into my pocket. Jacques keeps his own council, and he doesn't like questions.

I'll ask David Collins, though, before we go on his date.

I turn on the television to cover the noise from the bathroom, the clink of a hanger, the soft whisper of fabric, the buzz of a blow dryer. I'm already picturing too much, and in a perverse way, I anticipate what he'll be wearing. Something memorable, I'm sure.

There's a soft tap at the door. "Room service."

I wait a moment before answering, but all I sense is a single person whose heartbeat reads boredom rather than murder. I open the door. "Thanks."

A young man with residual acne pushes the wheeled cart into our room. I reach for my wallet to give him a tip. The cart is draped with a white linen cloth, and the tray on top has a silver domed lid. Nothing about the waiter sparks any interest, yet when he leaves, I eye the cart doubtfully. There's a sound or a smell I can't quite place. David didn't tell me what he ordered. I inhale slowly. Nothing savory or salty. Nothing grilled. No garlic.

"Is that my—" David comes out of his room at the same time I lift the lid.

The explosion throws us both to the ground.

CHAPTER FOUR

For the second night in a row, I'm stuck picking shrapnel out of my chest. Mostly nails, with a few ball bearings for variety. There's no silver, and nothing much hit David, but my shirt is wrecked. We're going to have to go by my condo, because my only other option is an old Mickey Mouse T-shirt.

David Collins does not need to see that.

"What the hell?" He's still on his ass in the bedroom doorway. There's a streak of blood on his cheekbone, and his hands have turned to paws.

I shake both my arms. A scattering of nails hit the floor. The room service lid is near the lanai window, and there's a scorch mark six feet in diameter on the ceiling. I lean over the cart. What's left of the tray is black.

"I think…" I poke at a cylinder in the middle. "Must have been a pipe bomb." I straighten, dusting away the rest of the debris. *Damn it.* "We need to get out of here."

Heavy footsteps pound up the hall, followed by voices at our door. "Hey? What's going on in there?"

The door opens under my hand. A man in a black suit with a hotel badge bulls through. There are two security officers with him, and a pair of sirens roar up from the street.

I tell the story once, and then again when the police arrive. David is gathering his stuff, his expression a postcard for rebellious teen. Too bad. His bio says he's almost twenty-three, so he can man the fuck up. Someone's shitting on his vacation, and it isn't me.

We waste way too much time hassling with the cops, and then with hotel management, but finally, we're in the Escalade. It's about eleven o'clock, and the dark has rolled down over the city. We're not too far from the airport, and on instinct, I head for the four-oh-five.

"Where are we going?" David's voice is pitched lower than his normal whine, with more growl in it. I slide a glance in his direction, but he's staring out the window.

I turn the AC on and roll my window down, because the smell of wolf has my mouth watering. I'm not hungry for him, exactly, but I've had to heal injuries for two days running. When you're hungry enough, even bad food smells good.

And David smells pretty damned good.

"I need to go home." I pull up to a red light, calculating how long it'll take us to get there. "We should be safe enough and can figure out what to do next."

David's hair doesn't have quite the swoop as when we first met, there's no kohl around his eyes, and his jeans are so tight, I wonder how he can breathe. He also wears a soft gray tank top and a darker hoodie; altogether conventional compared with his other outfits.

"You must have liked this guy."

"What?" He curls his lip but doesn't look at me. "Shut up. I half think you set that bomb off just to keep me from having fun."

Good thing the light changes so I have something to do besides tell this little pisser off. "Maybe."

"You're not thinking." He jabs his finger on the pad to roll his window up. "Which doesn't actually surprise me." Stroking his hair, he glares into the dark. "If whoever sent the bomb found us at the Travel-Dodgy, they'll likely know to look at your apartment."

I don't change course. We pass one of those rows of palm trees, the tall, perfectly matched pairs lit up from underneath. They make LA look classier than it really is, the stately palms and Art

Deco architecture doing their damnedest to distract visitors from the refuse of human ego.

He's got a point, even if he's being an asshole about it. Whoever is harassing us may know my address. I could call Sheena; in fact, I'll have to tell her we're not at the hotel and I'll need her to meet us wherever we end up

But where should we go?

I keep us headed for the four-oh-five, but decide that instead of going west to Santa Monica, we'll go east, through Hollywood to Los Feliz. Jacques owns several safe houses, and I pick one at random. They're all sturdy and secure, but Connor helped Jacques buy this place, so maybe my choice wasn't entirely random.

For the first time since I lost him, Connor's memory doesn't gut me. Instead, I get a bittersweet twinge because yeah, one time a real man cared about what happened to me. Rather than ruminate on the change, I glance at my passenger. "So who's after you?"

He gives a "tsk" of disgust. "Who's after you?"

I shake my head, tapping the brakes to avoid hitting a Prius with a speed problem. "No one I know about."

We sit in silence for the better part of two miles. "Yeah, you're right," he finally says. "It's probably me. I've got" — he turns his face to the ceiling, and

for just a moment, there's a crack in his armor—
"family stuff."

I barely keep myself from laughing at the cliché. Of course, the son of the American Were Authority Alpha would have family stuff. He needs to stop with the vulnerability, though. His one or two glimmers of sadness give me a perverse need to comfort him.

David's phone chirps, and he glances at it and fires off a response. "Wants me to live in her goddamn back pocket," he mutters. Straightening in his seat, he glares at his own knees. "Might be hard to believe, Guido, but even in the twenty-first century, some people don't think a gay can be an alpha."

His bitterness burns. When his phone chirps again, once, then twice, he ignores it.

I'm not sure if I should respond to his last crack or not. After a beat, I decide to shift our direction. "Let's not narrow our options too quickly. I've been thinking—"

"Be careful, hero. Don't hurt yourself." He flaps both hands like he's waving off smoke from my overheated brain. He's not quite smiling, but the bravado is back.

And just like that, I want to punch him in the mouth. "At any rate," I continue, fighting a grin, "Jacques knows we're together. Maybe he's got an agenda, either to make trouble with the wolves" — though if Jacques is taking a swing at the American Alpha, I'm not the only one with a death wish — "or take me out" — always a possibility — "or kill two birds with one exploding room service tray."

"S. M. H." David rolls his eyes. "I can't believe you fell for the old exploding-room-service-tray trick." His giggle edges toward hysterical.

With a sound that's half groan, half laugh, I merge into the high-speed lane on the freeway. "You're right about one thing."

"What's that?" he asks absently. He pulls out his phone and turns it around in his hands.

"Someone could know where my condo is. We're heading for a safe house."

"Mm? Where?"

Watching him inspect his phone is distracting me from the road. "In the hills above Hollywood. What's wrong?"

He gives me a bleak look. "They could be tracking me through my phone."

Before I can respond, he flings it out the window.

"Now they can't."

The silence returns, but shorter this time.

"I'll call Sheena and ask her to take you to get a new phone in the morning."

He blinks a couple of times, his youth showing through the bravado. "Thanks. If I go too long without responding to my sister's texts, she'll get the whole pack agitated."

We wouldn't want that. Keeping my mouth shut and my eyes on the road, I steer us to safety.

When a vampire is powerful enough to start siring other vamps, the results are halfway between family and a murder of crows. The sire is responsible for everyone's security; therefore, Jacques's string of safe houses with vampire-ready rooms.

I'd tried to talk Jacques out of buying this particular house, a big Spanish barn on the end of Wild Oak Drive. The neighbors are too close, for one thing, but he likes the view of the Hollywood sign and the rumors of a notorious history involving pretty young boys and lines of cocaine.

David surveys the marble floor, wrought iron trim, and spacious living room as if hiding out in million-dollar homes is his standard. We drag his bags to the closest bedroom, the only one on the main floor.

I wonder how long it's been since he had something to eat. "The kitchen should be stocked,"

I say, pointing him down the hall. "Well, there won't be much fresh stuff, but you should be able to scrounge something."

"Not hungry." He kicks off his shoes, slides off his hoodie, and crosses the living room. There's a lanai running all along the front of the house with a view down into the canyon. We're isolated, but not isolated enough.

I stop him when he tries to open the door to the lanai. "Don't go out there." The living room doesn't have near enough furniture for the space, but rather than crowd him, I pause next to the large leather sofa.

"Why? No one knows we're here."

He's right, but no one knew we were going straight from the airport to that gay bar either. "Don't want to give anyone a target."

Knocking the door frame with the side of his fist, he gives me a disgusted once-over. "I was supposed to get laid tonight, and instead, here I am with a guy with blood on his shirt."

I tug on my wrecked crewneck. At least my wounds from the nail-bomb have healed. "I'll go change."

"Where's the remote?" He gestures to the flat-screen television opposite the windows taking up most of the wall.

I shrug, irritated by his demanding tone. "Somewhere." I leave him in the living room, muttering curses. Those curses turn to laughter when I return wearing Mickey Mouse. A gift from Sheena, I brought the faded T-shirt for sleep, and it's the only other thing in my bag that hasn't been shredded.

"Well, look at the badass vampire now." David points the remote at me. "You look gay enough to watch *Dancing with the Stars* with me."

Great. He's found the remote. I should have disconnected the cable. The dancers on the big screen are spinning fast enough to make me dizzy, or maybe it's the volume, so loud the bass is pounding on my sternum. "I still need to call Sheena." Any excuse to escape.

"Can I borrow your phone first?"

"Why?"

"To text Abby, my sister." He stretches both arms over his head, showing off tufts of soft brown hair, and I'm caught by the urge to nuzzle against him, to burrow into his sweet and earthy scent.

"Might as well have hung onto your own phone." I hold out my iPhone. The last thing I wanted was a string of text messages from every member of the Collins Pack. "Have her delete this number after she sees your text."

After a minute, he hands the phone back. "You said you're going to call Sheena? Are you going to tell her where we are? Can you trust her?"

"Of course. She's an Amazon."

He crosses his arms, fingers tapping on skin, a hank of hair flopping down over his brow. "I never met any supe who wouldn't sell you out for the right money."

So much bitterness. He might be young, but he's not naïve. His messy hair makes me self-conscious about mine, and I run a hand over the top of my head. Maybe I'm escaping to call Sheena, or maybe I'm unsettled by my response to a man I shouldn't get involved with, who seems to have a target on his back, who's seen my Mickey Mouse shirt and lived to tell about it.

"If an Amazon swears loyalty, they don't falter, and Sheena and I go back a long way." We'd been taking turns saving each other's asses since I was a card shark and she was running gin.

The noise of the television is muffled in the dining room. There's a table long enough for twelve large chairs, and the windows look uphill toward Griffith Observatory. I talk to Sheena, but my mind is on the young man in the other room. He's cheering for someone named Darius, and I'm curious to see what kind of man he's attracted to.

Probably not an oversized Italian with unnaturally pale skin.

Sheena promises to arrive in the morning, and I give myself a moment before facing David. I need to keep him safe, which means I need more to work with than some bullshit about family drama. The guy came on a spring break vacation by himself, which all of a sudden feels like a big red flag. For all his talk about getting laid, I have to wonder if he's got some hidden agenda.

And I won't accomplish anything if my dick is hard.

So I fan my spark of curiosity to take my mind off the heat building in my balls. For a moment, the ghost of Connor stands in front of the window, joking with Jacques about the stories these walls could tell. Connor and Jacques had hit it off from the beginning, and a spike of remembered jealousy drags me down.

I don't like David. I'm just responding to physical cues because it's been so long since...

Admit it, man. So long since you had sex.

I'd have to be truly dead not to respond to his hints. Still, it doesn't matter. I can keep this professional. My goal is to get information out of David Collins. Nothing more.

Back in the main room, he's curled up on the couch, clutching a pillow. "Look"—he gestures at the screen—"Darius is leading."

Damned if Darius isn't a fair-skinned Italian-looking guy. "How much longer will this show last?"

"It's almost over, but I got it off Netflix, so there are six more episodes in the season." He punches the pillow. "Not like we got all that much to do."

"Except stay alive long enough to figure out who's trying to get to you." I perch on the edge of the couch, gingerly, because I can't trust myself to get to close to him. I have questions, and while I can persuade an ordinary human to answer truthfully with a little nudge of my mind, David is anything but ordinary.

"I told you. It's my dad or my uncle or one of their hoo-rah lieutenants."

"But what if it's not?"

He flaps a limp-wristed hand, giving me the full nelly. "It is." With a heavy sigh, he wiggles around till he's sitting. "How much do you know about Were politics?"

"Not much." I dare to ease back against the leather cushions. "It's like vamp politics, but with more body heat?"

David gives me a sly smile. "I like body heat. Do you like body heat?"

Before I can answer, he's coming for me, crawling up the couch. I put up a hand to stop him, but he laces his fingers through mine. "Is this okay?" he whispers.

I don't respond, but I don't push him away either. Over the last 175 years, I've tried just about everything, in every combination. Past and future fade in response to the heat of his now.

"I'm about to graduate," he says, "and that means it's time for me to get sucked into the machine." He draws my hand closer, till my knuckles are brushing against his chest. "I'll go to work for my dad, and I'll move on up the ranks." His grip on my hand is hot, but he hasn't grown fur yet. "He's the American capital-A Alpha, but he's also the small-a alpha of the Collins Pack. He says if I can take care of the family pack, he'll have more focus for national issues. That scares some people, because I'm flamboyant and I honestly don't give a fuck. There's not a wolf out there who can take mine in a fight, and there's not a man in the pack who wants a queer in charge."

I believe every word he says. "We can cross your father off the list, then. If he wants you to take over, he can't be trying to kill you."

His shrug doesn't have much confidence. "It might be his way of testing me, of making me prove to them all that I'm up to the role."

Talk about your tough love. I chew on that for a while. "But do you even want to take over?"

"I'll do whatever is necessary to keep my family safe." His conviction shines through, straightening his shoulders and raising his chin. "My mother, my sister, my cousins Marcus and Ben, they're my posse. If they need me to step up, I will."

"Why a solo trip to LA, then? Why leave your posse at home?"

"Because." He tugs on my hand, using it for leverage to climb up over my thighs. He smells good, like wolf and sandalwood and man. "This is my last chance, Guido. In Seattle, I'm the Alpha's son. Everyone knows it, and my life is planned down to how many shots of espresso I can order from Starbucks." He's hypnotizing me with his warmth and the sound of his voice.

"For this trip," he goes on, "I bleached my hair and bought tints for my eyes, and I want a man in every orifice by the time I'm through."

When his lips meet mine, I don't try to stop him. I can't. Connor was so long ago, and David is here and now.

He kisses me fiercely, as if someone's going to lob a bomb through the window any second. He tastes good, surprisingly sweet, with an undertow of cigarettes and wildness. I want more of that. More of him. We can talk later. I fold his strong, wiry body in my arms and lift, carrying him upstairs to the safe room.

"I'm not a damsel in distress." David nuzzles at my neck. My body is heating up, my breath coming short. All my hungers are clamoring.

We cross the threshold. The room is geared toward vampires, so there are no windows. I don't turn on the light. Don't need it. My vision works fine, along with my sense of smell. I have no trouble finding his hard body.

"Imma fuck a vampire." He sings the words, turns them into a chant. I know he's teasing, and I know we don't mean anything to each other, but it still makes me pause.

"What?" he asks.

I dump him roughly on the bed.

"Hey! What the fuck?" He scrambles up onto his hands and knees. "Why you mad, Tony?" He gets ahold of my shirt and crawls up Mickey, then flicks my chin with his tongue.

"Stop." I cover his mouth with my hand. He bites me, pushing the heat in my belly to the red zone. So what if he's just fucking me because I'm a vampire? I'm just fucking him because he's got an amazing ass. Giving in, I reach for that amazing ass and grind him against me.

His hard cock rams my hip. "Damn." I huff the word. With his fingers clawing at my chest, I wonder how long it's going to take me to peel these jeans off his body.

I set to work on his fly, stopping when he needs my hands to pull Mickey over my head.

"You're pretty for a dead guy." His voice has a growl in it, like he's close to losing control. He could, too. Unless he shifts, I can handle whatever he gives me.

To give him a taste, I grab ahold and yank his arms over his head.

"Tony." His voice is deeper still.

I loom over him, barely giving him time to get his legs around before I'm flattening him on the bed, one thigh jammed between his legs. "Don't move," I whisper.

He's breathing fast, little jerky breaths that take me even higher. I drag his jeans off, making him whimper when I catch the sensitive bits. Don't care. His tank shirt is even easier; I rip it down the middle and latch onto one nipple, sucking and biting, not gentle at all. My incisors ache with want, but I'm determined to scratch only one itch.

Feeding from someone, sharing their blood, creates a bond. The more often it happens, the stronger that bond becomes. Connor's death destroyed the bond we shared, and that destruction ripped me apart. Two years later, I'm still recovering. I won't make that same mistake again.

"Fuck." David gives a strangled cry, his hands tangling in my hair.

I grab them again, stretching him out till he groans. "I said don't move."

"God damn." He comes close to a whimper.

I pin his wrists with one hand and jam my thumb in his mouth, hips rocking against his belly. He sucks, his eyes blown black. "That's right, pretty baby," I say. He teases the pad of my thumb with his tongue. "You gonna suck me like that when it's my cock in your mouth?"

His cheeks hollow and the pull on my thumb has me gritting my teeth. For a second, I'm torn. I don't want to let go of his wrists, because I like the way his body's holding on to some tension, as if he's half tempted to fight. And I don't want to pull my thumb out of his mouth, because the way he's sucking it could make me cum in my jeans.

I decide there are better uses for his pretty mouth and reach for my fly. In moments, I've got both hands on his forearms, my cock poised at his lips. "You did say every orifice."

His grin takes on a wild edge. His lips part, and I thrust straight on in until I bump the back of his throat. He thrashes underneath me, and I almost lose it right there. I thrust again, zero to sixty in less than ten seconds.

He gags. Tears pool at the corners of his eyes. I could stop, but his wet heat feels too good. Besides, he's a damned werewolf. If he really wanted me to stop, I'd be lucky to get away with my prick still attached.

I fuck his throat, ramming him again and again, until my balls tighten and I jerk my hips back.

"Fuck," he screams. "Why'd you stop? That was so fucking hot."

Without answering, I grab his hips and flip him over. He scrambles up to his hands and knees, but I shove his shoulders down. Yeah. Now I got what I want: his ass in the air, all sweet and round and open.

I tease my fingertips over his pucker, drilling a tip in dry. "Oh yeah," he moans. "Do it, Guido."

I smack that ass, hard. He squawks and scrambles away, glaring at me from the head of the bed. "What the hell? Warn a guy before you do that."

I stare him down, gently stroking my cock. "Why? You gonna turn into a wolf or something?"

He bares his teeth and growls. His eyes, though, never rise above my waist.

"Now here's the deal," I continue. "You can be the werewolf princeling during the daylight hours, and tonight I'll be a notch on your lipstick case, but my name is Trajan, damn it. If you want me in that sweet little ass of yours, I suggest you remember that."

He catches his lower lip in his teeth, his expression somewhere between protest and mutiny. His debate takes too long. I tuck my cock away.

"Wait." He raises his chin, his attitude tinged with vulnerability. "Will you fuck me, Trajan? Please?"

I raise one eyebrow and shimmy the jeans over my hips. "Get back where I put you."

He crawls closer, slow and sinuous, then positions himself with his ass right in front of me. "Drama queen," he mutters.

I should swat him again, but his musky scent is making my mouth water. I reach for the nightstand and grab some lube - Jacques keeps his houses ready – then slide a slick finger into his hole.

His breath hitches when I add a second finger. I'm so hard, I might lose control if he bumps against me. Slicking myself with lube is a lesson in self-control, and pushing into his heat severely tests my restraint. He's clutching fistfuls of the linen sheets, and even better, he's loud, erupting in gibberish that includes the liberal use of the word fuck.

If he can let go, then so can I, and I whale on him, determined to fuck him so hard, he'll remember me for a long while.

My balls tighten to the point of implosion. I reach around and grab his cock. It takes only a couple more thrusts and he's screaming and thrashing, hot cum pouring over the back of my hand. A nice guy would back off, give him some time to come down, but I go harder, drilling him till my own release sears me. I'm drowning in white light and pleasure, but I keep myself standing upright so I don't bite anything on accident.

One taste of werewolf blood and the stuff in the plastic bag is likely to make me puke.

"You held out on me, sweetness." David's voice is languid, relaxed. I can hear his smile, though his face is still pressed into the bed.

I slowly withdraw, savoring the borrowed heat suffusing my muscles. "Sweetness? Try again."

He flops over onto his side. "Trajan's just so…so…"

"What?" I ease myself down next to him on the bed.

"I don't know." He curls himself around me. I stiffen. Never been one for cuddling.

He giggles and folds himself tighter. "Badass vampire."

I lie still for a moment, fighting the urge to force some space between us. Slowly, like a chunk of ice melting in the sun, my body relaxes. We're not snuggling, but I no longer want to bounce him out of the bed. "Let's get some rest. We're safe enough here, and tomorrow after sunset, we'll move again. Sheena will stay with you during the day."

"You told her where we are?"

It was a calculated risk. "If someone starts shooting, we'll know it's her."

"Nice way to set up a friend, Tone." His laughter is tinged with bitterness.

I stiffen. Our moment of sharing is over. "Good night, David."

CHAPTER FIVE

An hour after sunset, a chindi trots up to the living room window. I'm already annoyed because I woke up to a plumbing issue at one of my apartment buildings, and hunger has clawed through all my patience. I need to get to the few packets left from my last blood bank order. They'll be stale as shit, but I'm too hungry to be picky. We're leaving for my condo as soon as Sheena and David get back from shopping, and I do not have time for a coyote who's been possessed by an evil ghost.

Sharp claws tap on my window. I ignore the sound, but it won't give up. *Tap tap tap tap tap.*

I jerk the sliding door open. The coyote squats on his haunches, grinning at me, sending chills along my spine. If a chindi found me, then whoever sent it could, too.

"What?" I'd break the creature's neck, but don't want to chance the ghost jumping into me.

"Got a riddle for you." The chindi speaks in the harsh voice of an animal.

"Who sent you?"

"A friend, so listen." It barks, as if clearing its throat. "They're dark and always on the run. Without the sun, there would be none. What are they?"

"No fair, fleabag. I haven't seen the sun in a hundred years." Still, I memorize the words. A ghost doesn't just show up to tease.

"Get over yourself." The creature hops onto all fours.

I swallow some of my frustration. Don't want to chase the thing away before learning anything useful. "Sorry."

"Sure you are." It huffs, pausing to scratch at an ear. "Here's the deal. There's a lot more going on than you know, Gall. Make like the answer to my riddle."

Make like the answer…? "I don't know what you're talking about." *Something that's dark in the sun?* "You mean a shadow?"

The rudimentary intelligence fades from the creature's eyes, and I'm faced with an ordinary coyote. It growls at me, baring its teeth, and runs away.

"Well, shit," I say to no one in particular. I take a moment to parse the faint silhouette on the dirt cast by the living room light behind me. It takes a pile of cash to conjure a chindi. "And for an extra fifteen percent, they'll deliver a message that actually makes sense."

Whoever sent it must have only paid for the bargain version.

Voices come from inside the house, interrupting my moment of frustration. David and Sheena are back, and the city lights are rolling out below me. "Pack up. We're taking off," I holler to David without turning around.

"Sulking on the patio?" David strides out. His hair has a loud purple streak, and his heels are higher than his shorts are long. "I wouldn't have guessed you were the sullen type." He wrinkles his nose. "Oh, wait. You're totally the sullen type, Sal."

"Go pack your shit, and, um" — I flick a gaze at his obnoxious heels — "you might want to change into shoes you can run in."

Sheena comes out behind us. "Where are you headed?"

The chindi's words rankle. They feel like a warning, if nothing else. "Not sure. I'll call you with our location."

She gives me a hard stare, the planes and angles of her face drawn tight. "I hear you. If you need a babysitter tomorrow, I'm your girl."

In spite of myself, I reach for her hand. "Thanks."

"Sure." Her smile has a note of understanding. We've been friends for some seventy-five years, and while I know she'd be the last person to betray me intentionally, I don't want to take any chances. There are bigger things at stake than my life, or David's, for that matter. A war between the vampires and the wolves would be a disaster.

Until I figure out what's going on, David and I are on our own.

Sheena takes off, and while David packs his things, I clear away any traces of our presence. I'm still wearing my Mickey Mouse shirt, and besides the blood, I'll need to pick up some clothes when we get to my place. Packing takes David a lot longer than unpacking did, but finally, we're in my Escalade.

Through it all, he's so brittle and distant, I wouldn't believe we'd fucked if I hadn't been there myself.

I start the engine, and he immediately rolls down a window, his knee keeping up a steady pistoning. "Don't," I say. "The air conditioner is on."

He takes out a cigarette and flicks a match, giving me a flat stare.

"You can't smoke in here."

"Stop me." He inhales, tosses the match out the window, then blows the smoke out after it.

A werewolf is quick, but a vampire's quicker. I snatch the smoke from his hand and toss it out the window.

"Dammit." He scrabbles at his seat belt and flings the door open. We're doing about forty down a twisting road.

"What the hell?" I slam on the brakes. He takes off at a run, and as soon as I get the car pulled to the side of the road, I follow.

He hits a patch of scrub, an empty lot that opens into the side of the mountain. He's fast, hugging the ground, and I have the feeling if he didn't like those booty shorts, he would have shifted. That might have given me a problem, but he stays on two legs, so he doesn't get too far before I catch him.

"What is your deal?" I grab him by the shoulders, jerking him to a halt.

He yanks away from me, stumbles, rakes his hands through his hair. "I just want a fucking cigarette."

I highly doubt he jumped out of a moving car over a cigarette, but I give him a minute to get his shit together before I press him. The moon hasn't risen high enough to crest the mountains in the east, but the night sky has a silvery cast. I fold my arms across my chest and wait.

David's breathing hard, half turned away from me. "This was supposed to be fun, you know? Hit the big wicked city, dress pretty, do unmentionable things with men I'll never see again." His lips tighten. "I figured they'd at least give me till graduation before they started in."

God only knows why he gets to me, but I have to fight the urge to put my arms around him. "Might not be the wolves. Could be a vampire, either Jacques or someone working for him. Someone who wants to get at me and is willing to risk a war to do it."

"Didn't know you were all that important." He sighs, rubbing an open palm over his forehead. "If that's true, we're really fucked, because I'm pretty sure there are some who would just as soon see me dead."

He meets my gaze, and something between us clicks. Someone wants one of us dead, and we're each looking at the only guy who can help. Maybe I'm stupid to trust him, but that's what I see in his eyes.

"Look," I say, "I got to go by my condo and get some things. After that—"

"What?"

I shrug. A car winds down the street in front of us. The sage scrub surrounding us doesn't give much cover, and we both freeze. The car passes, and I stand. "Let's go."

"You still haven't told me where we're staying tonight."

"That's because I don't know."

The uncertainty lasts until we reach my condo.

"OMG. we should totally stay here!"

David spreads his arms and swirls around the middle of my living room like he's Maria von Trapp and the hills are singing.

I shake my head, still not sure how he managed to run through the scrub in those heels without breaking something. "Easy, princess. Don't get too comfortable."

"Why not?" He bounces over to my leather sofa. "This wouldn't be your lair if it wasn't armed to the gills. We're probably safer here than anywhere else."

I'm on the move, and he contorts himself to follow me. "And if I'm a princess, does that make you a prince?"

I let a beat pass. "I'm not compatible with any particular sign, baby."

He tilts his head, the purple streaks flopping like puppy dog ears. "Did you seriously just mangle a Prince lyric?"

My grin spreads slowly, at least until I realize I'm smiling, and I stop. "What can I say? I'm a fan. Now don't mess with anything while I pack."

I leave him doing dance moves while singing "Kiss" in a light falsetto. He's doing a fair imitation of the Purple One, but no one's been in my space since Connor. There's something about having a stranger—and yeah, even though we'd fucked, David is still pretty much a stranger—spreading his energy around my space that feels odd. Connor's scent has faded, but I want to hold on to the rest: his fingerprints, his breath, his life force. Maybe I'm keeping the place as a shrine, but I don't care. David's bright, vital presence turns Connor's absence into a stabbing pain, gutting me.

I toss a fistful of clean shirts, some jeans, and a blazer in an overnight case. I really do need to figure out a plan. We could keep hitting safe houses, I mean, Jacques has at least eight scattered around the city. But someone knew where to send the chindi. Sheena could have ratted us out, but a stab in the back isn't her style. She'd want to look me in the eye when she cut me down.

But if Sheena's the only person who knew where we'd crashed, and she didn't send the chindi, then there's a wild card out there.

And I only play poker in Vegas.

When I come back into the living room, David's wandering around touching things, spreading his stink of wolf and cigarettes. Those booty shorts are killing me. *Sonofabitch.* "I gotta grab one more thing, and then we're gone." I'm still not sure where we're going, but maybe it'll be better if I make it up on the fly.

I head for the kitchen and pull a small cooler bag out of an otherwise empty cupboard. I open the stainless steel refrigerator door for my stash; three one-unit bags of blood. There's about eight ounces in each, and they'll last me a week.

Seven days before I have to hit the blood bank again or come up with an alternative.

David, of course, has followed me into the kitchen. "What's that?" He points at the blood.

"Nothing." I stuff the bags in the cooler and tighten the Velcro closure. I'm half-starved now, but there's no way I'm going to eat in front of him.

"Wait." He grabs my wrist. "You really did hold out on me."

"Yeah, so? Come on. We gotta go." I pivot, jerking out of his grasp. The kitchen's smaller in proportion than the rest of the condo. Never bothered me much, but I'm a little surprised by how much space a small werewolf takes up. David's looming, way too much presence for me to pass by.

"You could have fed from me." He rams me with his chest, forcing me back against the counter. "Why didn't you? I could have had the orgasm of the century, and you denied."

I pinch the bridge of my nose. He's twenty-two. Of course he thinks with his dick. "Leaving now."

He huffs and backs away. Great. Now I'll get to see what pouty David looks like. He follows me silently — *thank God* — and we head for the car.

We come off the elevator, and the parking garage is deserted, a cavern of cement underneath the building. A few cars are parked in the stalls, each more expensive than the last, and the harsh fluorescent lights turn all their paint colors to gray. My SUV is to the left, and an open staircase is across from us.

The bullet catches me in the shoulder, next to the strap of my overnight bag. David and I both hit the ground. I cover him with my body till we figure out which direction the shots are coming from. The bullet's not silver, which is a weird stroke of luck I'll have to think about later. Even so, it stings enough to make me grit my teeth.

David gives a muffled squawk, and I ease off. I crabwalk both of us back to the elevator. We're too exposed, so our only protection is to stay low.

"We need to get to the car," he says.

It's at least twenty feet away, but we're both pretty fast. We should be able to make it. "Let's go."

A steady barrage of bullets pepper our feet, but neither of us gets hit. Using the driver's door as a shield, I scan the space.

A flash of movement catches my eye, from the direction of the stairs. I wait, watching between cars for whoever to give themselves away. There. In the light. Auburn hair. Broad shoulders.

Connor.

He runs up the stairs, moving fast, but not vampire fast. For a second, surprise keeps me still. For only a second.

"Get in and lock the doors." I toss David my keys and take off running. Connor's scent hits me at the row of cars closest to the stairwell. By the time I plant my foot on the first metal riser, I'm almost delirious with it. The hair. The build. The scent. How can it be Connor?

Connor is dead.

CHAPTER SIX

My run up the stairs is a waste of time. No Connor. No gun. Once I'm out of sight of the Escalade, I worry the gunman might have circled back around. Thinking of David, I run down the stairs even faster.

On the floor of the garage, Connor's whisky-and-smoke scent hits me so hard, I stumble. He must have waited behind the cars at the foot of the stairs. He can't be alive. I saw his body, still and cold and gray. My shoulder aches from the gunshot, but the wound is closing over. Mostly I'm angry that there's blood on my Mickey Mouse shirt. No, wait. Mostly I'm enraged by the appearance of my former lover.

Who shouldn't be shooting at me, even if he is alive.

"And when did he grow a goddamn beard?"

David's silhouette is visible in the driver's seat of the SUV. I get in the passenger side, figuring he can drive while I pull myself together. He might not know his way around, but I don't know where we're going, so we're even.

He eases the big vehicle up the exit ramp. "Which way do I turn?"

"Take a right and head for the 101." I've got half an idea. Maybe. "We'll go north to Thousand Oaks and stop at the first hotel we pass with vampire-ready rooms." It might be smarter not to stay in a place with a vamp room, because that's the first place anyone would look for us. But it doesn't feel right to leave David guarding my carcass all day long. At least in a vamp room, I can lock the door.

At the end of the block, the light is red. "Change of plans," I say. "Pull it into the Walgreens lot right here and get ready to move your stuff."

For once, he doesn't argue, doesn't debate. In fact, his ongoing silence is starting to make me nervous. I give him a look, but his eyes are on the road. This last round of pyrotechnics seems to have shaken the spunk out of his sassy bravado. His fingers tap a staccato rhythm on the steering wheel, and his change of mood makes me unhappier than it probably should. Can't be helped. I'll deal with him after I find us a different set of wheels.

David turns into the parking lot. "If you're worried about lube, I've got more than we'll ever need."

Somehow I doubt his silence meant he was planning sexcapades. "Didja ever hotwire a car?" I ask. His smile broadens, and he shakes his head.

"See if you can accidentally tap that CRV right there." I point to a red Honda parked in one of the darker patches in the lot.

David slows the Escalade to a crawl, turning the wheel just enough to kiss the CRVs bumper. No alarm. I scan the lot. No one's around. "Do it again, a little harder."

He does, harder but not hard enough to leave a mark. Still no alarm. I check my cell phone for messages, then stick it in the glove box, open the door, and hop out. "Okay, park where your headlights won't shine on me."

This whole thing is brazen as shit, and we've probably got even odds of being caught. My heart's jumping in my throat. Most human cops I can handle, but every so often, they send a vampire out. If I get busted by another vamp, no way I'll be able to talk my way free.

I run my hand underneath the running board on the driver's side, looking for an "emergency" spare key in a magnetized box. I check both wheel wells on the driver side, too. No luck. David's standing by the rear end of my SUV, waiting for my signal. Another car pulls in the lot. I duck under the flare of headlights and freeze.

Shit.

The other driver parks and jogs into the store. I move my search to the passenger's side. If there's no key, I'll break the window to get in, but that's a lot more obvious. I start with the rear wheel well because it's closest. No key. Then the running board. Still none. The front wheel. Nope.

Disgusted, I head back to the driver's side door.

"What are you doing?" David calls.

"Hang tight." I reach down one more time, and there it is. A small metal box stuck underneath the car. I pry it free and break it open to retrieve the key.

We're lucky that all the Walgreens shoppers are busy tonight. I get the car unlocked, and we transfer our luggage to the CRV as quickly as possible. I pop the license plate off my SUV and stick it in the CRV's back window, leaving the Honda's behind. In less than fifteen minutes, we're back on the road, this time with me behind the wheel.

"Well, damn, Tony. Who knew you were a pirate of the highway?" David's smile has more life to it, as if the rush of stealing a car restored his spark.

I don't want to get into how that makes me feel.

"It's not fancy" —between the sand, the dog hair, and the old In-n-Out Burger bags, it really isn't—"but it'll get us out of town. You got a new phone, right?"

He busies himself looking for hotels in Thousand Oaks. In a couple of blocks, I pull over at a Bank of America and withdraw the maximum amount the cash machine will give me, then ask David to do the same. I want to pay cash for as long as possible so we don't leave a trail of credit card receipts.

"So we've got a few hours till sunrise." David slides a smile my way. "How do you think we should fill the time?" He gives his own cock a blatant rub. "Looks like my dick thinks stealing cars is hot."

This grubby old CRV is about a thousand degrees all of a sudden. "I'm thinking," I barked a laugh, "I'm thinking it'll take at least an hour to get where we're going, and then we need to make sure you're going to be secure during the day, and—"

He leans across the seat divider, stopping my words with a nip on the ear. "We almost died. What better reason is there to fuck?"

I don't answer him. The main reason not to fuck just took a shot at me.

By the time we get checked in to La Manzanilla, a run-down three-story walk-up with a glorious view of the freeway, it's nearly sunrise. We hit the mini-mart at the gas station next door so David can stock up on cigarettes, semi-perishable baked products, and a lifetime supply of Mountain Dew. Our rooms are adjoining, and before I head into mine, I make him promise he won't leave the room or call room service or do anything else that might draw attention to himself.

And before he lets me go, he all but begs me for a hand-job. "Later, puppy." I've got some blood to drink, and not the warm kind. David complains about my refusal, but the shadows around his eyes tell a different story. We both need rest.

The last man I fed from was Connor, who is apparently not really dead. Don't know how that makes me feel. *Oh, wait. Yeah I do.* I'm angry.

Because it's easier to be furious than wallow in confusion or sadness or any other phony-baloney emotion.

I fish one of the units of blood out of the cooler. Stale. Cold. I poke the plastic with my thumbnail and suck hard. The stuff is so foul, it makes me gag. Tastes even worse knowing I could be drinking sweet, salty werewolf blood.

Though werewolf blood has strings attached, and I'm feeling pretty burned.

I double-check the door to make sure it's locked and sink down on the bed. The windowless room takes the coffin vibe a little too seriously, but it's a place for me to rest. I stretch out, eyes already drifting shut. I have to trust no one can get in, and I have to trust David will be here when I get up.

He is. I can hear him as soon as my body kicks back on. Well, it's not him I hear, but music, heaving grunge chords beating against the door separating our rooms. I finally pull off the ruined Mickey Mouse shirt and shower. My overnight case is full of denim and black crewneck shirts.

Black doesn't show the blood.

I toss some product through my hair and slick it down, and then it's time to face the werewolf. There's no point in knocking on the door to his room—the music is so loud, he'd never hear me. I let myself in, squinting against the onslaught of sound. He's draped across the bed, an arm over his eyes, and not a stitch of clothing on his body.

His tight, golden body.

I don't slam the door or shout over the music. He must sense me because his cock stirs, swelling against his thigh. Mine wants to answer, but I ignore it. Just because David's turned himself into a damned open invitation doesn't mean I have to accept.

Who the hell am I kidding?

"What's going on?" I speak without raising my voice.

David stirs, keeping one arm over his eyes and running his other hand over his chest, up and down, each stroke going lower and lower.

"Knock it off."

He shifts his arm far enough to squint at me with one eye. "You knock it off." His hand drifts lower, brushing the edge of his neatly trimmed bush. "Knock that chip right off your shoulder and suck me."

I allow my silence to answer him.

"Fuck you, then." He flops over on his belly, treating me to a look at his gorgeous ass.

With grim determination, I drag my gaze away. "How was your day?"

"Fanfuckintastic."

I cross to the window simply to have something to do besides stare. "You're lying."

"Nope." David sits up on his knees. "I'm using sarcasm. Did they do that back in your day? The phrase fucking fantastic suggests something good happened. Fanfuckintastic implies the opposite."

His hands are fisted on his thighs and there are notes of anger and fear in his voice. Something happened. Something bad.

Dusk is deepening to night, and the highway out our window is streaked gold from the stream of headlights. I have options here. I could sit on the edge of the bed, waiting patiently for him to trust me, the way I would for any other wounded animal. I could take him up on his invitation and fuck him till he talks.

About the only thing I can't do is leave.

My options aren't great, and while I'm sifting through them, I stand with my arms crossed. I guess my silence bothers him, because he flips around and glares at me. "I've seen walls with more personality."

"Maybe." He's close to breaking down. I can sense it and hold on for the blow.

"Damn it." He punches the mattress, hard. "Don't you believe in small talk? Hey David"—he uses a high, mincing voice—"how the hell was your day? What'd you do with yourself while I was, you know, dead?"

I don't respond. My silence is pissing him off, but anything I say will make him angrier. Several moments pass, then he straightens up, squaring his shoulders. "Not that you care, but I had a busy day. I had thirty-seven texts from my sister, another two dozen from my roommate back in Seattle, at least one from each of my eight cousins, and an email from my uncle."

His voice quivers on "email." "You seem upset."

"Very observant." He claps slowly. "Uncle Brendan is the family pack's Delta, and I'm supposed to meet him in the morning."

My knowledge of pack politics is rudimentary, but I think the Delta is the enforcer. "Why?"

He makes a disgusted "tsk." "Because word got back to my father that someone tried to kill me outside a nightclub, and now they all think I'm in danger."

Interesting. "No comment about the bomb in the hotel or the gunman at my condominium?"

He raises his hands and lets them flop. "Right, well, lemme email him back real quick and make sure he's got all the deets, 'kay?"

He's missing the point, but I let him carry on.

"He's going to cut my vacation short, reel me in under the pretext of protecting me."

"But you don't trust him." I'm stating the obvious, but I need to be sure.

The look he gives me is more complicated than what I was expecting. There's anger and fear, yes but also determination and an unshakeable confidence. "The only thing I know for sure about any of my father's sidekicks is that my wolf can take them."

Now I do approach the bed. I don't touch him, but I get a better sense of the mix of pheromones he's giving off. He may be dead wrong about everything, but he absolutely believes what he's saying. "If there's a chance that your uncle is behind all this bullshit, I don't think you should meet him."

The look he gives me is cold, leaving little doubt that he's the Alpha's son. "I have to. If I don't, it'll undermine my father's control, and then they really will kill me." He sighs, deflates a little. "I can take them. I can."

"But" — I reach out, brush a strand of blond hair behind his ear — "this was supposed to be your chance to have a man in every orifice." For someone so bold, he's achingly young. "Email him back and tell him you can't meet till nine p.m."

"Why?"

"Because you're not going in there alone. Your father hired a vampire, which tells me he anticipated trouble. Let me help you." My voice drops to a whisper, and I'm not even sure where the words are coming from. I'm too old, too bitter over the loss of a lover who might not have died. Instead of searching for Connor, I want to dress David up in his pumps and his furs, to take him out to some fancy club and give him his pick of the crowd. Then two of us can gang up on him and make his dreams come true.

But that's all a fantasy, and the reality is, I'm stuck in a shitty hotel room with a kid who's got a death wish of some kind. He leans into my palm, and I thread my fingers deeper into his hair, twisting the coarse blond strands.

"So where is this meeting supposed to take place?" He wouldn't have given them our location. Would he? Nervous energy surges through me. If he's told them, it's already too late for us to try to get away.

"The national organization has an office suite downtown." His dry lips brush against my skin. "I figure I'll take an Uber."

"You're not taking an Uber." I shake my head. "Tell them you can't be there till after sunset, and I'll call Sheena." The skin of his cheek is barely rough, like the finest grain of sandpaper. "Between the three of us, we'll make sure you get in and out safely."

"Don't assume the worst." He shakes his head, rubbing his sandpaper skin against my fingertips. "This is my family. I'll be okay."

I know in my bones he's wrong.

Before I can marshal another argument, David runs his tongue along the crease in my palm. We have the room for at least another night and, well, if this is going to be his last night of freedom, I guess I can't expect him to waste it.

I get a better grip on his head and pull him closer, pressing his face against my chest and running both hands over his bare skin. He's so warm. Even though I've fed, he still has fifteen degrees on me. His skin is smooth and velvety, his body compact, muscular, hard.

"Mm-hmm," he murmurs. He pulls up my shirt and puts an openmouthed kiss on my belly. "How's your stamina, vampire? Can you last as long as they say?"

I shove him down, jamming his face into my groin. "Try me." I'm not cocky enough to think fucking him will change his mind, but I'm hoping something will.

I pull my shirt off, and he works on my belt. His toenails are painted a deep aqua, the color of the ocean just before dawn, and for some reason, that makes me smile. Surprise. I'm not beyond feelings for anything or anybody. This pretty wolf-man has me by the 'nads in more ways than one. Then his mouth hits my cock, and I forget about details and colors and fear.

He takes me deep, the muscles of his throat massaging the head of my cock. I shift my hips, a tentative movement, and he wraps his hand around the base of my shaft. He uses his grip to set the tempo, and my hips fall in line.

This is good, so good my knees get weak. I thrust and his cheeks hollow, sending pleasure spiraling from my spine to my ass to my balls. He's taking me fast. Too fast. I pull back, and his gasp turns into laughter.

"So much for stamina."

"Shut up." I shove my jeans down and step out of them. "Why don't you show me that pretty ass up close?"

He walks backward on his knees, gets on all fours, and pivots around. I run my hands over the perfect round globes, kneading the dense muscles. He's shivering, and I brush his crease with my thumb, bringing a moan.

"Come on and fuck me." His voice is tight, twisted.

"In a minute." I bend forward and run my nose along his skin. He smells good, rich, his flowery lotion balanced by the wildness of his wolf. I flick his crease with my tongue.

"Shit."

I flick again, then lick, spreading his cheeks so I can hit his taint. I school my lips to cover my incisors, because one little scratch will blow my control all to hell. His balls are full and heavy, and except for the patch of pubes around his cock, he's shaved bare. I lick and suck and bite, working everything except his tight little asshole.

I'm teasing myself as much as I'm teasing him.

"Just fuck me," he whines.

"No." I rub the flat of my tongue over his hole. I don't know what I'm doing. I try to tell myself that when a naked man—a beautiful, naked, man—asks me for sex, of course I'll say yes, but in the pit of my belly, I suspect this is more than two bodies rubbing together.

And I know he's in trouble if he goes alone to meet the pack's Delta.

Once I start on David's hole, I can't stop. My tongue digs at the tight muscle, forcing it to relax.

"Come on." He's got that whine thing going on again, and I stab my tongue harder. The muscle is softening, so I add my index finger, getting it wet with spit and advancing to the first knuckle. He's rocking back and forth, whimpering. My own cock is hard, dripping precum on the bedspread.

"This feels so good, Traj, but I need your big dick, baby."

Traj? That's as close as he's come to my name. To reward him, I reach for the lube. I get myself all slicked up, then nudge his hole with the head of my cock.

"That's it, baby. Put it in there." His elbows buckle and his ass lifts. I ease in half an inch, then a whole inch, then two. He's so hot and so tight, for a minute I worry I may not be able to hold off.

But only for a minute. I start pounding, and damn, he feels good.

"Fuck." The word has a heavy helping of growl in it.

"Like that?" My dick's got a mind of its own, and it's moving my hips faster and harder.

Instead of answering, he reaches for one of my hands, breaking the bruising grip I have on his thigh. "Here," he gasps, and wraps my fingers around his cock.

I lean forward, which shortens my thrust and changes the angle. He's iron wrapped in velvet, and I stroke him in time with my hips. He grunts each time I slam into him, encouraging me to go faster, faster and harder, so fast and so hard, I really might lose it.

Hell, I'm already lost.

My climax comes on slow and sneaky, teasing my balls until I'm too far gone to call it back. "Jeee-sus." I spear him and hold on, pleasure pulsing through me. He drags my hand out of the way and starts stroking himself, his fingers burning under mine. I'm still in him when he shrieks, his body spasming around me. His heat makes me shudder, my fangs ache for contact with his skin, and for a few short moments, I forget myself entirely.

I bend lower and press a kiss between his shoulder blades. He arches his back, so I run my tongue along his skin.

"You're too good." His voice is soft, fragile.

I slowly withdraw from his body. "Yeah?"

He slides down onto the bed, landing with a soft "oof." "Thanks."

Sinking down on my heels, I can't decide on the right response. My body's already cooling, and I shiver, but not because I'm turned on. Something about David gets me naked in a way that has nothing to do with clothes. I don't care about him. I can't care about him. I haven't cared about anyone since Connor.

Even myself.

But Connor's doppelgänger is wandering around LA, and I just pulled my dick out of the son of the American Alpha. If I had a logical bone in my body, I'd realize this was all fucking crazy.

"Hey Tony. You know what I think?"

Fortunately, David's question interrupts my dive into darkness. "What?"

"You ought to take me out to dinner someplace pretty, and then you should come back and fuck me again." He rolls over, stretching, grinning down his belly at me. For once, he's not twitching.

Lethargy's sucking the wind out of my sails, and I slide down the bed next to him, close but not touching. "Oh yeah?"

"Come on, Guido." He reaches over and brushes the bangs out of my face. "It'll be good fun. I'll eat, and you'll get horny, and then we'll come back to this palace and…" He trails his gaze down my body, so hot I can feel it like fingers. He doesn't even need to finish the sentence.

I grab him by the scruff of the neck and kiss him, hard. "Get dressed."

Maybe if I get him drunk I'll be able to talk him into running away with me.

Getting dressed, the idea takes shape. Outside of Sheena, and possibly David, there's no one in this city I trust, and David only makes the short list because I've had my dick in him. Someone's tried to kill him more than once and included me by default. Or someone jumped him to get at me. My dead ex isn't, or maybe he is and I'm losing my mind.

Yeah, it's time to go underground until I can sort things out, and my gut's telling me to take David with me. He slips into a slinky black button-down shirt, the kind with random gold threads that probably started life in the disco era. I catch his eye, and he wets his lower lip with some seriously filthy heat.

Convincing him is going to take some work.

I'm buckling my belt when he clears his throat. "Your, uh" — he brushed the hair back from his own face — "hair."

"Need product?" I brush it back with my hand. Back in 1875, if someone had told me I was going to run across a vampire, I would have had a haircut first.

He smirks. "Yep."

I duck back into the vampire room, still strategizing. We'll pack his stuff and check out. I don't care that I've paid for two nights. I'd rather be alive. We can head out of town, toward San Diego or some little town out in the desert. Somewhere they'll have to work to find us. I'll ditch the CRV we stole and pick up something else. David's from Seattle; maybe we can head north instead.

Ideas are percolating, and so help me this is the most alive I've felt in a couple of years. The puppy is smart. Between the two of us, we can figure things out. Hell, we may even work things to our advantage.

I'm so far gone in my own head I don't notice the silence. I open the door, ready to ask David what he's hungry for.

The room is empty.

It takes several beats for me to make sense of things. There are two suitcases, each big enough to stash a body. There's a messenger bag, leather, sitting on the dresser, the flap open and cosmetics spilling out. The door is closed, the curtains drawn. The fur coat is hanging in the closet.

David's gone.

I cross to the door, fast enough to make the curtains flutter, panic fueling my speed. He's not on the walkway running along the outside of the building. I run to the closest stairwell. Nothing. No David. I stop and grab ahold of myself. Inhale deeply. Catch his scent. It's faint, but enough to give me a direction.

There's a parking lot between the hotel and the freeway. Three double-sided lights shine starkly over the crosshatch of white lines on the black pavement. Nothing's moving besides the endless stream of headlights on the 101.

The trace of David's scent leads me past the CRV, still parked in the spot closest to the stairs. I look through the windows, half hoping he's just come out to pick up his…I don't even know what. Nothing. I keep chasing the elusive scent before it fades away.

The edge of the lot is marked by a knee-high row of shrubs that grab at my trousers as I plow through them. Next door is another lot, another row of shops, but no David.

And I've lost the last trace of his scent.

Now what the hell do I do? I head back for our room and find David standing by the car, arms crossed, hands fisted. "Where have you been?" he all but snarls, his tone as pugnacious as his posture.

"Looking for you."

"You thought I'd walk out on two full suitcases and a makeup case?" He cocks his head, gaze drilling me. "And where the hell did you think I'd be going? On foot. Out here in the middle of"—he gives the area a quick once-over—"strip mall heaven."

I turn on my heel and head back to the hotel room. None of the words I want to say will help things in the slightest.

"Come on, Tony. You can't be that dumb."

I stop. *Don't tease a vampire, asshole.* Somehow, my voice comes out calm and clear. "Next time you want to go on walkabout, leave a note."

Footsteps behind me. I don't move. "I needed to think," he says, and when I don't respond, he keeps going. "Uncle Brendan agreed to a nine p.m. meeting."

"Good."

"He said you would be allowed in, since Dad hired you, but not Sheena."

Pick your battles, Gall. "Good."

"And…I'm sorry. I shouldn't have left without telling you where I was going." His voice holds true remorse, and my anger fades.

"I'm not your babysitter."

He reaches for me, his hand warm on my shoulder. "No, but I hope you're my friend."

I lay my hand on top of his. "Over dinner, you can tell me why you went for a walk here in strip mall heaven."

"It's a deal."

Over dinner, we clear the air. David says he left because he thinks best on his feet. I resist the urge to say he didn't appear to be thinking at all.

David blames all the shooting and exploding on *family stuff*, but I want to know what that means, exactly. That said, I opt for an indirect approach. "So, your father wants you to take charge of the family wolf pack. What does your mother think of that?"

His smile is brighter than the fluorescent tube lights overhead. "Not sure."

I use a smile and silence to coax more information out of him.

"Mom is great," he says. "She's…well, let's just say when Dad went national, she…didn't."

"What does that mean?"

He snorts a laugh. "She's not anybody's Mrs. Alpha. They're the happiest couple in the universe, but he's in DC doing his bit to keep the US government out of our hair, and she's in a cabin on Bellingham Bay, up in the northwest corner of Washington State. She writes poems and talks to the voices in the air and I don't know what all else. I haven't seen her in years, but she's quick with the email. If the weres have a religion, she's our high priestess."

"And your dad is okay with all that?"

"Didn't have much choice. Her wolf might not be able to take his, but she'd hurt him pretty bad."

"Huh. So, it's possible to refuse your father's request."

He makes a face at the obvious connection I'm drawing. *If Mom can say no, why can't David?*

The waitress swings by with his burger, which gives him a minute to compose an answer. After applying ketchup, he takes a bite and chews. Swallows. "Not bad. Overcooked."

"You're a wolf. You'd like it better if it was bleeding."

His shrug says I'm not wrong. "Now, about refusing Dad—"

I interrupt him. "You don't give me the impression that your heart is in it. Don't you have a brother or sister who could step in?"

He pours more ketchup, this time for his fries. "No brothers, and Abby isn't an alpha. She's younger than me, so it would be even harder for her to keep everybody in line."

I tap a finger on the table like I'll be able to shake loose a new idea. Should have picked a diner with a bar attached so I could have some tequila. "Still, seems like taking over a werewolf pack when you don't want to is a setup for problems." *Disaster, really.* "Maybe you should spend some time thinking about what you really want to do."

Raising his water glass, he gives me a mock toast. "Thanks for the advice, Grandpa. I'll be sure to take it under advisement."

O-kay. Time for a subject change. "So what's the game plan for tomorrow night?"

David is midbite. He chews and swallows and answers. "We're going in confident. We don't know what's going on, but whatever it is, between the two of us we'll handle it. There's no reason for Brendan to send me back to Seattle."

"Sounds good." I like this take-charge version of David, but I'm still tapping the tabletop, still looking for alternatives. "Be even better if we knew what he was up to ahead of time."

David points at me with a fry. "Now you're talking. I wonder who might know…"

I list everyone I can think of who might have heard rumors about the Collins pack. David texts his sister and a cousin or two, trying to figure out what his uncle is up to without actually asking. Neither of us comes up with much, although I do manage to line Sheena up as backup. Uncle Brendan said she couldn't come into the meeting with David, but he didn't say anything about keeping watch outside.

After a vigorous game of hide the pickle, David sleeps while I stand guard. We switch off at sunrise, and I spend the day in the hotel's vampire room while David keeps watch. Later, I rise and put on my very best hit man chic, but when I let myself into the main hotel room, I'm in for a shock.

David sits at the desk, typing vigorously on a laptop. He's wearing navy-blue trousers and a crisp white button-down with a light blue tie. His suitcoat is draped over the back of his chair, and his hair is combed into the approximation of a conservative style.

"Who the hell are you, and where is David?"

He smirks at me, closing the laptop lid. "I told you. Dad wants me to take over the pack, so I need to look the part."

I shake my head. It's David, the tame version. "Not even a little lip gloss?"

Grinning, David puts on his jacket and straightens his tie. "Let's go see what Uncle Brendan wants."

I follow him out, not at all sure his sudden transformation bodes well for the future.

We also drive past the Walgreens where we left the Escalade and *praise Jesus*, it's still there. We swap it for the CRV—with the gas tank full as a thank-you to the owner—and switch the plates. Restored to my monster truck, we're ready to rumble.

We pick up Sheena on the way. She takes one look at David and hoots. "Back in the day, we would have asked why you're dressed like an undertaker."

He tosses his head, for a moment giving us full diva David. "They say you gotta know your audience."

I don't entirely agree, but I keep my mouth shut.

We park in the lot next to the Harris Building in downtown LA. Our plan is simple. David and I will go in, and Sheena will keep watch from the ground floor. If things go sideways and David's uncle tries to march him out, she'll be there to interfere and presumably I'll be right behind them.

Better to have a plan for trouble than to have it catch you unawares.

Retail stores occupy the street level, and though they've all closed for the day, David knows the code to let us in the building's main door. Sheena reclines at a table in a coffee shop that opens into the lobby, her long legs outstretched and her phone in her hand. David leads me to an elevator that takes the two of us to the second floor, where the American Were Authority has a suite of offices. We're met at the reception desk by a young wolf who greets David like a brother.

"Traj, this is my cousin Marcus." David knocks a fist against his cousin's shoulder.

I offer to shake hands, and Marcus almost carries it off without letting me see his grimace. "Nice to meet you," I say without cracking a grin.

Marcus is also wearing a suit, though his is a deep charcoal-gray with faint pinstripes. "Come on. Dad and the others are waiting."

I can't wait to see how many *others* he means.

He leads us to a conference room with a long cherrywood table in the center. An older wolf sits at the far end of the table, with three younger wolves on the right-hand side and two on the left. There were only two other seats at the table. Logic dictates that David should take the one on the end opposite his uncle. That leaves me and Cousin Marcus fighting over the last chair.

I let him win, preferring to stand near the door behind David.

The meeting starts benignly. They're all related so had no need for introductions. Not that I would remember their names if they told me.

Uncle Brendan begins by rehashing David's first night in town. He also mentions a threatening note, a choice little detail David had previously left out of his narrative.

Brendan's voice has a soporific quality, and he rants on about David's importance to the pack and how he shouldn't put himself in danger and *blah blah blah*. From nowhere, Brendan pulls out a gun, but my reflexes are slow.

Then he shoots me, and everything gets slower still.

"What the hell did you do?" David leaps to his feet and heads for me, stopping only when his uncle makes him a target.

"Nothing permanent, unfortunately." His uncle sneers the words, his manicured hands holding the gun steady. "He's still with us. He just can't move."

That's the Lord's own truth. My limbs are heavy, stiff. I couldn't have moved if the walls came caving in on me.

"We need to talk to David privately, so you can wait here while we go upstairs."

"No." David speaks with calm determination. "Anything you need to say to me can be said in front of Trajan."

His uncle aims the gun at me again. "The first dose will wear off, but a second dose might not have such a happy outcome."

David grimaces, plainly unhappy with this turn of events. I'm in no condition to deliver wisdom, but I might have told him that if you want to take over the pack, here's your chance. Instead, he gives his uncle a long, hard stare, and capitulates.

The group of them surround David and file out. There's a disturbing undercurrent of excitement among the men who are supposed to be his family, his pack.

David is in trouble. Big trouble.

As soon as the door is closed behind them, I struggle to move my right hand. Breathing is hard. My chest is heavy and my limbs feel like lead, but if I can get to my cell phone, I can send Sheena a text.

Either they didn't correctly calibrate the dose of whatever they shot me with, or rage is a powerful antidote, because I manage to drag out my phone.

Upstairs.

That one word is all I can manage, but it should be enough.

Getting my phone back into my pocket takes some concentration. Sheena pops her head through the door, but my half-assed gesture toward the ceiling sends her off again. It's a good ten minutes before my body recovers enough to take a step. I stagger into the hallway. It dead-ends in a door about thirty feet to my right. Every step makes the next one easier, and if I'm not moving with vampire speed, at least I'm moving.

The door opens into a stairwell, the industrial kind with perforated metal risers and gray paint. A man's suit coat is draped over the railing leading to the floor above me. Dark blue. I catch the odor without touching it. David, but wilder. He must have stripped so he could shift.

Which means it's not a real emergency, because he was still worried about his clothes.

Climbing the stairs, my pace slows. The effects of the drug are fading, but lifting my feet takes work. Each step echoes, and I'm filled with the sense that there's something waiting for me. I taste the air. Cocoa butter from Sheena's skin lotion, as familiar as my own scent. Wolf.

I reach the landing for the third floor and keep going. Every instinct is aiming me up. I stretch my senses, touching on a frantic heartbeat. *Up.*

Moving methodically, I reach the third floor. The landing is a small space, maybe eight feet square. There's a narrow window set high in the wall, letting in the fractured glow from a nearby streetlight. A single door separates me from…whatever.

Something thumps on the other side of the door, and a low growl crawls over my skin. Tension spurs my hunger. My mouth waters in anticipation of sweet, salty blood.

Slowly turning the knob, I nudge the door open just far enough to catch a glimpse of the scene beyond. The room is a single large open space, an empty warehouse with windows along each wall. In the center, David and Sheena are standing back to back; well, Sheena is standing and David is on all fours. They're surrounded by his uncle and cousins and a tall, rangy wolf.

David's wolf is just as big and dark as I remember, and when anyone moves, David's lip curls in a sotto voce growl.

"You're being an idiot, David," his Uncle Brendan says, earning himself another subsonic growl. "Just sign the form."

Sheena snorts. She's got a dagger in one hand and a pistol in the other. Her black clothing is dark enough to suck up most of the light in the room. "Have you met David before? No way he's gonna do something he doesn't want to do."

No one notices my arrival, though David immediately homes in on my presence with a subtle shift of his head.

They say a vampire fights better if he's fed. I've never had to prove the corollary—that he fights best when he's hungry. And I am definitely hungry.

The others are jawing, moving closer to David, closing in. One young punk is still carrying a clipboard and pen, as if he'll somehow be making a wolf leave his paw print on whatever document they're after him to sign.

The rangy wolf has singled Sheena out, and she cuts loose with a warrior yell. It takes either titanium balls or a heavy helping of stupid to go up against an Amazon, and she's holding him off with a dagger and a scowl.

David's crouched on the floor, his low growl reverberating throughout the room. Another cousin—*Jesus, how many cousins does a guy need?*—has aimed a gun at David, right between his eyes.

Without thought, I dive into the mix, knocking the two-legged wolf with the gun off-balance. He shoots, the bullet lodging into the floor at David's feet, but he doesn't go down. Before I can wrestle his gun away, he takes another shot, pinging David in the haunch. My vision turns red, and I knock him out with one heavy fist.

Rather than slow David down, the bullet to the butt seems to convince him that these assholes mean business. David leaps, landing on Mr. Clipboard and getting a mouthful of his throat.

"No. Don't. He's pack." Uncle Brendan stands in the doorway as if he's ready to take off if things get really nasty. *So much for the pack enforcer.*

David shakes his head, worrying the guy's flesh.

The tallest of the two-legged wolves hauls off his own jacket as if he's getting ready to shift. "Seriously, David. If you kill him, it'll be *beurtielung*. You know that."

Beurtielung. The werewolf equivalent of a trial—without the impartial jury.

"Never. Stop. Hunting. You." The guy on the floor rasps the words, his cold gaze making a promise. "And when you're a lone fucking wolf, you'll be stuck on two legs, and it'll be even easier to take you down."

There's a pause, as if the whole group needs to process the threat that's just been made. They're talking about cutting him out of the pack, and then killing him. *So much for pack loyalty.* I take advantage of the lull to speak up. "If the rest of you guys take off, David'll let him up."

David's eyes flash, and I nod my head, hoping he'll understand what I'm after. "David's not going to sign anything, but he won't kill anybody either." I scan the room, deciding who to grab first if things go south. "Now get out of here before we get arrested for trespassing."

From the way Sheena's eyebrow rises, I can tell my attempt at a threat might not be the most intimidating thing ever, but it's all I've got. Killing half a dozen werewolves would spark a war none of us really want.

The shifted wolf backs away and the rest take baby steps toward the door. Brendan mutters a curt "let's go," and they all take off, pounding down the stairs. The room is empty of wolves—except for David and the guy he's pinning—and David lets go of the guy's throat, keeping one big paw on the center of his chest. The guy starts spouting bullshit about crime and punishment.

David leans forward till they're all but nose to nose. David growls. Mr. Clipboard buttons his lip. David snarls. The guy is barely breathing.

David swipes his paw across the guy's chest, leaving a trail of torn fabric and blood. The guy scrambles up, looming over David as if he's going to start something up again.

I remind him that he's outnumbered. "He might not kill you, but I didn't make any promises."

The guy glances from me to David. "Arrogant fucker." He spits the words, then takes off after his friends. I'm not sure who he's aiming the comment at, but it doesn't really matter. David and I are both pretty arrogant. The guy leaves, and that's what's important.

I follow him through the door, stopping at the top of the stairs. I listen hard to make sure they're really gone.

I'm also giving David a chance to shift back in private.

"Think they'll wait at the bottom?" Sheena comes up behind me and leans close enough to rest her chin on my shoulder.

"Don't know." I shift my weight, and she steps aside to give me space. Though we managed to clear the room of obvious threats, we're still not safe. They could tag us at my car or follow us out of here. "We need to get far away until we figure out what's going on."

A blast of heat and light from behind my back tells me David has shifted back to his human form. He's hunched over, gripping his ass cheek where a red mark is all that's left of the bullet wound. "Ryan shot me." He doesn't straighten, doesn't raise his eyes from the floor. "My fucking cousin shot me."

My bones are telling me we need to buy some time. I raise my chin at Sheena. "We need to get out of town."

She shrugs. "I know a place."

CHAPTER EIGHT

This is the kind of place they shoot horror films in, you know?"

David drops his cigarette butt in an empty beer can. He's sitting on the porch of our tiny cabin in the woods, somewhere near Idyllwild. The place has a kitchen, a bedroom, and a closet that locks from the inside. It's not perfect, but I figure we're only going to be here for a week or so.

Just long enough for the dust to settle.

"But then I'm sleeping with a vampire, which already has its horror movie connotations. At least out here, you're less likely to get shot again." He grins at me, because he knows it's still too bright for me to come outside and teach him a lesson in respect. Even though the sun's dropped behind the trees and left us in a pool of shade, my skin heats if I get too close to the door. And it's not the good kind of heat David gives me.

He's dressed in worn jeans and a lavender tee, his hair falling around his face because he hasn't bothered with product. I like it that way. It's sexy. In fact, I like it so much, I want him inside.

I get as close to the doorway as I can, then stop and laugh at myself. Wasn't so long ago I was ready to make a leap into the sun, and now I'm sweating when my toes edge to near the light. "Get in here, puppy." I add some snarl so he'll know I mean business.

He stands, smooth and graceful, the jeans pulling across his thighs and giving me nasty ideas.

"Sheena's not going to be here for an hour or so," he teases, running a hand over his tight belly. We both know I've got my friend's schedule committed to memory. She's been our primary source of news, new burner phones, and food — In-N-Out Burgers for David and bank blood for me.

I still won't feed from him, which still pisses him off. I tell him it's the phase of the moon. He rolls his eyes at that. He's also learned that not all of his pack mates can be trusted, a hard but valuable lesson.

He comes closer, and I back away from the doorway's glare. Even without his makeup and hair product, he smells good, sweet and healthy.

I get my arms around him and pull him close. "What are we going to do for that hour, do ya think?"

"Hmm." He ruts easily against my thigh. "I could come up with an idea or two."

I lift, and he takes the hint, wrapping his legs around my hips. From here, I can kiss him without bending down, so I do, deep, possessive kisses that get us both revved up. His dick is hard against my belly. "Trajan," he sighs, and I lose it completely.

We're both crazy, really, because soon we're going to have to leave this grubby little cabin in the mountains, and out in the real world, weres and vampires don't mix.

But we're not leaving yet.

I haul him into the bedroom. He slides down my body, and we both make short work of our clothes. I could look at him forever, his body glowing golden in the fading light. He bounces onto the bed, spread out for me, his dick hard, his cheeks flushed. I crawl over to him, going belly to belly, grasping both our cocks with one hand.

There's lube, but I'm too eager to reach for it. I want the heat of his body, the rub of his iron-hard cock next to mine. We're both thrusting, sticky with his sweat. We don't talk about this thing between us. We just take each other, night after night, waiting to see what happens next.

It doesn't take long for him to come, and the slickness of his release sends me right behind him. I'm pounding hard, my focus drawn down to this one thing, the heated pleasure between us. My release catches me off-guard. My body locks, and then I'm falling, David's soft laughter carrying me down to earth.

"Fuck you," I whisper, my forehead pressed against his neck. The restraint required not to sink my incisors into his flesh comes close to ruining the moment, and I roll to the side.

"Later." He cuddles in next to me. "Even you need time to recover, Tony my boy."

"That's fine, puppy." I pat his thigh.

"I talked to my sister."

Shit. So much for postcoital bliss. I stifle a groan and give him a "go on" gesture.

"There's no way she's on Uncle Brendan's side. No way. I trust her more than I do any of the others, and she'll stir up trouble if she doesn't hear from me."

"All right." I hope he's right about trusting his sister.

"Besides, Sheena's bringing me a new phone, so she can get rid of this one."

Another day, another burner. "Sure."

"I asked Abby to call someone at the university and withdraw me for next quarter."

"David." This is a big deal. I roll up on my side, facing him. We'd agreed to stay underground until we knew what was going on. I'd hit up the bank before we left LA, so we're flush for a while. Not that there's anyplace to spend money around here.

"Are you sure?" I meet his gaze. Turns out he'd lied about the contacts. His eyes really are as blue as the sea.

"Uncle Brendan wants to cut me out of the pack, and since he lost the first round, he'll hit harder next time."

"And I suppose it would be too easy to talk to your father."

"He might already know."

Ouch.

"About the only person I know for sure isn't trying to get me is the dead guy I'm fucking."

A real hero would say something dramatic, promising to protect him with body and soul. Instead, I say, "Oh, I'm trying to get you all right" in my best gangster drawl and kiss him again.

Soon we'll grab my Escalade from its hiding spot on an old forest service road and head back into the city. We'll figure out how do to an end run around his uncle and get David back to his real life. And somewhere along the way, I'm due for a conversation with my not-dead ex.

This thing with David won't last—can't last—

but right now, pressed against him belly to belly, he's everything I want.

I might not be able to say the words, but I vow to do whatever it takes to keep him safe.

Part Two: Golden Wolf

Chapter Nine

David

To tuck or not to tuck?

Not really a question. I turn sideways in the crappy mirror, an antique medicine cabinet with a thin band of chrome framing the crackled glass. All I see is a skinny werewolf with a thing for dressing like a girl. I mean, I've had two bodies since I was a kid. Maybe sometimes I wish was built like Scarlett Johansson, but this right here is not just a rebellious phase, thank you very much. Shifting taught me to be suspicious of limits.

Standing on tiptoe, I get a warped profile shot. My little silver mini doesn't leave much to the imagination, and while tucking would smooth out the front, if I package the jewels, any excitement and I'll be in serious pain.

And Tony-the-hot-vampire can be *very* exciting.

Dad insisted on hiring me a bodyguard, and now I'm stuck with him. Trajan — I call him Tony just to fuck with him — is not my type, but he's not ugly, either. And not straight. The opposite of straight, in fact. I'm not going to be losing my heart to a vampire, but since my vacation turned to shit, at least I'm getting regular sex. Very regular sex.

Even so, I'm not sure I should stick around. For now, we're together until Trajan decides I'm safe, and while I kind of hate relying on him, my big attempt at self-sufficiency didn't work out so well. I'm an alpha by nature, though, so waiting around for anyone's permission sucks.

Maybe I would be better off on my own.

Without answering my own question, I fumble through my pouch of lipsticks, happy it's here and not in Sheena's storage locker with the rest of my stuff. Carting two oversized suitcases and a messenger bag full of makeup and hair product all the way up here seemed like overkill, so I consolidated and stashed the rest. Ever since my uncle showed me how things really stand, we've been hiding in a cabin in the woods, about two hours out of Los Angeles. Trajan's friend Sheena's the only one who knows we're here. She's an Amazon, at least a foot taller than me, and I wouldn't want to take her on in a fight. Every couple of days, she brings food and plastic bags of blood, even though Tony-the-dumbass could feed from me if he wanted to.

Anyway, Sheena's our link to the city, and to keep me from going nuts, she raided my suitcases for some makeup, a couple of cute dresses, and my Fluevog boots. Glossy black, high chunky heels, blunt toes; scoring these babies on sale might end up being the high point of my life.

I slide into the boots and zip them up. It's nearly sunset, and my new favorite vampire will be up soon. I pull out a coral lip gloss with sparkles. Nope. Too gold for the dress. I go for a fuck-me red instead, amusing myself with anticipation.

Nothing quite like leaving blood-colored smears on a vampire's dick.

The cabin is in the San Bernardino Mountains, tucked into a pocket of cedar trees, Douglas fir, and ponderosa pine. The March air is brisk despite the fading sunshine, but I'm a damned werewolf, so I don't care. I want a cigarette, but if I smoke in the cabin, Trajan'll bitch, and anyway, I want to fix my makeup more.

When the sun sinks behind the tallest trees, the light in the cabin goes from daytime to dusk in about three minutes. I can see pretty well in the dark—not as good as a vampire, but close—but

I've just made a swipe with the red color over my lower lip when the sun checks out.

Lipstick is fussy work. I reach for the light switch, but my momentum is halted by a sound. The scrape of tires on a dirt road.

Sheena?

She'd shown up before lunch and left within twenty minutes. Said she had to be back in the city by four. No reason for her to have turned around.

I don't touch the switch.

The darkness thickens around me. I'm in six-inch heels and a skirt so short, my bits hang to the hem. Not fighting clothes, and there's no way in fuck I'm going to ruin these boots by shifting in them. The cabin's small—two rooms and a closet. Tray has the closet door barred from the inside, and it won't do me any good to try to wake him from his death sleep.

I slide out of the bathroom. Under the bed, there's a shotgun. I crouch, reach, come up again armed and, despite the heels, dangerous.

The front door is the only way out, and it's locked. I wait in the main room, finding a shadow where I can watch the porch. A car rolls up the drive. Not Sheena's silver truck. A sedan, dark gray. No headlights, despite the gloom.

The car stops, the driver gets out, and I flip the gun's safety. He's tall, broader than Trajan, and he moves deliberately, like he knows where he's going and who he's going to see. His footsteps are heavy on the wooden porch. The door rattles under the force of his knock.

He moves past my line of sight. The only sounds are the soft moan of a breeze through the evergreens, the crackle of grit under his shoes, and the heavy throb of my heart. The door handle jiggles, and I twitch, despite my efforts to stay calm. I only have to shoot if someone comes through the door. I raise the shotgun. Really, I could go either way. I don't like killing people, but right now I pretty much only trust the vampire and the Amazon.

Shit. There's a bad joke in there somewhere.

A series of clicks, and the handle turns. Despite my Fluevogs, the urge to shift comes close to wrestling away my control.

I raise the shotgun, slow, widening my stance, channeling my inner Black Widow. The door swings open. I sight down the barrel.

"Trajan?" The voice is soft, husky, warm where it brushes over my skin. I don't respond, my focus balanced between the man in the doorway and the dark closet door.

"Hey, it's me."

Me? Who? What the hell?

He steps into the room, and though I may regret it, I don't shoot. I can tell when he sees me. His posture stills, hardens, and he reaches for his inner pocket.

"Don't." I whisper the word, but he does stop.

"David? David Collins?"

I stay silent, busy cataloguing every detail. His smoky scent. Indeterminate eye color. Hipster beard. Curly brown hair. "Brown" isn't quite right, but it's too dark to get more specific. His single-breasted suit jacket fits him well, and he's wearing it over jeans. So, money, but casual about it. I'd need a better look at his shoes to confirm that impression.

"You two need to move." He shifts his weight, keeping his hands where I can see them. "I don't how yet, but this place has been made. When Trajan gets up, you need to go." He steps out onto the porch. "I'd offer you a ride, but…"

I growl in response.

"That's what I figured. Just tell *mo shiorghrá* what I said," —he fades into the darkness—"and I'll see you both back in the city."

By the time Trajan opens the closet door, I've changed out of my dress and Fluevogs and am wearing an old pair of sweatpants and nothing else. All my stuff is packed. I'd have packed his, too, if he hadn't locked it in the closet like a paranoid bastard. I'd also sent Sheena a one-word text.

Tuna.

It's the code word we'd agreed on for emergencies, and absolutely not a slam on her sexual orientation.

Trajan comes into the cabin's main room, his gaze darting between my bare chest and the suitcase by the door. "What's up?"

"We had a visitor." I stuff the last bag of blood in his cooler and zip it shut. "Someone who smells like smoke and called you mah heergrah, or something like that."

"*Mo shiorghrá.*" Trajan uses a more guttural accent and his always-pale skin turns sheet white. His eyes are sleepy, his hair is hanging at angles, and he's about as cuddly as a teddy bear in bondage gear.

"Someone you know?"

He doesn't really need to answer. The crease in his brow and the brackets around his mouth speak of loss, sadness. Whoever this guy was, Trajan knew him and probably loved him. I stifle the whimper of jealousy before it can really get started. "He said we needed to leave, that some unspecified person or persons knew we were here."

Trajan nods, still looking like he's seen a ghost.

"I packed everything into my one suitcase" — actually a duffel bag smaller than the one I take with me when I go to the gym—"and if you can carry the gear, I'll shift so I can move faster." I'm not exactly sure where we'll go, but as soon as Trajan comes out of his little funk, we can work that part out.

"I'll go get my…"

He's headed for the closet when the shooting starts.

Glass shatters and I hit the floor.

Hard.

Trajan crawls toward me on his belly. There are voices outside, yelling in a language I don't speak. Spanish? Swahili? I don't even know. What I do know is that if anything happens to my Fluevogs, a bad situation will turn into utter shite.

"I hear at least two of them," I whisper.

"Shh." He puts a hand on my shoulder and closes his eyes. "Two in the front, at least one behind us, and" — his brows draw together — "one down the trail a bit."

"Are any of them your boyfriend?" I don't even know why I sound so bitchy. It's not like I've got any claim on Salvatore-the-vampire.

His hand falls away. "Shut up."

Another bullet careens through the broken glass where our front window used to be, slamming into the wall over my head. "Maybe it's your ex-boyfriend. I don't know. The one who stopped by earlier." I guess I get mouthy under pressure.

Trajan doesn't respond, and I'd say he's taking the high road, except both of us are kissing the linoleum. Things get quiet outside, so I ease up on my elbows. He jerks me down.

"We're going to the bedroom." His voice is hot and hard, and I spout an inappropriate giggle.

"This really isn't the time, Guido."

"Shut. Up." He grabs my arm so hard, I wince. "I'll open the window, then I want you to shift and run. Keep to the shadows until you hit the trees."

There's only about twenty feet of scrubby grass between the house and the forest, so I should be able to get by one guy without too much trouble. Still, that leaves my favorite vampire dealing with three, or maybe four, armed men. If they're really men. I inhale as much air as my anxiety-twisted chest cavity can hold.

"Elf." I roll the scents around on my tongue. "And phouka."

"Doesn't matter. I'll slow them down, then track you."

Footsteps pound across the front porch, which keeps me from begging him to bring my boots when he runs. Instead, I thrust the shotgun into Trajan's hands. He hasn't wandered around much outside, but a couple of times during his death sleep, my wolf scouted the area. "There's an old shack on top of the ridge behind us, about a quarter mile south of here. Look for me there."

Someone hammers on the front door. We scramble into the bedroom, and as soon as he gets the window open, I shift. I manage to stifle most of the heat and light, even though it burns like fuck. Anyone outside couldn't have seen more than the glow from a cell phone, and even then for only a second. I nudge him with my muzzle.

"David…" His voice cracks, like he really cares.

I pause, coiled for the leap that will take me outside.

"Be careful."

You too. I leap out the window, land lightly in the dirt, and take off.

Normally, my wolf thinks in broad strokes. Run. Fear. Cold. Except tonight. All I can think about is that tiny crack in Trajan's voice when he said my name.

Oh no, I am not falling for a vampire.

My fur is dark gray, almost black, and once I hit the shadows, I'm difficult to see. I keep moving. I smell danger and fear, spread out instead of focused on one spot. I don't stop, I don't look back, and I don't get hit by a bullet.

I don't even pause when an explosion behind me sends a ball of fire into the sky. Jesus fuck, I hope Trajan got out of there.

After ten minutes' hard running, I reach the top of the ridge. The night smells like smoke. One of the lookout towers must have seen the flames, because the breeze carries a distant siren.

Fear.

Cold.

Guilt.

I slow to a trot, heading south to the old shack. Why the hell had I run? I should have stayed. Helped. *Damn.* I slow down further. When I'm the Alpha, I'll need to give directions, not leave my friends stranded.

I tag that thought for later, when I have the brains to figure things out.

I come to an old cedar, split nearly in two by lightning, the bark scorched and splintered, the dead half flopped over on the ground. I test the air. The shack is near.

And so is the sound of hoofbeats.

I stop in the shadow of the broken tree. Poised. Angry. A large black horse trots up from the direction of our cabin. The wind is behind me, so I can't catch his scent, but no normal horse would be following a wolf after dark. I'd guess either shifter or phouka. I bare my teeth in a growl that even I can barely hear.

He stops, shaking his mane, exposing his throat. I snap my jaws. That's what I'd aim for. The throat. He paws the ground. Twice. Three times. If this is a code, I don't speak it.

Our standoff lasts…some time. My wolf doesn't carry a watch. I mostly bristle and growl, and the phouka stamps and shakes his mane. Then the crash of heavy feet through the underbrush interrupts us, and he takes off at a gallop.

I crouch, ready to chase.

Heavy breathing, lots of effort, but downwind so I can't catch the scent.

Wait.

Recognition kicks me in the belly. It's Trajan.

He's empty-handed, his clothing is charred, and I squash the impulse to throw myself in his arms. Even my wolf knows leaping at an injured vampire is dumb. Instead, I bark. He stumbles to a halt. The skin of his arms and hands is a fiery red, his cheeks are hollowed, and he smells like smoke and burnt meat.

"Fucking elves," he mutters, and his knees give out.

I shift, because the wolf can't help him now. It's barely ten o'clock, and the air is close to freezing. Even my werewolf ass will notice that kind of cold sooner or later. "Is there anyone coming after us?"

"Nope."

I debate telling him about the phouka. I probably should, but I can do it later. If the horse comes back, we'll hear him before we see him, and I'll shift. First priority, though, is getting Trajan back on his feet. We have about eight hours till he either needs to be in a vampire-safe room or dug into the earth.

And right now, he is messed up.

He hasn't moved since he hit the ground. Why is there a "we" anyway? I could shift again, and run, and if ol' Tony-baby fries at sunrise, it won't be my problem. I can even put together a reasonable argument, saying the only reason he stood up to my uncle was knowing my father'd kill him if he didn't.

Except, what kind of person dumps an injured ally, especially one who got hurt saving their ass? A shitty person. That's who.

Besides, I've still got *vampire bite* on my bucket list.

I get down next to him and shake his shoulder. He groans, his flesh cold as death. "Come on, Tony. Rise and shine."

His head wobbles, and with a grunt, he digs his fingers into the dirt.

"Yeah, baby. See if you can sit up." I put an arm around him and help. He ends up sitting. I'm carrying most of his weight, but that's okay. I bring my wrist in range of his teeth. "You're so cold, Trajan. Feed some, and then we'll get out of here."

He grabs my forearm with a grip so tight, it's like his hands have turned into claws. "No."

"Come on, dude. Don't be an idiot." He's freezing, he's injured, and we've got to move. Feeding only makes sense.

"Get me…" He rasps the next word into the dirt.

"What?"

"Something. An animal." A rough cough stops his words. "Please," he whispers.

"Oh for fuck's sake." This is crazy. No, wait. We've gone past crazy into some alternative reality. Tony would rather feed from a rat than from me. I shut my eyes and bite down on some really unkind words. The fastest way out of this mess is to get him on his feet, and if there's some magic vampire provision against feeding from wolves, I'll just have to deal.

Okay. I lower him and scan the area. There's stuff scuttling around out there, easier for my wolf to catch than me. The wolf perceives all living things, picking up their scent and quivery pulse. Other weres ping like a burr in my fur. Pack calls to my soul.

Shifting back and forth is exhausting, but I guess I'll be able to sleep when Trajan is tucked away. I poke him. "I'll be right back."

He grunts. My bones are weary, but I squash my bitching and shift. I don't bother stifling the heat and the light. I can't.

My senses snap into place. The dark is brighter. The breeze tells the story of every life it's touched. The ground echoes with footsteps. I trot around the broken tree, past a mound of huckleberry, then back around, widening my circles until I almost trip over a goddamn raccoon.

A raccoon.

Peering through its black mask, it rises on its haunches, little black hands curled against its chest. Its snarl is meant to be fierce. My wolf is not impressed.

Not a fair fight. Not a fair fight at all. I snatch the creature, break its neck, and run back to Trajan. Tossing the masked bandit within his reach, I turn my back. He groans. There's a scrape. A slurp. Then he strains. Gags from someplace deep. Vomits. I don't turn around.

More slurping. More retching. The process continues well past when I'm ready to hurl right along with him. Finally he rises, his footsteps scuffing through the dirt.

"Do you think we can make it past the cabin?" he asks. "There's that hotel about two miles down the road."

I glance at him, making no move to shift. If he leads, my wolf will follow.

I wake up next to a dead guy. A resourceful, persuasive dead guy, who scored us a hotel room despite looking like a burned-out bum with a large "dog" at his side. I'm calling him Rocky now. Because raccoon.

Our hotel room is small and barely clean. It smells like mold and old cigarettes, and it beats the hell out of the great outdoors. I might be a wolf, but sleeping in the dirt sucks.

I can't remember if I shifted before I fell asleep or passed out and then made the change. Trajan pulled the drapes, locked the door, and covered himself completely with the mottled orange bedspread. I'm lying on top of the spread, naked and starving and pretty much alone.

Dead guys don't make the best company.

For one slamming second, I'm lost without the pack. They've always been around, either in my home or in my head. I might have lived in a dorm at school, but I texted my cousin Marcus half a dozen times a day, and my sister twice as often. We were bound by more than blood.

Trust is built into the bedrock of the pack, which is why I didn't stand my ground when Uncle Brendan escorted me out of the conference room. The memory sends a flare of embarrassment across my skin, though I could be just chapped from this cheap-ass bedspread.

The pack's Delta, our enforcer, had asked me to meet him, and his deputies—including Marcus, ffs—caught me off guard. I may never really get over having Ryan shoot me in the ass. The memory catches me a hundred times a day, and every time, it's like a punch to the belly. I should have stood up to Uncle Brendan. I should have stood up to them all.

Because in the mix of scents that Trajan brought with him out of the burning house, there was wolf. And it wasn't from me.

Fortunately, a cell phone's chirp drags me out of the latest chorus of *Isn't David an Idiot*. I pry my eyelids open. The room is dim, with just a skinny line of yellow framing the window. It takes some fiddling, but I manage to turn on the squat little lamp in the bedside table. Its twin sits on the table by Trajan's head, and underneath the lamp, I catch the red flash from the phone.

Moving hurts, but nothing that a couple of downward dogs won't cure. I may well be the only werewolf who likes yoga. I don't know. I haven't asked around. I check the phone, and it's a text from Sheena, asking what the hell is going on. Trajan's lying there like a corpse, shrouded in orange, and I reply to Sheena because it's going to be a while till my favorite raccoon fiend wakes.

They tried hard but they didn't get us.

I only had to wait a few seconds for her to respond.

WTF?!!!

Instead of texting her, I call. "Can you talk?" I ask as soon as she picks up.

"Tell me what's going on." Her words are clipped, harsh, the kind of no-bullshit attitude I can deal with.

I give her the bullet points: the visitor, the shooting, the explosion. I skip the raccoon. "And now he's dead in the bed, and I'm naked."

She doesn't answer right away, and I get distracted by a bag of corn chips, a package of tiny chocolate donuts, and a Mountain Dew. *And* a pack of smokes. Damned if Rocky hadn't thought of everything.

"The only way anyone could have found you is by following me."

Sheena interrupts my scavenging. Her conclusion is obvious, and one I've obviously been avoiding. I mean, Trajan trusts Sheena, so I trust her. Whether someone followed her or she sent them, I can't deny we got set up.

I stuff my mouth full of chips as if somehow the crunching will help me come up with a plan. When Trajan rises, we need to move along, and though it would help if I had a pair of jeans, I can always shift. Not boasting, but most wolves can't go back and forth more than once in a day. Mine can. It almost makes up for being continuously underestimated.

I end the call, promising only that Trajan will be in touch later. I finish off the chips and donuts, wash them down with Mountain Dew, light up, and resolve to spend the afternoon thinking things through. Trajan will bitch about the smoke, but I need to reevaluate my approach. My father wants me to be the family pack's alpha. Might be time for me to start acting like it.

CHAPTER TEN

It's hard to win an argument when you're naked. Especially when one look at the dude you're arguing with gives you a semi. I have a towel around my waist, left over from my shower, but there's only so much cheap terry cloth can hide.

I'm in the doorway to the bathroom, hanging on to the towel with both hands. Trajan's sitting on the edge of the bed, looking all bulky and sleepy and hot. His shirt sleeves are scorched black, the cuffs burned away, and there's a splatter of raccoon gore down the front.

He's flipping his cell phone around like he can make it play back the conversation I had with Sheena.

"I didn't tell her where we were." I keep insisting, and he keeps stabbing with me with his vampire stare.

He opens the phone—because of course it's a flip phone—and runs his thumb over the numbers. "You're too smart to have done otherwise."

Wait. A compliment? I try to parry his stabby stare with a helping of wolf glare, but my stomach rumbles instead.

"Didn't you eat?" He scans the room, and I have to stifle a snicker. Only the bottle of Mountain Dew is still sitting on the table.

"Yes, a couple of hours ago. The snacks were awesome, though."

A worried crease between his brows softens his glare. So much obvious concern turns me on. *Fuck.* Everything about Trajan Gall turns me on. It's like in a week, he's trained me so that one brush of a hand through his thick dark hair has me salivating like Pavlov's dog.

And yes, I do always think about sex. I'm twenty-two. It's my life.

"We'll have to get you something else."

Yes, yes we will. "And you're going to need to feed, too, Rocky."

The glare is back, shutting down any hint of concern. "Sheena wouldn't give us up on purpose." He says it flatly, as if it's the one fact he can hang on to and I should probably go with the flow on the subject change.

"But someone figured it out," I say, going along with him even though I usually suck at taking hints. His gaze caresses my bare chest. "Stop that." I give him a profile view, but there's not anywhere to hide when you're naked. "So…" Because two can play the subject change game. "I think we should go back to LA."

Trajan jerks like I've flicked him between the eyes. He doesn't speak right away, holding on to his strong, silent type image. He doesn't say no, though, so I take the opportunity to give him some bullet points. "Look, odds are that Uncle Brendan's little 'sign the severance contract' party and all the various life-threatening events are related. He's determined to get rid of me, one way or another." Chicken skin crawls up my neck at the memory of the guns and the bombs. "We need to figure out a way to shut him down, and we can't do that hiding in the woods."

He rubs his chin, gaze fixed on the ratty tan carpet. "Well…"

Ready to push the issue, I cross the room and straddle him, climbing up high on his thighs. I run my hands over his upper arms, which leaves the towel basically draped over my lap.

"Don't." He flinches under my touch. "I'm foul."

"You are pretty rank." I keep up my massage. "'S okay, Rocky. If we can't hide in a place as big as Los Angeles, California, we deserve to get caught."

"Hm." Tentative, he slides both hands under the towel. "I don't know." He grabs me, digging his fingertips into my thighs hard enough to hurt, then flips us both so I'm on my back on the bed, he's plastered to my front, and the towel's a fading memory.

Holy fuck, I love it when he tosses me around, but for once, I can't let myself give in to him. I squirm, trying to get away, but he catches hold of my wrists. He grinds against me, the thick seams of his jeans giving my erection a reason to grow.

"I'm thinking I'll shift." I gasp the words, determined to keep us on task. "Since I can't very well hike naked to where you parked the Escalade."

"You should wait here. I'll get the car, get our stuff out of storage, then come back for you." He nuzzles my neck.

As if his breath's going to distract me. "No. I will not be left behind." Every so often, I have to remind people of who and what I am. He may be a bossy vampire, but I'm the son of the Alpha.

He freezes, likely affected more by my tone than my words. "If I do not keep you safe," he says, murmuring the words against my skin, "then my life is forfeit."

"And if you leave me here alone" —I force him to stare at me so he'll know I'm telling the truth— "I won't be here when you get back."

The silence between us grows, and the way he's pinning me to the bed becomes less about sex and more about domination. Not a problem. I have plenty of experience topping from the bottom.

"We're either equal partners here, or I'm out."

While he's chewing on that thought, I slide out from underneath him. He ends up sitting back on his heels on the bed. I stand on the floor next to him, lightly tracing the bulge of his bicep. "You know, your shirt looks like something from *The Walking Dead*."

He snorts and shakes his head. "That's a dumb show."

There's an argument I won't win. "When you're ready, I'll shift, but I'm probably going to need a steak sometime real soon."

His shoulders sag, and I know he's given in. I'd be happy except I'm tired and naked and shifting's going to burn like a bitch. The combination stifles my fist-pump of victory.

"We should go by the cabin first," he says, "and see if there's anything we can salvage."

"Sure. Maybe my boots made it through the firestorm."

And maybe wolves can fly.

My Fluevogs did not survive the apocalypse. My suitcase, however, did, but if shifting to my wolf had burned, shifting again so soon will feel like diving into a pool of battery acid. I opt for the wolf, rationing my energy so I don't become an even greater liability.

Because this is, without a doubt, all my fault.

Our cute little hideaway cabin is now three walls and some rubble, festooned with strands of decorative yellow police tape. We stay long enough to collect what we can, then drag everything along a narrow trail to the old Forest Service road where Trajan left his Escalade SUV. And thank the sweet baby Jesus, it's still there.

I put off the shift as long as possible, riding shotgun and pretending not to hear Trajan muttering about lupine insanity. The hum and sway of the big vehicle makes my wolf queasy. When Trajan finally pulls off the freeway, the best I can do is an irritated yip.

He parks at a strip mall, a low white rectangle with black glass and neon signs. Yum Yum Donuts. Teriyaki. $8 Hair Cuts. Words in a script I can't read. We're not far from the road, and it's not like I can shift in the car. "Hang on," he says, and climbs out.

He goes to the door between the donut shop and the hair salon, his cell phone stuck to his ear. He doesn't knock, but after a minute, the door opens. I can't see the person he's talking to, the glass door reflecting headlights from the street behind us.

When Trajan finally comes back, I'm pissed. I snap at him, and he tells me to shush. "Stone is cool." He steps to the side, putting himself between me and the street, and opens the door. "Go on. I'm going to grab your stuff, and I'll be right behind you."

Which means I have to walk into a strange place on his word alone. I growl at him, hackles bunching.

He shakes his head, a hank of hair falling into his face. "It's okay. If I was going to kill you, I'd have done it before now."

He has a point, but I still can't quite keep my upper lip from curling up over my teeth. I give him another snarl and leap out of the car. I cover the distance to the open door in about three steps. Once inside, I come to a dead halt.

A fucking troll is standing right there.

Seven feet tall, maybe 280 or 300 pounds, he's got a moon face and black hair pulled up in a knot.

I crouch, haunches shifting to find traction. Can't help myself. He's a fucking troll.

"David," Trajan snaps at me from the doorway. "Chill out. Stone is my friend."

The thing about LA is, every one of the three and a half million people in the city moved in with their own crazy traditions. I haven't been in this town long, but tripping over kelpies and cait sidhe and golems is part of the deal. But a troll? Standing in what looked like somebody's janitorial storeroom?

Not what I expected.

The door whooshes shut behind me, and I pivot, snarling. Trajan drops my suitcase, sending up a puff of smoke. "Oh for gods' sake. David, this is my friend Stone." He strides forward like he's afraid I'm going to jump at the human mountain. "Stone, this little asshole is David Collins. We need a room where he can shift"—he glares at me hard—"and I swear he's got manners when he's on two legs."

Stone chuckles, a sound that rumbles lower than the foundation of the building. "Sure, Traj." He jerks his thumb toward a doorway in the corner of the room. "My guys went home already. Just go do your thing and lemme know what else I can help with."

Wondering how I hooked up with a vampire who had a troll on speed dial, then wondering again at the craziness of the situation, I pad past both of them, refusing to skulk around the perimeter of the room. The door opens at the touch of my paw. The back room is an office of sorts, with a desk and a couch and a flat-screen TV. Porn plays soundlessly, two men working over an enthusiastic blonde. I turn my back and grit my teeth.

This is going to hurt.

Ten minutes later, I'm curled like a fetus, on fire from my soles to my sinews to the straggled remains of my expensive haircut. Three complete shifts in just over twenty-four hours could kill a wolf. Mine just got pissed, and had no problem letting me know about it, clawing at my bones like he could force me back to his form.

"Shh." I can't get my finger to my lips. Hell, I can barely pucker.

"What?"

The voice startles me, causing a flinch that brings tears to my eyes. *Fuck. This sucks.* If it's not Trajan on the other end of that word, I'm in a world of shit. Pretty much my only option is to play dead, so I do, hoping whoever it is will go away.

"David?"

Damn. It's Trajan. He's concerned. I blink to let him know I heard him.

"Stone sent a guy out for a steak. Should he bother to cook it?"

My mouth waters, and even that stings. I inhale. Just gotta get one word out. Exhale. "No." Yes would have been easier to say, but really, just give me meat.

Footsteps. Trajan comes closer. His knees creak when he squats, and a single bubble of laughter leaves my throat as a croak.

"I brought you some clothes," he says. The metal buttons on my jeans hit the floor with a click. "Can I help…?"

The phrase drifts off, as if the vampire really doesn't know what to do. Hell, I don't know what to do either. I've never actually shifted so many times in quick succession. I didn't have a choice, though, and now I'll just have to suck it up.

"Here." He wraps an arm under my shoulder. "Let me…" He lifts, setting off a round of muscular screams that damn near escape from my mouth.

I plant my teeth in my lower lip. He lays me on the couch, and a hiss leaks out, but at least I'm not sobbing.

"You want me to help you get dressed?"

No. I want you to leave me the fuck alone. My breath hitches before I can speak. "Give me a minute."

He does, standing weirdly still, because vampire. A conversation starts up in the other room. The low, rumbly voice must be the troll. I don't recognize the other. I close my eyes and just breathe. Crack a lid when I hear Trajan's voice with the others. Let myself fade until his fingertips trace lines my forehead. Cool. Comforting. Color me confused.

"Here." He taps my ankle. "Lift."

Eyes still shut, I lift one foot, and he slides fabric around it. My jeans. They stink of smoke. When he taps my other foot, he doesn't even have to speak. I lift, and he drags denim up over my knees.

"Now your ass."

I want to ask why he's being so nice to me, but instead, I lift my hips. A new scent catches my attention. Meat. My mouth waters. The wiggling and shifting feels more like stretching unused muscles than the agony from before.

Trajan tugs and adjusts, and I can't help but notice the location of his knuckles when he buttons my fly. I also can't help but notice how damned loose the waistband is. I must have lost ten pounds in the last two days, and the smell of food becomes more pervasive.

"Help me up." My lips are dry. Cracks pull open when they move, and my eyes water at the sting. "Gotta eat something."

He reaches around, his forearm solid under my shoulders. My head spins, but he gets me sitting. He sits on the couch next to me, lifts a hunk of beef from a bowl in his lap, and places it against my lips. If he didn't have a vampire's reflexes, I'd have bitten his fingers.

I chew the raw meat. Beef and blood and salt. *Best. Thing. Ever.* As fast as I swallow one mouthful, he feeds me another, until I finally catch hold of his wrist, wordlessly asking for a break.

Trajan slides close enough for his knee to rest against my thigh. "Talked with Stone while you were out. He used to date a shifter, a cat or something, and she told him she couldn't shift, go from one form to the other and back, more than once in a day."

I'm listening, but I'm also wondering if he'll let me lick the blood off his fingers.

"I figure you went to your wolf and back, what? Three times in a day and a half?"

I don't want to have this conversation. "Hey Rocky, you must be hungry, too."

"Nope." His tone should have warned me some caution was in order.

I'm not that bright, I guess. "Come on. Just drink the blood from the bottom of the bowl."

Trajan plops the bowl in my lap, stands, and crosses to the doorway. "Sheena will be here in a little while. Finish eating and come out when you're dressed."

I keep my mouth shut, strangely unhappy that my *piss him off to change the subject* strategy has worked.

"You could have died." Trajan's grimace is cold, hard. "If you could keep from taking stupid chances while my life is at stake too, I'd appreciate it."

He manages to make the act of closing the door sound pissed off, and I flop over on the sofa. I really am kind of an asshole.

CHAPTER ELEVEN

So, what are our priorities?" Sheena addresses the question to Trajan, but I'd like a chance at answering. My priorities are a shower and another couple of pounds of beef. A beer. A cig. Maybe an orgasm.

Yeah. None of that's happening any time soon.

We're sitting around a conference table in a second small office off Stone's big storeroom. The whiteboard on the wall is covered with scribbles, either a diagram for rewiring a house or instructions for performing an autopsy. Makes me curious about what kind of business he's running here.

Trajan clears his throat, drawing everyone's attention. In front of him, there's a flattened blood bag, and he's got a hint of color in his cheeks. His hair's still a mess, though.

"Someone keeps trying to kill David," Trajan says.

"That's a problem." Stone looks at me like he's trying to figure out why someone would bother.

"It's either Uncle Brendan…" I give them all a bitchy smirk. "Or else they're trying to kill you, and I'm just in the way."

Obviously ignoring me, Trajan turns to Sheena. "Have you heard anything? Anything at all?"

"Rumors of someone on a vampire hunt?" I don't really think anyone's after Trajan, but playing that card is easier than owning that my uncle wants me dead. I pick at my faded gray T-shirt, wishing all the clothes I had left didn't smell like smoke.

"So what's the deal with"—Stone looks me up and down—"him?"

"Good question." Sheena's blond hair is pulled tight in a no-bullshit braid. Her all-black outfit carries a hint of danger.

"Definite issues with his pack, but your uncle, what? Wanted you to sign a contract? That's not the same level as blowing up a cabin." Trajan has his hands clasped on the table, resting on his forearms, the whiteness of his knuckles showing he's somewhere between frustrated and angry. "I mean, those dudes outside the nightclub the night you landed weren't all that great a threat, and the hotel bomb was so weak, it had to be an attempt to fuck with us rather than do any real damage."

"What about the guy who shot at us in your condo's garage?"

The look Trajan gives me is so heavy with…something…I regret bringing the incident up. Which makes no sense. I hold his gaze steadily, willing him to explain.

"Connor," Sheena says, one quiet word sending a ripple of reaction across the table. Stone's eyebrows lift, mine furrow in confusion, and Trajan goes rigid.

"What?" Stone breaks the tension. "You got dead guys shooting at you now?" Shaking his head, the troll scoots his chair back far enough to plant his fists on his knees. His thighs are huge, his knuckles like rows of rocks. "Oh, wait. Vampire."

Trajan drags both hands through his hair, rubbing like his head hurts. "Yeah, well he's not dead." He shuts his eyes and I lose my link to whatever's going on in his brain.

"The guy in the garage looked right and smelled right," Trajan continues. "Then yesterday, he showed up at the cabin and warned us to leave, right before the shooting started."

"*Mah heergrah.*" I'm mangling the accent and don't even give a shit. "Your ex found us in the cabin?"

"*Mo shiorghrá* was his name for me, yes. No one else would use it."

Stone cracks his knuckles hard. "Fuck, man. Soul mates?"

Soul mates? Well, I guess I didn't figure Connor was calling Trajan cutie pie.

Trajan shoves away from the table and stalks out of the room. And I didn't figure Trajan for a drama queen either.

"Give him a minute," Sheena says, and I glare at her. It's not like I was going to go running after him. I drop back into my seat. *Oh…*

"So." She lets go of a breath so deep, it's almost a sigh. "Sounds like Connor is not only alive, but he's made a habit of showing up in awkward situations. Since it's not clear whether your uncle's trick and all the other incidents are related, maybe Connor's the first question we should answer."

"Yeah, man. Some of my guys probably remember him. I'll put the word out." Stone rises to his full seven-whatever feet. I glance at Sheena, not sure if I'm supposed to stand or not.

She flips me a pair of new burner phones. The dull gray devices are still in the packaging. I pry one open, then the other.

"Call me."

I start to obey her immediately, then stop and glare. She's used her dom voice on me, and I don't like it. Her expression doesn't break, though, so I go back to the phones. When I've got her number loaded in both contact lists, she rises, too.

"Tell Tray to keep in touch," she says.

I'm left alone at the conference table, with the phones and the whiteboard's weird diagram. *I bet my cigarettes are in the car.* Finding Trajan's ex may be the key to all this bullshit, but it doesn't sound like any fun at all.

We leave Stone's place without telling everyone where we're headed. Not that I recognize anything anyway. As near as I can tell, Los Angeles is an endless confederation of strip malls linked by slow-moving freeways.

We end up at a three-story walk-up Trajan tells me is in the city of Pasadena. The hotel room is decorated in shades of pink and green. Seriously. Someone back in the day made that fine decision. Now the carpet is minty except for the gray paths cut by uncountable pairs of dirty shoes, and the plaid bedspread sags in line with the mattress.

I don't care as long as there's a shower. That's my first stop. I scoop up every sample bottle of shampoo and body wash and whatever and leave Trajan to settle himself in the attached vampire room. I hope his room is orange and brown and we can have an ugly comforter contest.

After the shower, I feel slightly more human — or as close as I get. Trajan has emptied my scorched suitcase and spread my clothes all over the room, and I'm the only thing in the space that doesn't smell like smoke. "What the hell?"

He shrugs. "Gotta air things out." There's half an apology in his voice. "You should sleep. The sun's going to come up in a couple of hours, and one of us will need to stay awake." He rubs his eyes, looking as tired as I feel. "I don't want to tell anyone, even Sheena, where we are."

The air-conditioned chill battles with the exhaust-heavy air from the doorway. He's right. I'm going to have to pack in a good eight hours between now and sunrise. It's a physics problem, or something. All the drama has me wired, though. "Not sure I'll be able to close my eyes."

He moves, smooth and fast, pushing me back against the saggy mattress. "Let me help you."

"Wait."

But he doesn't wait. He tugs on my jeans. They're so loose, they slide right down. Then he slides down too, landing on his knees. I want to protest, but the best I can do is twist my fingers in his hair, holding on while he pulls my hips to the edge of the bed.

His lips trail along my inner thigh, but as my pulse races, I hear *soul mate soul mate soul mate* with every beat. He tongues my balls, sending shivers up from my belly. He's been so good. Loyal, protective, kind. And I can't figure out why.

"I'm confused." The words come out all fragile and whiny.

He sucks on a tiny bit of skin, hard enough to scratch with his incisor. After laving the nip with the flat of his tongue, he grasps the base of my shaft and gives it a stroke. "Not all of you is confused."

His eyes are dark and warm, and it wouldn't take much to lose myself in them for a good long while. *Soul mate.* "Why are you blowing me if the love of your life is out there somewhere?"

Trajan jerks away, a hank of black hair falling across his face. "Don't." His fingertips dig into my thighs.

"Don't you." I scoot my hips away from the edge. He's moved into the gray zone between "adventure fucking" and "oh shit my heart's involved" and I don't like it. "Things are complicated enough."

Because I might talk a bunch of bullshit about a guy in every orifice, but I know what it means to be deeply connected with another man. And I know how hellacious it is when things end. I may or may not have a mate out there somewhere, but he's not going to be a vampire, and I can't afford the feels ol' Tony is bringing up in me. "You chose a raccoon, Rocky." It's a lame defense, but it's pretty much all I got.

Sighing, he rests his forehead against my thigh. "I don't know what we're caught up in, David, but I don't see the harm" — he tips his head so his lips brush my skin — "in taking care of each other."

Chills spread in his wake, and my dick bobs. *Fucking traitor.* Trajan takes that as a sign and kisses his way to my bull's-eye. For a second, I worry about unruly hair, because the current shenanigans haven't left time for manscaping. In the end, though, I'm warm from the shower, and his lips are cool. The body gel sample reeks of lavender, clean and astringent in a room full of smoke. When he swallows me down, I drown in waves of relief and joy, sadness and regret.

Despite all the emotional bullshit, my dick's an iron rod. The vampire sucks, hollowing his cheeks, and I send up a keening cry. So good. He works me, bobbing and swallowing. Heat builds, coalescing between my hips and the small of my back. Part of me still hates how he gets behind my defenses.

The rest of me is ready to go off like a rocket.

I've got one hand in his hair and the other clutches the bad plaid bedspread. My hips rock in time with his motion, driving deeper and deeper. So warm. So wet. The scratch of his fangs tightens my balls. I glance down, and for one second, I see behind his walls. There's affection and confusion and white-hot desire. I can absolutely relate, and the realization is the spark that sends me off.

I let go and fly down the cataract of pleasure, my body rocked by the storm. I thrust hard, shooting down his throat. He takes it all.

I fold to the side, my cock slipping from his mouth. I've got no reserves, no energy. He helps me get my head onto the pillow and covers me up.

"I'll set the alarm," he says.

I curl up on my side, tugging the bad plaid up to my chin. I don't answer him.

CHAPTER TWELVE

Order whatever you want." Trajan's stretched across his side of the white vinyl booth.

He wants me to think he's relaxed. I'd believe him except that he's tapping the table with one finger. Tick, tick, tick, tick, tick; steady as a metronome. The menus are black and heavy, and the tabletop is covered with white linen under glass. We're at The Darden, an old Hollywood hangout. Think Gary Cooper and Rock Hudson in boxy suits, Marilyn or Katherine in silk chiffon and pearls, and Lew Wasserman chasing down a deal.

These days, the customers still talk about scripts and contracts and *what's your next project?* but they're as likely to be wearing shredded denim and a man bun as tailored trousers.

The glass globe candles are dim, the place smells like garlic and perfume, and we're waiting for Sheena. She called Trajan and said she had some ideas about Connor, and asked us to meet her here at nine p.m. It's almost nine thirty, and I'm pretty sure Trajan is losing it. *Tick, tick, tick, tick, tick.*

The waiter comes over, a thick gold septum piercing sitting oddly over her wide, Disney smile. I respond to a text from Abby, bringing on Trajan's glare. He doesn't want her to have the number of today's burner, and he refuses to take me at my word that ignoring her texts would stir up a whole lot more trouble.

Tucking my phone away, I order chicken-fried steak and mashed potatoes. My mouth waters in anticipation of the crispy fried meat, and I gulp, suddenly guilty that Trajan's only had a little stale blood since this latest round of smack the werewolf began.

To keep his mind off Sheena, I decide to talk blood. "So, if you feed from me, what's the worst thing that could happen?"

The ticking stops. He leans forward on his elbows, his flat predator's glare getting my dick so hard, I'm lucky I don't burst through my jeans.

"You. Could." He clasps his hands, as if he needs to stop himself from grabbing me. "Die."

"I figured." I scratch my chin, going for casual but not too casual. Don't want to piss him off any more than necessary. "But short of me dying, what's the worst?"

He doesn't answer, and for a moment, I'm distracted by a man in a hot pink suit. The fabric is light and shiny and he's holding hands with a woman old enough to be his mother. The look they're exchanging is absolutely not maternal. *Oh my.* I blink and turn away. "Seriously."

"We should probably talk about your uncle."

His glare sends tendrils of desire whipping over my skin. I'm kinda sick that way, and I'm tired of how he keeps dodging the blood question. "Look, if you feed from me, you know my metabolism will go off like a rocket. I'm not afraid of you hurting me."

He clasps his hands together so hard, the knuckles crack. "No."

The waitress interrupts us. She probably has trouble setting my dinner down through the layers of tension zinging around the table. I slice into my steak, trying like hell to remember some bit of vampire lore that could explain why he's being such a stubborn ass.

"Do your father and your uncle get along?" He stretches back out in the booth, obviously deciding the food is enough to keep me occupied. He starts tapping again. *Tick, tick, tick.* The edge of his nail hits the glass.

For a moment, the savory meat overwhelms me, and all I can do is chew and swallow. He waits, tapping, until I catch his gaze. "Well enough, I guess." I swirl another bite of steak through the mashed potatoes. "At least they did until Dad took over as the big, big dog."

"I don't know much about your politics. How did he become American Alpha?" Dark hair falls into his face, and the combination of red meat and hot vampire has me thinking of all kinds of inappropriate behaviors. I'm wondering what Miss Disney would think if she came back and found me under the table.

Instead of sucking, I chew and swallow. "It's like a presidential campaign. In the olden days, they had to fight it out in the ring, but too many family packs ended up without their alpha, so now it's just shaking hands and finding votes."

Trajan ponders that for a minute, then scowls and flips open his phone. "Where's Sheena?" He mumbles the words, so I don't answer. With a grimace, he shoves the phone away. "We need to find Connor, and we need to force him to tell us what he knows."

I wash down the steak with a sip of tasty red wine. "I'm sure there's a reason your ex came back from the dead just in time to warn us that our secret hiding place wasn't so secret." There's a bitter taste in my mouth that has nothing to do with the food.

Trajan's jaw clenches, cheeks hollow and cheekbones jutting, and for a moment, I can see how hungry he is. "Look," I say, "if Sheena doesn't show, we'll have to find her. You must know where she hangs out, right? And if we don't, we'll go back to the hotel and you'll feed before you lose your mind."

I lay my forearm on the table, palm up, my wrist bare and vulnerable. "We don't have to fuck if you don't want to mix things up" — though I really, really want to — "but I need you hitting all cylinders, dude."

"I am just fine." His scowl is a thing of beauty, and there's a tiny bit of acquiescence in his tone.

His hair flops forward again, and I'm glad he didn't have any product to slick it back. He's got that big Italian thing going on — the nose, the cheekbones, and underneath his jeans, the cock. I'm infatuated with that cock. I never had much appreciation for the hit man type, but Trajan Gall does it for me.

"Finish your dinner." He waves brusquely at my plate. "There are a couple of clubs we should check out before we go back to the hotel."

A skinny hipster in thick black glasses almost trips over our extra chair because he's so busy staring at Trajan, he can't walk straight. I lift my chin with as much "back off" as I can muster. I don't care that all hell's breaking loose around us.

This one's mine.

An hour or so later, we're the only men in a cramped pub in a strip mall off La Brea. The air smells of equal parts old beer and teriyaki from the plate lunch place next door. The bartender's wearing a bra and black stretch shorts, and I swear she sweats more testosterone than I've got in my whole body.

The place is empty except for a pixie at the bar who might be the bartender's girlfriend and a pack of wolves in the corner. Yeah, a wolf pack. About seven of them. All chicks. All done up in black leather biker gear. All of them glaring so hard, it feels like we're walking past a wall of pitchforks.

"Sorry, you guys are in the wrong place." The bartender's got an accent I can't place, though from up close, her sheet-white skin can't have seen the sun in a couple hundred years.

Trajan stops behind a barstool and crosses his arms. "We're looking for Sheena."

The bartender's lips thin, allowing the needle-sharp point of one incisor to show. "You're in the wrong place."

They're flinging vamp mojo at each other so hard, it's making my skin crawl. The pixie on the barstool must feel it too, because her glamour starts to crack, her gossamer wings fluttering just on the edge of my vision.

Then, because shit's not weird enough, a couple of the wolves stalk over. One's tall and lanky and the other's about my height with lots of curves, and I decide their names are Batman and Robin.

"Y'all need to go," Batman says, a magnolia lilt to her vowels.

Robin just growls.

I try to get Trajan's attention, but he's too busy glare-wrestling the bartender. The pixie's gaze is bouncing between the two vampires, and the other wolves are getting restless, belts and chains jangling. I take a deep breath. Time for the alpha to take charge.

I straighten to my full five feet five inches and let my wolf out just enough to buzz along my skin. No fur, no claws, but even without a mirror, I know my eyes have gone full lupine, amber gold with a wide black pupil.

There's a reason my family's run our pack for five generations. Power is hereditary, and while this pack's alpha might be able to keep a pack of rowdy bikers in line, my genetics say I could control every wolf in this country if I applied myself.

Robin drops first, with Batman right behind her. "Sir," one of them whispers, but I'm too busy staring down the leader of their pack to respond to them.

Between the tats and the dreads and the leather bustier, the pack leader's a walking stereotype. She comes forward and stops behind the two who are kneeling. She wants to fight, but it only takes a couple of seconds for her to bow her head. "Sir."

"What's your name?"

She lifts her head but keeps her gaze on the floor. "Lydia."

"Cool. Nice to meet you, Lydia. I'm David Collins, and my friend and I do not mean to trespass. You're the boss here, okay?"

She meets my gaze, her uncertainty apparent. I raise my hands, palms up, and tell my wolf to sit the fuck down.

"I'm nobody's alpha yet. I'm just trying to stop a fight. Obviously, you've got your little chicks' nest going on in here, no sausages allowed or whatever, and that's cool, but we're looking for our friend Sheena."

"She comes here all the time." Trajan pivots so he's standing at my elbow. "Sheena's an Amazon, blonde, works at the Rectory."

"Does that sound familiar to any of you?" I don't try to force too much authority into my tone. I want the truth, not just whatever pops into their head because I compelled them.

"She was here," the leader says, not quite up to the level of arrogance she had when she walked over. Close, though, so she heard me when I said she's the boss. And honestly, this is a parlor trick compared with what my father can do. For me, power comes shrouded in ambivalence; a useful skill, but not something I want to do all the time.

Batman lifts her chin and manages to meet my gaze. "She said she was going to meet somebody, and we saw her talking to some dude in the parking lot, so we figured that's who she meant."

The bartender smacks a rag down on the bar. "Would you guys shut the fuck up? What happens in here stays in here."

Makes sense, actually. A small place like this, with such a specific clientele, probably has to keep a pretty tight lid on things. Doesn't stop me from glaring at her, or from being surprised when she shuts up.

"What'd he look like?"

None of the weres answer Trajan, so I repeat the question.

"Didn't get a good look at him. He had brown hair, maybe about his size." Batman points at

Trajan. Her description isn't much help. Easily half the men in LA are about Trajan's size.

"What time did you see her?"

This time, I don't have to prompt them to answer.

"'Bout seven thirty." Robin's twisting her fingers together like I'm causing her pain.

Aw shit. That's not what I meant to do. Time to break up this little party. "Come on." I nudge Trajan. "Let's go."

He gives the bartender another mean look and nods to me. We head out, the swell of the wolves' voices chasing us through the door. Trajan hits his key fob, and the big SUV lights up.

"Get in," he says, all overbearing vampire.

I stifle a grin. Under the right circumstances, I can be a badass too, and I like knowing he's seen that side of me. I climb in and buckle up. "Drive on, boss man."

CHAPTER THIRTEEN

So, I don't know Trajan Gall all that well. I mean, I met him at LAX at the beginning of what should have been my one-week spring break sexcapade. My agenda was interrupted by gunshots and explosions, and Tray and I hid out after that, waiting for the crazy to fade. We were together a week, maybe ten days.

And in all that time, he never mentioned his kinky side.

I mean, my family would have a collective shit fit if I brought a vampire home, but still, how disappointing.

We pull into a parking lot outside a plain three-story stucco building. The door is wide and black, and there's no signage to identify what kind of establishment we're entering. The doorman's human, and he and Trajan bristle at each other so hard, I can smell the bad blood. Somehow we get inside, and my jaw drops past my knees.

The big room is done up in black and red and chrome. A glossy bar runs along one wall, and the strip lights shining down on the shelving make every bottle sparkle. Everything gleams except the shadowy corners. My skinny jeans aren't skinny enough. My Chuck Taylors are too flat. Hell, given the crowd, I should only be wearing leather.

Because yeah. The crowd looks like The Gap made a bondage ad. Leather chic. I'm totally underdressed. Trajan strides over to the bar as cocky as if he owns the place. Or at least like he's been there a bunch of times before.

He grabs a barstool, but I'm too excited to sit. I know we're supposed to be looking for Sheena, or maybe Connor, or something, but damn. I came to this town to get dirty, and this place—despite the cool glossy décor and the artfully distressed customers—is filthy.

Trajan's drawn some not-unexpected interest, and I lean against him so everyone knows I'm first in line. "This is crazy." I pitch my voice low, half of my attention on a couple of men sitting on a low black couch right across from us. Their relaxed sensuality fires my imagination.

So does the collar the blond one is wearing.

"Sheena works here." Trajan's not paying any more attention to me than I am to him. He's trying to catch the bartender's eye, and I'm watching the couple. The blond guy is younger, dressed in booty shorts and that collar, and his broad pecs and flat nipples are making my mouth water.

His friend is older but still trim. Distinguished. He's dressed in black, more slumming billionaire than leather daddy, and he waves at a third man who's standing near us at the bar.

Trajan picks up a conversation with the bartender, and as soon as I hear Sheena's not working, I tune out. My couple is standing now, laughing with the third man. The older man has his hand resting in the small of the younger man's back. Then the third man brushes a thumb over the younger man's lower lip, and the older man whispers something in his ear.

With a smile that tightens my balls, the younger man sinks to his knees. All around us, people are playing. There are more collars, some with leashes. Bare skin. A pretty black woman's straddling a platinum-haired man, her hips rocking steadily. But when the guy in the booty shorts kneels down, I lose sight of everything else.

I lean harder against Trajan, or maybe my knees go weak, but he reaches out and wraps an arm around my waist. He and the bartender seem to know each other pretty well, so I leave him to his private detective work and watch the scene unfold.

The older gentleman steps up and with gentle hands, he pulls the kneeling man's arms up and back, grasping him tightly around the wrists. The third man faces them, one hand on his fly. He's polished, even by Hollywood's standards. Dark hair slicked in place with product, expensive tailoring. He lowers the zipper on his trousers and draws out his dick.

He's hard, long and narrow and cut. Either I make some sound or Trajan's psychic, because the vampire tightens his grasp. My own cock is swelling, all my blood headed south, and I rub my belly against Trajan's arm. The dark-haired guy strokes his cock, brushing the tip against the kneeling man's lips. Trajan and the bartender laugh. The older man's knuckles grow white.

Then, without any more preamble, the guy thrusts his cock into the kneeling man's mouth. One stroke. All the way in. The kneeling man swallows without gagging, his nose brushing perfectly groomed pubic hair. The older guy says something, and the third guy laughs and begins thrusting.

This living porno is so hot, it might kill me dead. My hips start rocking in time, and though I'm not exactly aware of when it happened, Trajan's big hand drops down and covers my dick. Which is so hard, my jeans are excruciating. Trajan rubs, and I rock, and across from us, one guy fucks another guy's mouth while a third guy restrains his hands.

I want to be the guy on his knees so bad, I almost lose my mind.

A single tear trails down the kneeling man's cheek, but he barely gags despite the pounding.

"You want to play?" Trajan asks, as if he's read my mind without looking away from the bartender. I nod, and he slides my zipper open and wraps my cock in his cool fingers.

Holy shit. I sag against him. My dick is out where anyone can see it, so hard I could put someone's eye out. Guess I'm an exhibitionist at heart. Or maybe fucking two men at once is right at the top of my bucket list.

My belly starts quivering, the first hint that I'm getting close. The older gentlemen bends down, murmuring in the kneeling man's ear. He moans, and the guy fucking his mouth thrusts even faster.

My hips lose their rhythm, but right as I'm about to have my first public orgasm, Trajan grabs hard down at the base of my cock.

"Nope." He shoots me a glance and chuckles in the face of my whimpers. "We've got at least one more stop and no time to clean up." He shifts so he can brush my neck with his lips. I feel pressure from one of his incisors, a tiny scratch that draws every ounce of my attention. The tip of his tongue quivers against my skin, and if he didn't have a lockdown on me, I'd have shot my load right there.

He better not be making promises he doesn't intend to keep.

Trajan tucks me away and stands, and even though the trio across from us haven't hit their peak, I force myself to follow him. This visit has given me plenty of jack-off material, but I have no idea if we're any closer to finding Sheena.

Ten minutes later, we're in the Escalade, heading from North Hollywood to God-knows-where. Another club to connect with another friend.

"So you knew your way around that place pretty well."

Trajan doesn't react to my comment. His jaw is tight, his expression hidden in shadow. I keep pushing, though, because between my alpha moment, the live porno, and the interrupted hand job, I'm ready to explode.

"Do you, like, hang out there?" I can't imagine him tied up or chained to the wall or anything. No, if anything, Trajan's the guy behind the whip. This doesn't bother me at all. "Do you have one of those leather harness things?" I squirm, trying to find an angle for my dick that doesn't hurt,

He's silent for long enough that I figure he's not going to answer. We pull to a stop at a red light, and I decipher the signs out in front of a strip mall on the corner—or at least identify the language they're written in.

"Yes."

I jerk my attention back to the vampire. "You have a harness?"

"Yes, I've been to the club before. I own it." We move off in the flow of traffic. "Mostly I let the managers run things, but Sheena is a dominatrix, and she invites me when she has a sub who would benefit from my skills."

Whoa. I have no idea what that means, exactly, but I've never been more turned on in my life. "You do have special skills." Wait a minute. He won't feed from me, but he'll bite some trussed-up pigeon? Irritation kills my hard-on faster than a bucket of ice water.

"It's not what you're thinking." He brushes my chin with his knuckles.

So he's psychic now, too. "Sure."

His chuckle makes me even angrier.

"When she has a client who would benefit from exploring...other facets of his sexuality, she'll sometimes call me."

"For your magic cock?"

He laughs, and his hand lands heavily on my thigh. "You like my cock well enough."

My snotty response is lost when he gives my dick a squeeze. I grab his wrist but can't pull his hand away.

"Now, puppy" — he rubs hard — "the bartender hasn't seen Sheena since the staff meeting this afternoon, but she was said she was meeting someone at Fashion. We'll retrace her steps as far as we can and see what we see."

Made sense. Sheena supposedly has information about Connor and isn't the type to pull a no-show. Besides, Fashion's one of the clubs on my spring break wish list. I'd heard it was three levels with multiple dance floors, lots of secret corners, and an open policy. Gay, straight, human, supe; everyone went to Fashion. I wasn't dressed right, but at least I could check it off the list. And I wouldn't need to find a date while I was there, because I'd be going home with a vampire.

"From what the guy at the club said, Sheena might have been meeting Connor." Trajan still caresses my crotch, but his expression has gone distant.

"That's convenient."

"Isn't it?" He moves his hand closer to my knee. "There are a couple of vampires working security at Fashion. You can go dance while I talk to them."

More foreplay. At this rate, I'd shoot like a thirteen-year-old as soon as he gives me permission. Permission. Yeah, my experience in the land of kink is limited, but this works.

Fashion is just as glittery and shallow as the name implies. I'm absolutely going to have to come back sometime when I'm dressed to play. As it is, Trajan waves me over to the first dance floor we pass, and I dive on in. The beat is heavy, tribal, and the crowd is thick. For a second, I try to remember what day of the week it is, but it doesn't matter. At a place like this, every night's a party.

Bodies close around me, and the air is slick and sweaty. I'm not catching anyone's eye, but they're bumping me, brushing against me. Time slows down or speeds up. I can't quite tell. Someone's wearing spicy cologne. A girl dressed in '50s drag backs into me, her ass firm in her dark blue dungarees.

I let it all go, the fear, the exhaustion, the Uncle-Brendan-wants-me-gone. I know my pulse and the beat and the scents of human and were and elf. Just one big throbbing ball of life, with me at the center of it.

A body moves in behind me. A Trajan-sized body. Hands wrap around my waist, big, strong, and masculine. My eyes are shut, and if I don't smell vampire, it must be because there's too much competition.

My head tips back, resting on the vampire's shoulder. He must have found what he needed faster than either of us expected. Good. Time to fuck or be fucked.

Ready to drag him down for a kiss, I pivot and reach for his face. Shock destroys the mood. It's not Trajan. My hands close on air.

"Hello, David."

The guy from the cabin pulls me against his body. The one who called Trajan *mo shioghrá*.

Soul mate.

Connor.

CHAPTER FOURTEEN

Connor's not just dancing with me, we're belly to belly on the dance floor, his big hands around my waist, holding me close. The thing is, I don't mind at all. His scent is smoky, a little bit leather, a touch of horse. And whisky. I'm pretty sure he's the phouka I saw the night the cabin burned.

He's watching me, letting me take stock of the situation. My hands are spread flat across his chest, where I can push away. Or maybe pull myself closer. It's not like Trajan and I have a commitment.

Okay, that justification gives me a twinge, but still.

He leans toward me, his eyes burning amber in the flashing lights. I tip my chin in case he needs a kiss, but he dodges, stopping just shy of my ear.

"Good to see you," he says, his voice tripping something in my chest.

I inhale more of his smoky scent. "Surprised to see you."

My scattered thoughts are climbing out of my dick, and I realize I somehow need to get this guy to Trajan. My next logical thought has to do with Trajan's likely response to seeing his soul mate.

Probably there won't be enough room for me in that bed.

Well, damn.

It takes me a minute to wrangle my priorities. Connor keeps his hands on my hips, heavy, strong. If you'd asked me about my type before I met Trajan, I'd have sketched someone like Connor. His combination of confidence and polish pulls me in like a shift in the space-time continuum.

Though even as the mystery man draws my interest, my attraction to Trajan tethers me. The scratch on my neck from his incisor stings.

A reminder of promises made.

Dragging Connor over to Trajan will fuck everything up, from my perspective at least, but I try to do it anyway. I rise onto my toes, close enough for my lips to brush the lobe of his ear. "I have an idea." I don't really. I need to make something up on the fly. "I think" —I slide my hands down his chest and interlace our fingers— "maybe you should come talk to a friend of mine."

Because wouldn't it be wild if he and Trajan wanted to help me live out my porno fantasy?

"I don't think so." He draws his hands away, but slowly, stroking my fingers. "You and Trajan keep your heads down and you'll be okay."

He eases back a step. I grasp his shirt, crushing the silk in my grip. "You know what's going on." I jerk him closer. "You need to tell us."

"I can't. Not yet." He disentangles my grip. Something—a noise, a feel, a shift in the dense air—pulls his attention and he scans the room. Before I can stop him, he fades into the crowd still packing the dance floor.

"No." I scramble after him, but he's too fast, too determined. It's not long before I'm on a different level, a different dance floor. All alone in a crowd of strangers. I can feel eyes on me, but I don't know where they're coming from. Guys with a thing for twinks? Connor? My cousins come to finish the job?

I've got to pull it together. I'm being pummeled by scent—were, shifter, elf, human. My body's been teased and denied and I'm still queasy from shifting a dozen times in a day. I can do this, though. I straighten and scan the crowd. No sign of either the vampire or his soulmate.

At the opposite end of the dance floor, the DJ's on an elevated platform. There are dancers on either side of him, club kids tricked out in black and neon. I'll stick out, but if I can get a look over the room, it might be worth it.

I worm my way through the mass of dancers, perhaps tossing an elbow or two along the way. Scrambling up to the platform, I ignore dirty looks from the club kids. Dance. That's all I need to do. The beat finds me, and I move. Eyes brush over me, but I'm an underdressed go-go boy so it's expected.

A darkness at the edge of the room draws my attention. Trajan. He's tall enough to see over top of most people, and it's not long till our gazes cross. It's almost physical, grabbing hold of me. He dives into the crowd, and I track his obsidian hair. He's coming for me. For a moment, I lose the beat and whatever I'd felt in Connor's arms drifts away like a retreating wave.

I've done some stupid shit in my twenty-two years, but falling for a vampire has got to top the list.

My dad's already bitter because I won't give him grandchildren the old-fashioned way. There's no way he'll let it slide if I bring a vampire home. I'm already struggling to live up to his expectations. Years ago he decided I'd be the one to replace him because I'm ballsy and I can kick ass. Fighting is only one of the skills he claims I possess. I'm not sure what the others are. Like I said, it's a struggle.

He's got a woman picked out for me too, a fierce, beautiful wolf. I met Jocelyn once, and in a ten-minute snarkfest, we established a friendship and determined we'd never be married. I don't know what she's looking for in a mate, but it's not me. Maybe our fathers should mate with each other.

I haven't mentioned Jocelyn to Trajan because the whole arranged-marriage thing feels uncomfortably medieval. It makes perfect sense to a wolf. Not so much to the rest of society.

My flight of ideas is interrupted when Trajan hops up onto the ledge. The go-go dancers were barely tolerating me. He pushes them over the limit and the closest dancer gets all up in his face.

"Stop." Trajan's voice carries over the machine-gun beat. He grabs my wrist, commanding, proprietary. "Let's go."

We hop off the ledge. He's still got ahold of my wrist, and he pulls me to the edge of the dance floor. Our departure has drawn attention. Eyes. I can still feel them. I stumble after him, down stairs, through crowded hallways. By the time we reach the main entrance, I'm spent. Too much up and down. I'm craving steak.

Halfway to the Escalade, Trajan spins around. He walks backward for a couple of steps, then takes my wrist again and starts jogging. I'm too fried to get freaked out. The eyes have been tracking me for so long, I'm used to them, can barely feel them anymore.

Trajan hits the key fob. Lights flash and his SUV beeps. "There's at least two of them behind us. Get in quickly."

I do as I'm told…mostly, pausing only to taste the air. Is it Connor back there? No, not a horse shifter or a phouka. Is it? I clamber into the vehicle, unsure whether I've identified our tail or not.

He puts the car in gear, leaning over the seat, his gaze raking the darkness. I buckle in. This isn't the time for idle reassurance. The vibe is bad, like the scene in the movie where the hero thinks he's home free and Chuckie jumps out of the backseat waving his butcher knife around.

We pull out into traffic. I'm not sure where we are, nor how long it'll take us to get back to the hotel. It's three in the morning, which means we've got a couple of hours before Trajan has to be inside.

But what if they follow us? What if we can't shake them? I start marshalling my arguments. If I'm the one they're after, Trajan will just have to let me out. My chances won't be great, but better than a vampire in the sun.

He makes a quick left, and then a right. He speeds up. Slows down. I'm watching out the back window. There are no headlights matching us. He turns one more time and drives close to the speed limit.

"Would Connor follow us like that?" Apparently dodging a tail disconnected my filter.

Trajan shoots me a glance. "Connor?"

I rake a hand through my hair, pissed that it's all floppy and not held in place by product. "He was there." Trajan's expression stops me. I swallow hard and keep going. "Tonight. He came up to me on the dance floor."

Trajan tips his head to check the rearview mirror, then the side mirror. His lips are tight, like he's trapping the words inside. "You should have brought him to me."

"Yeah." Another rake of my saggy hair. The SUV's speed is accelerating. "He said we should lay low, and things would work out."

We hit a freeway on-ramp at about seventy mph. "You heard the part where we all decided we needed to talk to him, right?"

I smack the door with the side of my hand. "Guess you should have taught me the vampire mind-meld thing."

He shakes his head, not at all impressed with my snotty-brat voice. Any hope I have for raunchy fun dies a ragged death. We're doing about ninety, darting around other vehicles.

"Look." I turn in my seat so I'm facing him. "If we die on the freeway, we never will figure out what's going on, because it won't matter anymore."

He inhales, solidly aggrieved, but he does ease up on the accelerator. It's just a few more minutes till he says we're almost there. Either we weren't that far away or Tony-the-drag-racer broke more than the speed limit.

"I'm worried they're following us." Trajan mutters his concern to the hotel room door, sliding the key card into the slot. "We probably shouldn't stay here."

I tap the hall's glossy wallpaper with my knuckle. "Sun's coming up pretty soon."

He scowls at the door. I reach around him to push it open. The room is just the way we left it. Dirty mint carpet, slumping mattress, discouraging comforter. The contents of my surviving suitcase draped over every surface. The air is foul with old smoke.

"Seriously. I didn't see anyone, but what if they hit us when I'm down?" He braces himself on the plywood dresser, obviously frustrated. "Maybe we'd be better off in one of Jacques's safe houses."

Jacques. Trajan hadn't mentioned his maker in a while, and something about him tweaks my gut. Trajan and I had stayed in one of those safe houses, up in the Hollywood Hills. It'd be more luxurious than a shitty Pasadena hotel, but there are so many pieces to unravel in this mess, I'm not sure we want to be drawing any more into the mix.

"Not unless we can get in without letting him know."

Trajan gives me a measured look, and I like that he's thinking things through instead of just blowing me off. "Okay." He straightens. "Let's pack. We won't go through the lobby, and we'll use separate exits."

"Sounds good." I pretend confidence I don't quite feel. "Move the car a couple of blocks away. Text me, and I'll meet you."

There are lots of ways things could go wrong, but I jam my clothing into the duffel bag anyway. Trajan spends a few minutes peering through the gap in the window drapes, then disappears in the vampire room.

A few minutes later, we're both in the SUV, the pink-and-green hotel room fading in the distance. No one accosts us as we make our escape, and it takes most of my self-restraint not to wonder aloud if we really needed to leave.

The traffic is light, and if I close my eyes, the smell of the street drowns out the smell of smoke from my bag. When the silence starts to weigh more than I do, I break it. "Where are we going?"

"Pacific Palisades."

I squint at him, unsure of how far is too far. "We'll get there before sunrise, right?"

Headlights flash over his face, highlighting the planes and angles. He really is handsome, in a classic Italian kind of way. Against all odds, I'm still holding out a faint hope we have some fun before he crashes for the day.

I know. My priorities are screwed, right?

"It's the most remote of all of Jacques's houses." He speaks slowly, like he's still uncertain about his decision. "I think it's our best bet."

I'm going to have to take his word for it. After all, he's the one who'll burst into flames if the timing's wrong. He makes a few random turns — at least they feel random, and I assume he's trying to make it harder for anyone who might be following us — and then climbs up onto a freeway.

He's driving like a demon and the silence starts to squash me. "So..." I should keep my mouth shut. "What's up with that Connor guy anyway?"

The air between us hardens, crystalizes. I'm almost convinced he's not going to answer.

"He's dead."

Two words say so much and don't explain anything at all. The memory of Connor's hands wrapped around my ribs turn his statement to a lie. Or does it? Could he be a zombie? I mean, I would have expected less expressiveness. Less warmth. I'm still puzzling when Trajan continues.

"Two years ago, he was shot outside my club." He chews on his lower lip, and I'm torn between offering him comfort and leaving him alone so he'll keep talking.

"I saw him, David." The words ring with such anguish, for a moment I'm stunned.

Neither of us speaks, until Trajan rubs his mouth with an open palm. "We'd been together for five years, so the cops came to me to identify the body."

"Oh, man." Because when faced with real pain, I'm true to my college boy roots. I put a hand on his knee. Can't help myself.

"Yeah."

He goes silent again, and I figure touching him was the wrong idea. Even though I don't want to do anything but sympathize with him, I can't help but wonder how a vampire established enough of an identity for the cops to slot him in the next-of-kin roll.

There's a puzzle here, and I'm pretty sure I don't have all the pieces.

"Anyway." The raw edge to his voice startles me as much as the fact that he's still ready to talk. "I went to the morgue. I saw him on the slab. He was dead." He grips my wrist hard enough to hurt. "Dead."

A car comes buzzing up behind us, so close the headlights disappear from our rear window. Shit. Is this our tail? Trajan curses and changes lanes. The asshole drives on. It takes a minute or two for me to draw a deep breath.

Just an ordinary LA asshole.

The distraction gives me time to think. "I never knew a phouka could imitate death like that."

"What?"

He glares like I'm barking instead of using words, but I don't let his hit man demeanor discourage me.

"I smelled him, Trajan. The guy's a phouka."

"No." He digs his nails into my wrist. I shake my hand, trying to break free. "Connor is human."

I escape from his clutches. "Dude, he's a supe. He is. Maybe he put a spell on you or something." I mean, there had to be a reason for his state of denial.

He shakes his head, obviously unwilling to take this any further. I could tell him about the horse I saw the night of the cabin fire, but I let it go. If we ever do catch up with Connor, his nature will be made clear.

It's all pretty fucking odd, though.

I check my phone. Three thirty a.m. The sky is still uniformly black, well, dark gray, really, from the city lights. The eastern edge might be a shade lighter gray. "How much farther?"

Trajan waits a couple of beats before he answers. "About half an hour." The silence gets heavy again. I reach for the radio and find some bad pop music. Ariana Grande might make me want to stab someone, but she's better than moody vampire.

"Wanna know something weird about this place we're going?" His tone is deliberately light, like he's picking up cues from the music.

"What's that?"

"There's an abandoned Nazi camp about a mile away."

I give him my best "you're shitting me" look. "No way."

"I'm not lying. We'll be up on the top of Pacific Palisades, and back during World War II, this crazy couple thought Germany was going to win and built a compound to support the Nazi war effort."

I start to say something. Stop. Wonder if he's gone crazy. Open my mouth to speak and give up again.

"There's still one or two bunkers standing. I'll point it out to you when we get there."

I raise a finger. "You do that."

After a while, we leave the freeway and crawl up the side of the hills above Santa Monica. I lose track of the turns, of the street names. When he finally stops, I can no longer see the eastern edge of the sky, because of the hills. We're in front of a gated drive. He climbs out and presses a code into a touch pad. The gates slowly roll open.

The driveway is shorter than I expect, and from the outside in the dark, the house is at least as grand as the last safe house. Turning vampire must be good for the cash flow. He parks in front, and we both get out. I go around back to get our bags, and he presses a code into the touch pad by the front door.

"Dammit." He cranks on the door handle. Nothing happens.

"Try it again."

He does, but the door won't open. "Jacques must have changed the code."

Jacques again. I knew I didn't like that guy. I toss my suitcase back into the SUV's rear hatch. Trajan tries the code one more time, slamming the side of his hand on the door when it won't open. "We can head back to the hotel, I guess." I scan the sky. We've got another hour or so before sunrise. I think. I hope.

The driveway is a big loop. He pulls us forward, but the gate doesn't open. Trajan gets out and keys in the code again. Still nothing. Through the gate's poles, three pairs of headlights in close succession wind up the road.

"Well, damn," I say, mostly to myself.

"Yep. What do you bet they're heading up here?"

CHAPTER FIFTEEN

I don't want to know who's in those cars or why but they're headed in this direction. Every instinct in my bones is telling me to run. Run fast, and run far. We've got about an hour till the sun becomes a problem for my vampire companion, and a lot less time than that to get away.

"So you said something about a bunker?" It's a struggle, but I keep my voice from cracking.

Trajan's leaning in the driver's side door, the dashboard lights outlining his profile. "They'll track us."

"Damn. I guess we better just sit here and wait for them to come get us, then."

Despite my words, I climb out of the SUV and take a few steps along the fence. It's about chin height. I could be over it and shifted before ol' Tony makes up his damned mind. I crouch, preparing to leap.

"Wait." He heads to the back of the SUV, shoves our gear out of the way, and lifts the hatch. Instead of a spare tire, there's a small black bundle. He teases a pair of wires out of the end of it, twists them together, pushes a button, and sets the thing on the driver's seat.

He meets my gaze, fierce and determined. "Now let's go."

I hoist myself up on the fence, gulping a twinge of jealousy when the vampire leaps over in one move. The ground underneath is hard and covered in brambles. Despite that, I kick off my Chuck Taylors and hand them to Trajan.

"Ouch." I lift my foot off a thorn. "Hang on to these."

"What are you doing?" He stares at my shoes like they might take off on their own.

I gulp hard because this is going to hurt. "Shifting. The wolf scent will blend more with the wild, and a vampire's scent fades quickly. They'll have more trouble tracking us that way."

"Don't."

We don't have time for an argument. I shift before he can come up with a bunch of bullshit rationalizations. And before I can talk myself out of it.

Because yeah, shifting back and forth this many times is killer.

As soon as I can keep on my feet, I take off. Trajan's right behind me, then he passes, a sleek shadow in the night. I pick up my pace and follow. He's dropping down the side of the hill, going through sage scrub and dodging gnarled live oaks. After a few hundred feet, we pick up a path and move even faster.

We're stopped by a yellow hazard gate held in place by a padlock on a chain. Trajan grabs the chain. I scoot under it and glare at him.

"Yeah. Don't want to leave any — " An explosion from the direction of the safe house makes both of us jump. The chain breaks from the force of Trajan's response. "Fuck," he mutters, and pushes the gate open.

Then he charges down the trail. I keep up with him — barely — until he reaches a set of stairs. I get better traction in the dirt beside him, and it's a race to the bottom. We should probably slow down enough to listen for pursuers. We don't.

Finally, he slows to a stop. We're in front of a cement structure, and even in the fading moonlight, I can see it's covered with graffiti. "This place is pretty solid," he says. "I'll burrow in and hopefully you can grab a nap or something before I shut down."

While you're guarding both of us. He doesn't say it. He doesn't need to. The slope of his shoulders and the depth of his frown show his regret. I tip my chin up, hoping he'll read confidence instead of faked determination.

"Come on."

I follow him into the one-story building. In the main room, windows break up the crude slogans and swastikas painted on the walls. To the left there's a door leading into a large closet. Old wires and pipe stick out from the walls, but as long as no one opens the door, no sunlight will get in.

Trajan props himself in a corner. I don't know if I should stay in the room with him or guard the door. I wander in and out a couple of times and decide I'll be more use by keeping anyone from opening the door. I go out and, after one more look at Trajan, I close him in.

There's an old blanket in the corner. From the smell of it, someone lived and possibly loved on it. I drag it over in front of the closet, then scoot in so it's covering most of me.

I hope my shift back will kill the lice.

Exhaustion rolls over me in waves. Trajan will be conscious for a while, which gives me time for a nap. I can't even shut my eyes. That explosion was likely the SUV, which means the few clothes I had with me are gone. Trajan's maker has to be mixed up in the crazy somehow too, though for my wolf, it's a gut sense rather than anything rational.

And blaming Trajan's maker doesn't explain why my cousins nabbed me, or what's happened to Sheena.

I doze, almost despite myself. The change in light rouses me. The sun's up, so Trajan's out. The door to the bunker swings open, brightening the room further. A shadow falls across the floor, and then a man walks in.

Connor.

Can't stop myself from growling, even though if I kept quiet, he might not notice me. The sound in the back of my throat starts tiny and swells.

"David?" He takes another step inside. "It's me." The door swings shut behind him.

I bark, one single warning sound. He freezes. "Okay, so I'm just going to" — he slides down the wall in a squat — "sit right here."

The smell of horse and the supernatural compete for my attention. My rear haunches lift, ready to spring. There's no sound from Trajan's closet, so he must really be down.

"Look, I get that you're protecting him, but hear me out, okay?"

I don't answer, but I don't lunge at him either.

For a minute, he stares into his hands, like there's a cheat sheet for him to crib from. "Okay, I'm an agent with the Elite, the Securitas." He pauses, but I don't respond. Because I can't.

"Trajan doesn't know. I had an assignment two years ago and…well, never mind. Jacques and your uncle are up to something, but I'm not sure what or why. Tonight, I just happened to be watching a bunch of Jacques's thugs at that club. They took off, and I followed them and recognized Trajan's car."

He's oozing so much sincerity, I almost need a shower, but there's enough truth in his tone that I relax into my blanket. He's dressed in an ordinary-enough pair of jeans and a hoodie, but cold black metal gleams from his waist and from a holster on his thigh. I'm not sure what I thought an agent of the Elite would look like, so I guess he'll do. The Securitas is like the supernatural FBI, and the Elite is just what the name implies.

"I didn't figure you and Tray would be dumb enough to get caught by a bomb like that, so I took a look around after the other guys left. And here I am."

His eyes glow amber in the semi-daylight, and his hair is closer to auburn than brown, his beard a shade darker. He raises both hands and lets them flop onto his knees. "We'll just keep each other company till Trajan wakes up, okay?"

Something scrambles through the bushes outside. My ears twitch, but neither of us moves.

"Yeah," he says. "We'll just sit right here and wait."

Connor's alertness drains me. Not that I had much in the tank to begin with, but rousing myself every time he wants to go outside to scout around or take a leak or whatever gets to be a drag. My body finally wins, and I sleep. Not very long and not very deep, just enough to be befuddled when Trajan rockets out of his closet and shoves Connor up against the wall.

"Who are you?" Trajan spoke through clenched teeth. "And what the fuck do you want?"

"Trajan."

The thud of a fist landing on meaty flesh cuts off his words. Connor's knees sag, and Trajan punches him again.

"What." Thud. "The hell." Smack. "Do you want?"

Connor's on his knees. Trajan grabs a fistful of his shirt and yanks. Connor never lands a punch, nor does he go for any of the weapons he's carrying. It's almost like he wants Trajan to beat him.

The vampire's fist lands, this time in Connor's face. His lip splits, and when he whispers Trajan's name, he sends out a spray of blood. Somehow, that makes Trajan even crazier. He roars, louder than any animal could. The sound chills my blood. He drags Connor close and latches on to his bare throat.

As much as I've been after Tony to feed from me, this is not what I'd imagined. Connor moans, low and pitiful, as if he can barely tolerate the pain. One of his fists smacks weakly at Trajan's arm. Still Trajan drinks.

Connor's eyes slide shut. The wrongness penetrates my wolf's brain, and I jump up. If Trajan kills this man, we'll never know what the hell was going on. I bound across the room, and grab hold of Trajan's calf. I bite hard enough to taste blood, then worry the wound.

It works.

With another earth-rending shriek, Rocky-the-raccoon-eater drops Connor and turns to me. Fear turns my belly to water. Fuck. If I was smart, I'd get the hell out. Instead, I crouch, growling. I'm good in a fight, but facing a vampire in a blood lust could well be the last thing I do.

We're in a damned eight-by-ten-foot cement box. There's no place to run, nothing to hide behind. Trajan approaches, and I strap my weary ass together and face him. He lunges. The dense thwak of a pistol's silencer distracts us both. With a cry, Trajan goes down, dark red blood pooling on the floor at his feet.

"Fucking silver." Trajan lands on his knees. The pistol slips out of Connor's hand and hits the floor with a clank.

I end up tugging and prodding till they're lying side by side. It's early evening. I can't shift because I have no clothes. Well, I could shift, but then I'd have to shift back to travel, and…just no. After this, I want to go at least a year without dropping to all fours.

Unless there's a hot guy behind me and we're having fun.

I settle down between the two of them, afraid if Trajan wakes up, he'll take another run at Connor. I'm not sure I can stop him, but I'll try. The smell of blood teases me, and I'm grateful, because if I worry about being hungry, I might not have time to freak out over what's going to happen when Trajan wakes up.

I wait a while, maybe a few hours, until Connor stirs. His face is the color of the cement. He sits with a soft groan and holds his head in his hands. "Is he…"

His whisper draws my attention to Trajan. I nudge the vampire with my paw. Again. Harder. He grunts, and I catch Connor's gaze.

"Silver bullet." The man's lips are dry and cracked. "His body'll kick the casing out, and he'll come around soon."

I can't respond, so I shut my eyes. I'm still pretty tired, and if Connor wanted me dead, he would have let Trajan do it. At least this way, I can get some rest.

Or not. Trajan's arms flail out, and his body goes rigid. He yells, and with a snap like a breaking twig, a bullet's shell lands on the ground. I lurch to my feet, ready to hold him off if he makes another move at Connor.

Instead, he struggles to his feet. "What the hell, man?" His voice is raw. "What the hell?"

Connor looks like ass, or like he's just had half his blood volume forcibly removed. "We can talk later, Traj. For now, I just need you to trust me."

"Right." He uses almost as many syllables as a middle school girl. "I saw you dead."

"Later. I promise."

They go on arguing, but now that Connor's moving around more, I can pick up his scent. I'm almost sure he's a phouka. They're rare, but he doesn't match anything else I've experienced.

They're still arguing when Trajan's phone chirps. He drags it out of his pocket. "Sheena."

Connor manages to get as far as his knees. Trajan taps out a reply to the text message. "She says she got beat up." He speaks to me, cutting Connor out of our conversation. "Says she spent the night and most of today in an ER, went home and fell asleep, and just now woke up."

"We should get moving," Connor says. "My car is parked by the safe house. I'll give you a ride wherever you want."

"Okay." A flash of vulnerability crosses Trajan's face. I try to put myself in his shoes: a long-dead lover returns, and all hell breaks loose.

Yeah, that'd totally suck.

"We'll go get Sheena, then find a vamp-safe hotel. And you" — he points at Connor — "are with us until we figure out what's going on."

CHAPTER SIXTEEN

Sheena lives in the Jefferson Park neighborhood, south of the10. I know the lingo because Connor and Trajan bitched at each other about how to get here pretty much from the time we hit Connor's Prius until we pulled into her driveway. I'm dying to get out of the backseat, because being trapped in a sardine can with arguing alphas is no fun.

Once inside Sheena's old Craftsman house, all I can smell is pain. The place is all dark wood and clay tile. Her face is bruised, and she's moving like someone took a hammer to her ribs. She manages to close the door behind us, then settles on the couch in the front room. If she's surprised by Connor's presence, she's grimacing too hard to show it.

"Do you have any steak?" Trajan asks.

I jerk a glance at him, and yeah, he's staring back at me. I guess it's flattering to know I'm the first order of business.

"I need you to shift," he says, and my whole body shudders. This is going to be rough.

Connor more or less collapses in an old leather wingback chair. It's in the corner where he'll have a view of the whole room and the front door. Trajan's still standing near the door, his body rigid. The front room is small, overcrowded with emotion.

"Does he have clothes?" Sheena asks the room.

"No," Trajan answers for me.

Connor lifts his head. "I might have—"

"Borrow something of mine." Sheena cuts him off.

I trot over to a small hallway. Three doors open off it. One's a bathroom, and the other two are bedrooms. I pick one, and, judging by the clothes tossed everywhere, I get it right. For a minute, I have to fight my wolf. He doesn't want to give up control, or maybe he's just afraid it's going to hurt like hell.

Can't be helped.

I do my best to center myself, and shift.

The next thing I know, Trajan's kneeling next to me, shaking me gently. "David? Puppy? Are you okay?"

My mouth's so dry, I have to unpeel my tongue to talk. "Don't know."

"You howled like a banshee, and then nothing. I've been trying to wake you for like half an hour."

A shadow crosses the doorway. Connor again. "Is he okay?"

Trajan tenses but doesn't speak. "Yeah," I say, though likely I'm fooling nobody. "Just give me a minute, and I'll get dressed."

Trajan helps me sit, his hands steady and sure. Connor watches, and though I don't like it, I can feel his compassion. Whatever this guy is up to, I don't think he means to hurt us. I mean, beyond letting Trajan think he was dead.

I manage to get to my feet, stark naked, in front of two attractive men. One who is not my type, but that I'm kind of attached to, and the other who would be my type under different circumstances. *Well, howdy.* At least one part of my anatomy recovers quickly. I lean against Trajan, both for support and to hide my semi. "I need a shower."

"Sure." He helps me toward the bathroom, moving Connor out of the doorway with the force of his glare. Soon I'm under a cascade of warm water and covered in lavender bubbles. *This is good.*

I don't have the gear to shave and Sheena's selection of product is pretty limited, but I do my best. She's much taller than I am, so I make do with a pair of baggy peach shorts and a white mesh tee.

On her, it's probably a crop top, but I only have an inch or so of skin between where the shirt ends and the shorts begin. Even so, it's been so long since I had anything even remotely cute on that I'm happy.

I go back out to the living room. Trajan's just come back from the grocery store with steak and some vitamin-fortified something for Connor. Sheena is resting on the couch, and Connor's in a wing chair, head tilted back, his eyes closed.

Trajan brings me a bowl of raw beef and chucks a bottle of juice at Connor. That draws an oomph when it hits Connor's gut, loud enough to rouse Sheena.

"So." She rises on one elbow and swings her feet to the floor so there's space for Trajan to sit. "Where are we?"

I'm sitting cross-legged on a braid rug, my bowl set on the heavy mahogany coffee table. Trajan even remembered to bring me a napkin. I feel a little like a kid among grown-ups, but until I get some protein in me, I don't care. If Trajan and Connor are going to work things out, we'll have to start right now. I want us all on the same page before one of us gets killed.

Everyone goes quiet except for my slurping, like there's too many words to say and no one wants to throw the first ones out there. I already know part of Connor's story—he's from the Elite, and something-something mysterious something Jacques and Uncle Brendan—but I can't see any of that going down well with Trajan. Sheena's got a protective arm draped along the back of the couch around Trajan's shoulders, and her expression could freeze testicles. I concentrate on chewing and swallowing, trying to conserve strength.

Connor swigs another mouthful of juice, his attention somewhere above all of us. "So do you guys want to ask me questions, or should I just start talking?"

Trajan shakes his head like he can't even believe he's hearing the guy's voice. Sheena breathes. I slurp.

"Okay." The phouka—because of course the Elite would recruit a phouka—pinches the bridge of his nose between his thumb and forefinger.

When Connor says the words "I am with the Elite," Trajan goes completely stiff, as if he's using every ounce of self-control not to attack.

Sheena's protective arm becomes more of a restraint.

Trajan's voice comes from somewhere deep. "We were together five years and you never bothered to tell me?"

"I couldn't." Now Connor's talking to the floor.

"So what? I was just a convenient cover?"

Sheena flinches, and even I pause in licking my fingers. With one question, Trajan has made this very, very personal, and I glance at the Amazon, raising my eyebrows to ask whether we should leave. She ignores me, and until I'm sure Trajan's not going to lose it again, I stay put.

"No." Connor glances up from under his brow. His eyes are copper against his pale skin and bloodstains show as dark patches on his black hoodie. He clears his throat like it hurts. "No, what we had was separate, and very important to me."

"You let me think you were dead." The words crash out in a chasm of grief.

Connor flings himself up from the chair. "I had no choice." He stands, facing the fireplace, his back to the room. "I swear to you, *mo shiorghrá*. A job went sideways, and I had to disappear. It was the only way I could keep you alive."

Silence deadens the air, interrupted by the soft ticking of an old clock. Because every Craftsman house must have an old clock somewhere. I finish off the last bit of beef, still exhausted but functioning. Trajan sits with his arms crossed, his scowl fierce. Connor rests his hands on the mantel, frozen, waiting for the judge and jury.

Finally, Trajan speaks. "I don't know if I can believe that."

Connor's shoulders sink. "I swear." His voice trails off to nothing. "I swear."

"What does any of this have to do with someone jumping me outside the club last night? Or with the shit that's gone down with David?" Sheena's question acts like a blast of cold air in a dark room. "Because getting the jump on an Amazon takes a lot of planning, so this"—she points at her face—"was no accident."

"True." Trajan straightens, making a visible effort to pull back from whatever ledge he'd found himself on.

"Tell us what happened." I find I can speak now that the atmosphere isn't so tense.

"I went by the pub, and then I was supposed to meet you." She pointed at Connor. He raises his eyebrows, but doesn't confirm or deny her claim.

"We said we were going to meet over in La Brea, by the tar pits, but when I got there, two guys came out of nowhere and beat the shit out of me." She shifted like her body hurt. "Some people found me…I don't know, club kids or whatever…and they got me to an ER."

"Human?" I ask.

She curls her lip, then winces. "Yeah. Armed with baseball bats or something."

We still haven't dealt with my shit, but that's okay. We're talking, and no one's dead. This is good. I'm fading a little, but it's not even midnight. Connor looks so tired, he could fall on his face. Sheena's not much better.

Trajan, though. Trajan's up and pacing. "I want to check out La Brea, see if I can pick anything up. Come with me?"

He raises his chin at me. I blink, inhale deeply, and nod. Yes, I'll go with him, but the whole time, I'll be hoping like hell Connor's still here when we get back.

Hours later, Trajan and I roll back into Sheena's house. We cruised La Brea, and while we found the place where she'd been hit, we didn't see anything labeled "clue." Connor's sleeping on the couch. Sheena's bedroom door is closed, so she's likely asleep, too.

"Come here." Trajan draws me into the second bedroom. This one has blackout curtains and a big dead bolt on the door. All through our travels this evening, he's been distant, cold, so even this little gesture reassures me. Though it's mildly irritating that I need reassurance.

There's just enough room to walk all the way around the queen-size bed. Trajan pulls me closer. "There's really no other place to sleep." His cool fingertips trace the mesh patterns in my shirt. "Unless you want a blanket on the floor."

I lean into him, inhaling the dusty, electric scent of vampire. I'll sleep with him, but I don't want to talk. We've spent the last few hours in the kind of silence that forms when there're too many things to say. Touching is easier, anyway.

I catch hold of his shirt and rise on tiptoe, brushing his lips with the lightest kiss. He catches my ass with both hands and lifts, so I swing my legs up and wrap them around his waist.

We start kissing for real, hard and edgy. He nips my lower lip, bites the tip of my tongue. I'm rock my hips into him for all I'm worth. The last few days have been so stressful that this, forgetting myself in pleasure, becomes an absolute necessity.

He pivots and lowers me to the bed, pressing himself on top of me. He's thrusting, I'm thrusting, and this damned sure isn't going to take long. I swear I'm about to come when he lifts, sitting back on his haunches. I wail in protest.

"What's wrong?"

"So close." I can barely get the words out.

He chuckles and pulls his shirt off, unzips his fly. "I want to feel your skin."

I'm all but sobbing, I'm so turned on. He crashes down on me, and we get to it. No finesse. No grace.

Just two men taking what they need from each other in the most basic way possible.

It's easy to slide out of Sheena's baggy shorts, and the mesh top is barely there anyway. My skin is covered with cool vampire. His hands on my body are strong and sure. He spits in his palm and reaches down, grasping both of us together.

Yeah, this really isn't going to take long.

He mashes his mouth against my neck, and for a second, I'm distracted. Will he bite? He doesn't, but the orgasm rolls me anyway, drawing a yell from me that probably wakes the whole house.

And it wasn't even on purpose.

He follows me, though his cry is more of an aggressive hiss. Afterward, we lie together, our cum pooled on my belly.

"Nothing makes sense," he murmurs, nuzzling my ear.

I flinch. "Ticklish."

"Sorry."

I stroke his shoulder, scratch lightly down his arm. Comfort given, and comfort taken.

"I mean," he continues, "why the secrecy? Why the mystery? Why not just be honest?"

I'm not the guy to answer those questions, but I do my best. "For what it's worth, I think he's telling the truth." Because of course this is about

Connor. I snuggle in closer. "He was trying to keep you safe."

"Yeah."

Dawn is a cold gray shadow on the eastern edge of the sky. I sense the shift in the light, the change in color behind the blackout curtains. "You guys need to talk," I say. "Because for sure there's unfinished business between you, and I don't want to interfere with that."

Look how noble I am, falling right on that sword.

He pulls me tight to his chest. "Right now, it's all about you, puppy. It's all about you."

He's either lying to himself or to me. But he's lying.

CHAPTER SEVENTEEN

Before I get out of bed, I engage in some petty theft. My burner phone is lying in the pocket of a pair of shredded jeans from the last time I shifted. Somewhere near a Nazi compound? I need to google that and make sure Tony wasn't pulling my leg. At any rate, I swipe his burner and sneak out of the bedroom.

I want to text my sister and tell her I'm alive. I'm pretty sure it's a bad idea, because clearly there are problems in the pack. On the other hand, I'm closer to Abby than anyone else. She's not the conniving type.

Locking myself in the bathroom, I send a four-word text. *It's David. I'm okay.* I can't resist taking another shower, and by the time I get out, there are three messages from her. I struggle over how to answer. I could say I'm still in LA, but I don't want to give my location away. I could say I'll be home soon, but I don't know that's true. I could make some shit up, to lie.

But…not to Abby.

I end up begging her not to worry and leave the bathroom.

The front rooms are dark, their windows covered with wooden louvers. The smell of coffee tugs me into the kitchen. Yellow checkered curtains, white subway tile, and linoleum are way too cheerful for a six-foot Amazon who looks like she just went a dozen rounds in an MMA ring.

And Connor, whose pale complexion would make a vampire look healthy.

Judging by the sun, it's late afternoon, which means we have an hour or so before we see Trajan. The coffee pot is steaming, so I make that my first agenda item.

"Did you get any rest?" Sheena's in black running shorts and a ragged white hoodie, and she's clutching a mug in both hands.

"Enough." Not really, but I don't want to get into it. Faced with Connor, I'm suddenly a little ashamed of my early morning caterwauling. I can only hope he was too far gone to hold having sex with his ex against me.

He's sitting at a small wooden table under the window. There's a second chair. I could join him. I lean against the counter instead. "We didn't find anything useful last night."

Sheena takes a thoughtful sip of her coffee. "I didn't think you would." She's kind of a blank slate, but I read tension and maybe some anger in the set of her shoulders.

Connor pulls a smart phone out of his pocket. He drags a finger across the top and starts fiddling with it. "No hits yet," he says softly.

"What are you looking for?" I kind of want to take the second chair, but I hold off. Despite having spent the night with my hands full of vampire, there's something about Connor. He's got that whole fresh-from-the-shower-hipster vibe going on, a scruffy masculinity that's hard to resist.

He picks up the phone, taps it with two fingers, then slides them apart to enlarge the image on the screen. Holding it up, he shows me the burned-out hulk of a building. "That's what's left of the safe house where I found you. Unless Trajan's emergency blast was a whole lot stronger than it used to be, someone went in behind you guys and torched the place."

"What was up with that anyway?" I ask. His scent is doing strange things to my belly. "Who carries around an emergency blast?"

Connor and Sheena share a glance. Her lips curl, like she'd smile if things didn't hurt so bad. "A paranoid vampire," she says.

"He used to say he might need the distraction sometime."

He used to say… I get his point. Connor knew Tony first. I try not to pout. "Well, it worked for him, I guess."

"True." Connor goes back to messing with his phone. "I also posted a query on an encrypted page, poking at connections between Jacques and your family."

The coffee turns in my gullet. I don't know whether to laugh because the Securitas apparently have a LISTSERV of their own or freak out at his suggestion. "I'm not sure I want to know." But he's right. Some of the bullshit directed at me has vampire fingerprints, and some is coming from the pack. Though it makes me queasy to admit, it's unlikely I'd be lucky enough to have two separate schemes working against me.

"I hope you don't mind. Trajan mentioned that there had been incidents in addition to those I witnessed."

"You might say."

"Maybe nothing will come of it." He shrugs. "I do wonder, though, whether you might be better served to address the issue with your father directly."

"What? How? Dad's in DC. I can't just call him with something like this."

Sheena shifts in her chair. "Why not?"

"If I only had to tell him about those guys outside the Fubar or the cabin, that would be one thing, but I can't tell him about the scene with my uncle and cousins downtown over the phone." I pause, warming up to the idea. "We need to be in the same room when I tell Dad that his brother, my uncle, tried to force me to sign a severance contract. That way, he'll catch the scent of truth. If I'm on the phone, he'll have to choose whether to believe me or his brother."

"Severance contract?" Connor asks.

"That night when he asked you to meet him downtown?" Sheena says.

"He tried to make me a lone wolf." That's the first time I've said the words out loud. They leave a disgusting aftertaste.

Connor's gaze narrows, and he nods decisively. "Then we'll brave the wolf in his den."

"I don't know, Davey." Sheena's uncertainty makes me nervous. "Your dad could be involved with this somehow."

"True." It hurts, but I have to be honest. "But if he is, or if this is some kind of *let's give David a test* thing, he'll respect me more if I confront him directly."

"Or it could get you killed."

Connor's bald statement brings me up short. "No."

"Just want to make sure you understand the risk involved. Look," he says, "we can hang around and wait to see what your uncle does next, or we can address this directly." He pauses, foot tapping on the floor. "If there is a link between the weres and the vampires, it would be useful for me to interview your father, to identify how far the rot goes."

I'm still trying to fit the concepts of family and rot together when Trajan's voice from the dining room makes me jump five feet in the air. He comes to the edge of where the light from the kitchen windows can reach. "I agree with him. Confronting your father makes sense, and we're coming with you."

"All of you?" My voice squeaks, which pisses me off even more. "We're all just going to hop on a plane and go visit Dad?"

Sheena's staring at the floor, and I begin to wonder how bad her injuries are. I know her well enough to guess that she'd be the walking dead before she'd admit she couldn't help.

Connor doesn't look up from his phone. "I'm arranging for three tickets, one with vampire accommodations, and we'll fly tonight."

"I want you here in case things go sideways, Sheen." Trajan layers on the emphasis, giving her an out but at the same time begging her not to fight him.

She sets her mug down with a wince. "Yeah."

The situation is racing out of my control. "But what if someone comes after her here? And how the hell will I explain a vampire and a phouka to my father?"

"I'm not a phouka," Connor says, like somehow that answers everything.

"And I'm the guy your father hired to keep you safe, which, despite myself, I've managed to do. I don't think we need any more explanation than that."

Connor looks up from his phone. "We'll need to leave as soon as it's dark enough to travel."

The weight of the vampire's stare is comforting, though I try to ignore him. And honestly, Connor's efficiency is reassuring, too. I've never called a meeting with Dad before, and I've never been to his DC offices. All these moving parts make me nervous, so I guess having bodyguards while I figure out what's going on makes sense.

Not that anything in the current situation really makes all that much sense.

Nevertheless, I call my father's office and make an appointment with his receptionist, and I text Abby to let her know I'll be traveling. Then I turn the phone off so I won't be tempted to tell her anything else.

Abby would never sell me out, but someone close to her might.

Two hours later, I've got a new set of casually professional threads and a wallet with ID and a credit card. The Securitas works quickly. My suit didn't survive the meeting with my uncle, and while I do have stuff in Sheena's storage locker, none of my party clothes are really Dad-appropriate anyway. Now, my trousers are slim and show off my ass, my shoes are Doc Marten thick-soled oxfords, and my silky crew-neck shirt is the perfect color teal for my eyes. They even brought me an overnight bag with a cute pair of plaid pajamas.

Someone did their homework.

We've congregated in the front room, waiting for a pickup to go to the airport. Connor's in his brooding chair, Sheena's leaning in the doorway, and Trajan and I are on the couch. Connor checks his phone for the 4,576th time, and fixes Trajan with a glare.

"Have you fed from him?"

Trajan flicks a rando clump of hair out of his face and glares right back. "Not your business."

I'm busy trying not to look too mortified. *I mean, come on, Connor. Why not just ask how often I take it up the ass?*

Connor worries his lower lip, like he's not sure if his next idea will light a powder keg or not. "Look," he says, "that tracking thing. You can still do that, right? With me?"

The fierceness of Trajan's scowl could be measured on the Richter scale, but he answers. "I didn't bother trying because you were dead."

"I get that." Connor ducks his head, massaging the back of his neck with one hand. I know what he means. The tension is killing me.

"But you fed from me last night," Connor says. "If I took off now, would you be able to find me?"

A long pause. "Yes."

Sheena mumbles something that might be derogatory, but I'm not sure who she's aiming at.

I start picking at little pills in the couch's brocade upholstery. As much as I wanted Trajan to feed from me, not here, and not now, and not for this reason.

"Do it." Connor's tone doesn't allow for any wiggle room.

I freeze. Trajan scowls.

"I'll be in the kitchen." Sheena's departure feels like a betrayal. "Connor's right, Trajan," she calls over her shoulder.

Connor turns his formidable attention to me. He's the first member of the Elite I've met, and Jesus fuck, he's scary when he wants to be. "Roll up your sleeve and give him your arm." His expression softens for just a moment. "I know this is weird, but since we don't know what's really going on, the tracking thing could be important."

"You're not really giving me a choice." My voice has more balls than I would have expected.

"No, I'm not."

Trajan scoffs, his frown cutting deeper, but I do as Connor asked and roll up my sleeve. I extend my arm so it's within Trajan's field of vision, but he doesn't move.

"You don't know what you're asking," he says.

"Yeah." Connor nods, his expression the very definition of regret. "I do."

Our little tableau freezes until slowly, drawing out every last breath, Trajan raises his hands and wraps them around my arm. He lowers his head. His lips brush the bare skin of my wrist. He never once looks at me.

"I'm sorry," he whispers, and then he bites.

It's like being scalded with bliss. My dick is instantly so hard, it could cut right through these cute corduroy trousers. He pulls, swallows, and pulls again. The pleasure/pain thrusts into me, again and again and again. I'm making a wet spot on my pants and I don't even care. This is the most erotic thing I've ever done, and I should hate being forced into it, but I don't.

Through it all, Connor's there. Warm. Sure. A copper heart to Trajan's moonlit soul. Yeah. Fuck. If I'm spouting poetry, things are really screwed.

With a single lick, he closes the wound. He might have kissed me, too, but I'm too flustered to care. I don't feel any different. Maybe a little itchy from the wet spot. I'm just glad I didn't come. When it comes to clothing, I can work a lot, but plaid pajama pants on a cross-country flight might be pushing it.

"Our ride will be here in five," Connor says. I sag against the couch. Trajan sits with his head in his hands.

Way to make a guy feel wanted, Rocky.

Our ride can't come soon enough.

It's dark when we leave LA and broad daylight when we land. A windowless van picks us up from some underground transit spot at Dulles. More evidence of Elite efficiency. Trajan's groggy, but we get him to the hotel before he completely passes out.

We're booked into a suite in the Hotel Omni. Two bedrooms—one vampire-ready, the other with two queen beds—and a living area. The space is bland and lovely, and from our window, the swimming pool sits like a turquoise jewel fourteen stories below. We don't get to enjoy any of it because as soon as we get Trajan tucked away, it's time to visit Dad.

I'd feel better if Trajan were with us, but our appointment is for eleven a.m. Connor calls an Uber, and we're good to go. I figure I can talk Dad off the ledge and be back before Trajan wakes up.

"This should be interesting," Connor says, his forcibly light tone an attempt to diffuse my tension. We're in the elevator, and for some reason, he's standing close enough for me to feel the heat of his body. I catch the woodsmoke scent of phouka.

I tip my head so he'll get the full effect of my flirty smile. "Thanks for being here with me."

Our gazes clash. Hold. The temperature in the elevator car rises faster than the car is dropping.

"I didn't realize how much trouble you were in. I should have stepped in earlier, but…"

I shrug. "Coming back from the dead has it's challenges."

"Yeah."

I'm not convinced that's his only reason, although whatever he's tied up in is likely more complicated than a junior alpha were getting spanked.

"There's something else I want to do, too." Connor's whisper tickles my skin. Before I can reply, he leans over and kisses me. One minute I'm standing there like a slightly travel-worn preppie, and the next I'm crushed against the wall, his lips giving me a lesson in wanting what I can't have.

Our kiss is hot and sweet. His tongue teases me, and I stretch on my toes so I can get more. Deeper. We don't stop till the elevator does, and then he steps back, his fingers caressing my cheek. "That," he says. "I really wanted to do that."

"I…" Have no idea how to respond. It takes a lot to leave me speechless, but Connor the maybe-phouka-turned-Elite, has done it. *Damn.* The elevator door opens and I step through in a fog of confusion. *What the hell just happened?*

On the way to meet my father, we're silent. Between feeding Trajan and kissing Connor, I might have whiplash. And DC is DC. Classier than LA, but just as crowded. Too many people holding the fate of the world in their cell phones.

We get out of the Uber at the right building and jog up the steps. Connor's probably armed, which could be a problem, but it's not. We head up to the twenty-seventh floor, and I lead the way to the American Were Authority offices. The receptionist looks familiar, but I can't remember her name. Doesn't matter. She's pack. I don't care how crazy things get, the sense of having allies, confidants, friends, is good.

Pack is trust.

Connor follows me back to my father's office, keeping half a step behind like a good bodyguard.

Dad's secretary, Melissa, greets me like a long-lost nephew. "David Collins!" Her Deep South accent does funny things to vowels. "You come right on in."

She opens the door to Dad's office, but when Connor moves to follow me, she stops him. "You understand, don't you, sir? It's a family thing."

I glance at him over my shoulder. "I'll be okay. Just…um…wait here for a few. This shouldn't take very long."

He doesn't stop me—he can't. If he tries, he'll bring the whole pack down on himself. But his body language is telling me all kinds of shit. *Don't go. Be careful.*

Danger.

I should have listened.

PART THREE: COPPER HEART

CHAPTER EIGHTEEN

CONNOR

Tá mé ag siúl fear marbh.

Dead man walking.

Me. When the vampire finds out what I've done.

I'm sitting on a couch in the lobby of the Alpha Wolf's offices. The seat is uncomfortable, the office impersonal. Across from me, a receptionist is typing at a streamlined, silver laptop. She's wearing an earpiece with a wire mic, but no one has disturbed her concentration. Twenty minutes ago, David went in to talk with his father. Nineteen minutes ago, my gut started pinging.

Now, I'm ready to crawl out of my skin.

Something chimes, setting off sparks of anxiety, and the receptionist speaks. "Be right there, sir."

She avoids eye contact, picks up her laptop, and disappears through the double doors into the office.

Then, nothing.

She doesn't come out, and no one else enters. I wait, schooling myself for patience. Connor MacPherson can handle anything, right? Honorable member of The Elite. Famed fighter. Heartsick romantic fool.

All part of my CV.

Despite my best effort, my knee starts bouncing, a hyper staccato rhythm. Where is David? Why doesn't the receptionist return? He'd greeted her by name, and she'd known him. This couldn't be some kind of setup.

Could it?

I shift my weight, and the small envelope in my pocket crinkles. Impervious to heat and to moisture, it cannot be torn or burned. It's holding a slip of test paper that contains a sample of David's DNA.

The kiss in the elevator served more than one purpose. The DNA sample gave me a safeguard, a way of tracing David if he got into trouble, and it gave me a taste of something I've been hungry for ever since I first saw him.

In another ten minutes, I can't sit still any longer. David's been gone a good half an hour, and maybe he and Dad are having a heart-to-heart in an office with a view of the world. If they are, I'll have to beg their pardon. My gut's telling me they're not.

I stand, reaching for the gun in my shoulder holster. The tap is a ritual, a reassurance. If I acknowledge my weapon, then maybe I won't have to use it. Magical thinking.

The heavy door to the inner office swings easily. It opens into a hallway with a dim, unused feel. The building's at least 100 years old, the walls covered with a thick coat of plaster, and the air smells of stale lemon cleaner. Four doors open off the left-hand side. The only light comes from the fluorescents overhead.

I take a second to orient myself in space. The double doors at the end must be the corner office. If I were an alpha werewolf, that's where I'd make my den.

The only noise is the muted buzz of the ventilation system. No chatter from office workers, no beeps or rings from cell phones or computers. Nothing. I stop long enough to peek into one of the hallway doors. It opens into an empty room. Shite.

I pick up my pace, but I already know what I'll find. The big corner office at the end of the hall is empty. Deserted. No furniture. No receptionist. No nothing.

And shite again. "David?" I call his name, knowing it won't do any good. My pistol is no longer in the holster. I've drawn it, and I move down the hall, opening each door, searching for how they got him past me. There must be another way out.

There.

One of the empty offices has an inner door marked by an unlit exit sign. The door opens into a stairwell. Everything's painted a glossy gray, except for the danger-yellow handrail. I stop on the top stair, eyes half-closed, tapping my other sense, the one I keep secret. Even from the vampire I love.

Just one of many secrets I keep from him.

High windows give the stairwell a silvery cast. I reach out, seeking the residue of the living beings who have passed this way before me. I see auras, the shrouds of light surrounding all life. With luck and concentration, I can detect the echoes of those who're no longer present.

David came this way. I can feel his golden light.

I head down the stairs, alert for any signs of wolf. On some floors, I hear the normal voices or low music associated with business. The stairwell is dead quiet. I go all the way down to the parking garage at the bottom.

The stairwell ends in a small, glassed-in foyer. There's a window in the door. A neat row of identical Honda sedans are parked along the far wall. The place appears to be deserted, but a scent catches me.

I give the area a quick scan and see a spray of red on one of the windows. Taking another piece of test paper from my pocket, I press it against the droplets and return it to its envelope. It'll be useful if the DNA matches David's saliva sample, and if it doesn't, I'll use it as evidence.

I'm certain David was brought down here—faking an aural residue is nearly impossible, even if his abductors had guessed at my ability—but I'll need help to figure out where he's gone.

I pull out my cell phone and make a call, reaching my contact on the second ring. I rarely work with a partner in the field, instead relying on the hands and eyes and intellect of a wizard named Dante.

He sounds sleepy and annoyed, neither of which is out of character.

"The son of the American Alpha is missing, and I need a pair of bloodhounds and a courier ASAP." I spit out the address, waiting till he grunts to continue. "The courier will bring you two samples. One blood, the other saliva. Some of the saliva is mine. The rest belongs to the missing man." After the kiss, I'd distracted David long enough to lick the sample paper, leaving traces of us both. "I need a selection of tracers keyed to his DNA. The blood may be a match, and if it is, use it to strengthen the trace. If it's not a match, I want a profile on whoever it belongs to."

Dante harrumphs. "Anything else?"

"That's it." I bite back some less-affectionate responses. "As soon as you have the tracers, message me, please."

"Whatever."

I end the call before my juvenile side rises to his bait. Dante is difficult, but he's very, very good at what he does.

I'm going to need a combination of luck, magic, and good detective work to catch up.

But first I need to tell the vampire.

The courier arrives first. A stocky middle-aged man, he accepts my samples and tells me he'll let Dante know what he found. On his heels, the bloodhounds arrive, a pair of shifters who work as a team. Tall and lanky, dressed in marathon gear, they look human enough, but I know better. Their nickname comes from their keen sense of smell. While they won't have a lot to go on, they're my best chance for finding clues about David's location.

I take them up the stairway to the empty office, giving them every opportunity to catch David's scent. We exchange cell phone numbers, and they promise to call. I've never worked in the DC office, but members of the Elite are marked in a way that's impossible to duplicate. I trust them.

I must.

After sending the bloodhounds on their way, I tour the empty offices again. Nothing. Whoever is responsible had to have marched David out as soon as he came through the door. I tried to reassure myself that if their goal had been to kill him, a bullet through the head would have done the trick. No, they have a different game in mind.

I just don't know the rules.

I leave the empty offices, cut through the waiting room, and head out into the main complex. The scene hits the same level of banal everyday office activity as on our way in, but this time, I look closer. Weres, most of them wolves, walk alone or in small groups. Office doors are open, and there's chatter, laughter, busy work. No one stops me. No one seems to notice me at all.

I take the elevator to the ground floor. There, a security guard presides over a glass-topped desk. I catch his attention.

"Can you tell me where the American Were Authority Alpha's offices are?"

He doesn't miss a beat. "He moved two months ago. There's still wolves up there, but the big kahuna's over on O Street."

I make a note of the address and thank him. It's barely noon, so I've got several hours before Trajan rises. I could go back to our hotel and wait, or I could face the wolf in his den. It's possible he'll slip up, and I'll be able to retrieve David before the vampire wakes.

Unlikely, but possible.

I cab it to the O Street address. The building is the same nineteenth-century vintage as the first offices, but this time, I need to flash my credentials before they'll cooperate. I'd hoped to avoid doing that, but if advertising my M-status is what it takes to get David back, I'm in.

The security guard in the front hassles me about my weapon, so I end up flashing my badge before I'm through the door. I follow the signs to Randolph Collins's office, bringing out my company smile when I'm stopped by his secretary. She's older, her brassy black hair warring with the lines around her eyes and the soft skin of her jaw.

"I'm sorry, but Mr. Collins is in a meeting and can't be disturbed."

Of course he is. I pull out my badge a second time. "I understand he's busy; however, I'm dealing with an emergency, and I need to talk to him now. Please notify him that Connor MacPherson, M17, is waiting."

She punches a button, turning away as if she thinks I won't be able to hear her conversation. Her tone is clipped and unforgiving. If she gets her way, I'm going to have to find another angle.

"Okay," she says. "Yes, sir. Yes, sir."

I'm readying my next pitch when she punches another button and the door gives an angry buzz.

"You can go through." She's obviously unhappy with the decision, but I smile politely and get moving. I didn't really have another pitch, so I'm thankful this one worked.

I have mixed feelings about my job, in part because the Securitas have a reputation for high-handedness and secrecy. I might dislike being *that guy*, but given the situation, I intend to work that reputation for all it's worth.

I knock on the door to Collins's office, and at his gruff command, I enter. The American Were Authority Alpha is seated at a large wooden desk, an impressive setting for the man who oversees every were in the country. The office itself is dark and warm, the walls lined with bookcases, a console behind the desk covered with framed photographs. I catch a glimpse of a skinny, teenage David, but then his father clears his throat.

I blink, and his aura flares. Green for truth. Red for anger. Blue for sincerity. I fix the image in my mind so I'll have something to compare with after I tell him about his son.

"This really is an inconvenience," he says, arms crossed over his chest so I'll know exactly how much trouble I've caused.

I start to apologize, then stop myself. I can't afford to be intimidated by him. "Your son is missing, Mr. Collins, and I need to know if you've got any information regarding his whereabouts."

He drops his arms, hands landing flat on the desk. "What? How can he be missing?" He's dark and grizzled, the kind of man who needs to shave twice a day or face a permanent shadow. "He was supposed to meet with me today."

"Yes, and I escorted him—"

"Why is the Securitas escorting my son anywhere?"

His aura flickers, the colors shifting, but without the sick yellow-green indicating deception.

I explain the events that brought David to my attention, or at least a version of them. "This morning at just before eleven a.m., we went to a building on M Street. We were met by a receptionist David recognized. She brought him to your office, and when he failed to return, I went after him."

"That makes no sense. Why would he go to my old offices?"

I judge his gruffness stems from fear rather than anger. The colors in his aura shift, but still there's nothing to indicate he's lying. "How often do you talk to your son?"

"I've been distracted. There was a were attack in Sarasota and a series of thefts that have disrupted our supply chain." His grudging response tells me they talk about as often as I'd imagine a powerful man would want to talk to his rebellious child. I grill him on his knowledge of David's habits, of his lifestyle, all the while wondering whether any of the Alpha's distractions are connected to what's happened to David. Or if he's behind the whole thing and I just haven't asked the right question yet.

"Yeah, I know about the gay thing." Collins takes on the indulgent tone of a parent describing a toddler's phase. "He'll be ready to settle down after graduation, though. His fiancée is a lovely girl. She'll straighten him out."

I'm pretty sure Trajan doesn't know about a fiancée. This keeps getting better and better.

"Do he and his Uncle Brendan get along?"

Collins gives me a puzzled look. "Brendan holds David in high regard. He's the one who suggested I hire a driver from Jacques Bettencourt for David's vacation."

There's absolutely nothing suspicious in his aura.

"Brendan took the initiative to fly to Los Angeles, too, when he heard rumors that David was having trouble."

Still nothing. "How did that meeting go?"

"Well." He shifts in his seat, as if his patience is wearing thin. "Brendan said David convinced him that he'd be able to handle anything else that went on."

Clearly, Brendan had given his brother an altered version of events. In light of his dwindling attention, I shift to the other stuff he's got on his plate. "You mentioned thefts?"

His eyes narrow. "Yeah, and if I need your help, I'll ask for it."

All righty, then. I ask about the wolves' properties in the DC area. Collins provides me with a list, and I text a photograph of it to my bloodhounds. They can do some of the legwork, and Trajan and I can explore the likeliest places after sunset.

He straightens, as if the breadth of his shoulders alone will intimidate me. "I still don't understand why you're involved with David. Maybe he just, I don't know, took off without you. He's capable of looking after himself."

"True, but David was barely out of the airport in LA when someone started shooting at him, despite the presence of a bodyguard. You can't tell me that if anything happened to your son, you wouldn't blame the vampires, just as they'll blame you if Trajan Gall is murdered."

Some of the bluster fades from his expression, so I keep talking.

"I will admit that I discovered the events surrounding your son in the course of a separate investigation…" *or thereabouts*, "…but right now, this seems to be a more pressing situation." I stand because I'm running out of things to say. "We need to find David while he's still alive, sir."

The color fades from Collins's face. "Yes. We do."

CHAPTER NINETEEN

The sun hasn't quite set when Trajan wakes. I'm hunched over my laptop on the bed, researching the locations on Randolph Collins's list. One minute, I'm alone in the hotel room. The next, there's a vampire hovering over me. I jump but manage to stifle a startled squawk.

"Where's David?" He sounds more confused than concerned.

Even though I'd had a few hours to prepare, the question still catches me flat-footed. I owe him the truth, even though he'll likely take out his anger on the nearest punching bag. I just had to hope I'll be man enough to take it.

Trajan looms over me, and again I'm caught by the desire to wrap my arms around him and drag him closer. Time has changed nothing. He's the same dark, sexy man with the same strong, sexy body. Despite everything, I want him. Somehow, I can't bring myself to say David's been taken, so I ease into it. "It's been a busy day."

He stares, his hands loose at his sides, and the energy of his aura brushes against mine. I scoot my chair to the side, away from him, though still within his reach. "I went with him to his father's office, but it was a setup."

Those loose hands turn into fists. I try to ignore his response and keep talking.

"Someone must have been waiting for him to show. He went in to see his father, but never came out."

"You let him go in alone?" His tone is primed to hurt.

"Yes." If I say anything else, it'll sound like I'm making excuses. I keep going. Excuses are easier to deal with than silence. "He knew the receptionist. There was nothing suspicious about the place."

I half expect him to come at me. To throw a punch. Something. Anything. Instead, he stands still, but his eyes drill into my core. There's anguish in their depths, and I am the cause.

"There were wolves present in the office. The receptionist was a wolf. Obviously, we need to find him, and I thought we could start with were-owned businesses. I spoke with the Alpha, and he gave me a list of properties owned by the pack." Talking grants me a reprieve. "I sent bloodhounds to check them out, and they've come up with a couple of possibilities."

"Bloodhounds?" The word is flat, unnaturally restrained.

"Agents who are cultivated for their tracking ability."

"Yeah…that's right. The Elite. That detail you forgot to mention."

Here we go. Pain sluices through his words. For a moment, I really do hate myself for keeping secrets. For lying. For leaving him. There are parts of myself I barely acknowledge—the shifting, the history, the talents. Despite all that, I can't conjure a wolf out of thin air.

We need to stay on task here. I tamp down my jumbled emotions and continue. "I've also got a set of tracers, so when we do figure out where they're holding him, we can fine-tune our approach."

He grimaces, looking anywhere but at me. "How do we know…" His voice trails off, and he clears his throat. "How do we know he's still alive?"

I have to be honest with him. "We don't."

He rakes his hands through his hair, his aura shooting sparks of fiery red. I want to keep talking. Hell, there are so many things I should say, I can't figure out where to start. Trajan won't meet my gaze. He makes a deliberate move to the bathroom. He's shutting me out, and there's nothing I can do to stop him.

I catch him before he closes the door. "The bloodhounds have narrowed the list down to three sites. As soon as you're ready, we'll start looking."

He pauses, resting his forehead against the doorjamb. "We will? You seriously think we're going to find anything?"

His obvious animosity cuts me deep. "What choice do we have?"

"You could go on back to wherever." He straightens, staring up at the ceiling. "And I could find the wolf."

"It'll go faster if we work together." Laying the laptop on the bed, I stand. His body is calling to me, even if his words hold me at a distance.

I close in, resting a hand on Trajan's shoulder. "Let me help you with this, *mo shiorghrá*."

His body turns to stone under my touch. I let go, but don't move away.

"I mourned you," he said. "For two years, I grieved." He jerks away from me. "For nothing."

The bathroom door slams between us. I reclaim my seat on the bed, return to the laptop and the list of possibilities. My heart isn't in the search, though. My heart is in the shower.

So many emotions pound at me. *Sadness. Regret. Love.* Leaving Trajan killed part of my soul, and for two years I'd lived with the loss, an amputated limb sending flashes of phantom pain. Now he's here, breathing the same air, and all I want is to have his hands on me. To hold him. To beg his forgiveness.

My work with the Elites had defined me, at least until I met Trajan. The bond we shared gave me an alternative. For the first time in many, many years, I had something for myself. Something real, something warm, something good.

And then, in the middle of a case involving a missing fae princess, I *got made*, as they say in the biz, and for Trajan's safety, I had to disappear.

I stare at the laptop until my eyes blur. The shower goes on with a squeak. I fist my hands in the musty olive bedspread. That night in the bunker, Trajan would have drained me dry if it hadn't been for David. Trajan has feelings for the young wolf, and if I had any common sense, I'd leave them alone. Leave him alone. But it might be too much to ask of my heart to leave him again.

I'm more than a little tempted to join Trajan in the shower. We'd made showering together a habit, before, stolen moments for us. For his own safety, Trajan had to believe I was dead, and now if I can prevent a supernatural war, I'll have some level of satisfaction. But it'll be cold comfort for losing the man I love.

He turns off the water, and my breath catches. I know without seeing that he's shaking the water from his hair, toweling off, then folding the towel in half and draping it around his shoulders. He'll comb his hair straight back from his face and squeeze gel into the palm of his hand. His hair's an awkward length and poorly cut, but there's no point in getting a trim because he always rises with the hair he had when he left his mortal life.

Those small memories work on me, and without conscious thought, I find myself facing the bathroom door, gripping the knob. Silence from the other side. I should leave him alone, but I'm not strong enough to step away.

He flings the door open, knocking me off-balance. I stumble, brace myself with a hand on his chest. His bare chest. Skin warm from the shower. I swallow hard, try to right myself. He catches hold of my wrist. "Why?"

He jerks me forward, and before I can answer, we're kissing. His lips fuse to mine, his tongue possesses me. From the frisson of his aura to the dusty-sweet smell, he's exactly as I remember. I get a hand in his wet hair and another around his waist and cling to him like my life will end if I let go.

After his one-word question, we don't talk. I'll attempt to answer him later. Right now, I'm too busy kicking out of my sweatpants and pulling the crew neck over my head. He loses his towel at the same time, and then we're on the bed rolling over and over, skin on skin.

His kisses are fueled by anger. I can taste the fire. I melt into him, so thankful he's in my arms that tears threaten. He's rough, bruising me with the force of his grip. He latches onto my neck, and for a moment, I panic. I've barely recovered from his last feeding. I can't lose any more blood. His fangs stay sheathed, though the way he pulls my flesh between his teeth will leave a mark.

My dick is so hard, it hurts, and he's just as bad, so I reach for both our cocks. Roughly, he grabs my arm and slings me over on my belly. "Like this," he mutters, and I nearly do start to sob because I've wanted to feel him inside me ever since I left.

He spreads my cheeks and spits on my hole. A blunt finger spears me, rubbing in the slick. We've probably got lube somewhere, but I don't want him to stop. I want his anger. I want it to hurt.

Maybe down deep, I hope he'll purify us both with his righteous fire.

Wishful thinking.

He works a second finger in, his other hand planted between my shoulder blades, shoving me onto the bed. I'm barely ready when he pulls out. The head of his big cock nudges me, and then he shoves himself in.

I'm bearing down, using every trick I know to stay relaxed. It burns like hell, and I love every second. Trajan Gall is in me. Again. After so long. I rise up on my elbows, forehead resting in my hands. I can't look at him. I can't let him see my face. I can't let him see the tears.

He starts to thrust, a slow corkscrew that hits my gland and drives me wild. His hands hold my hips so tight, I'll have fingertip bruises. It feels so good, so right, I open myself and let him strip me raw.

He's grunting with every thrust, skin slapping against skin. His hand on my back softens, and he reaches up to thread his fingers through my hair, as much a caress as a means of control. Soon, too soon, he stills, and with a deep groan, he finds his release. He collapses on top of me, pressing me down into the mattress.

My cock is an iron bar trapped against my belly. He sighs and rolls to the side. I'm afraid to move because I don't want to break the spell. Hate sex works for me, as long as we don't go back to the frozen distance we had before.

"Come here." His whisper is raw, broken, and he draws me into his arms. I ease myself closer, so happy to be at his side, I can barely breathe. He strokes my arm with languid fingers. "So this is where we have a 'come to Jesus,' right?"

I stifle a laugh. "If you want to."

"Not really."

I'm hypnotized by the feel of his fingers tracing patterns on my skin. "We can defer until after we find David."

He gives a sharp inhale. "David."

Just that quickly, the spell is broken. Trajan stiffens; the biceps I'm using as a pillow jerks away. Though I do my best to hang on to the mood, my erection softens.

"David's the first guy who made me smile since you left."

I shift away from him. It's one thing to deal with his anger, another to hear him talk about his new man.

"Hell, he gave me a reason to keep living."

I wince, the guilt clawing at my heart.

"I know you and I have history, but I don't want to hurt him."

I clear my throat. "I don't either." I really don't. The young wolf is easy to like. "I won't interfere with the two of you."

I slip off the bed and go to the bathroom for a towel and some space. I clean up, leaving Trajan to his thoughts.

When I come out, Trajan's dressed and standing in the middle of the room. "Ready to go?" he asks.

I nod. Time to find the wolf.

CHAPTER TWENTY

This might be the world's saddest cliché." Trajan is hunkered down next to me, all dark clothing and pale, pale skin.

I lift my brows in lieu of asking why.

He snorts a laugh. "Look at us, man. We're hiding out in an empty office in a deserted building, watching a bunch of mysterious dudes bag who knows what from an unlit warehouse."

I rub my chin to disguise a smile. Trajan's attempts at slang didn't always work. "They're mysterious, all right."

They are. Four men, dressed in black, hustling unmarked boxes out a side door of a supposed storage facility and into the bed of a dark pickup truck. Their auras are muted, as if they somehow managed to hide even themselves.

A second small vehicle, a Mini Cooper or one of those little Fiats, is parked in front of the truck. The Alpha's notes aren't terribly clear on what was stored there, but I can hazard a guess that if this were a legitimate action, they'd have turned the lights on.

Trajan has his hair pulled back in a rudimentary nubbin of a ponytail, so for once I can see the whole of his face. His expression is somber, his features embedded in my mind. Allowing the vampire to believe I was dead is far and away the hardest thing I've ever done, and by rights, he should look at me with something close to hatred. Instead, my ass is still raw from his lovemaking.

"It's like, how many movies have a scene where the good guys are hiding out trying to catch the bad guys doing something bad?" His voice is pitched just above a murmur. "All of them."

"True." I catch myself before nudging his shoulder. I'd lost the right to do something as simple as that.

I do want to touch him, though, to reassure myself that we're really in the same place at the same time. Instead, I busy myself with night-vision goggles. The building we're watching is a three-story box with a set of double doors directly in front of us and a smaller side door on the north end. Something moves on the far end, and I focus my glasses there.

The block is mostly deserted. The only living things are on two legs, their auras colored with excitement and suspicion. "Damn," I whisper.

"What?"

He leans over my shoulder, and, as if we've rehearsed the choreography, I shift away. His weight, his heat are too distracting. He and the little werewolf are a thing, and I promised myself I'd leave them alone. And I will, as soon as I know they're safe.

Another movement, this time closer to the door. "It's a wolf in his fur."

He grunts, a surprised sound. "I see him. Wonder if he's wearing a white hat or a black one."

"A white hat or a black one?" I can't control a grin.

"Like in the old cowboy movies." His smile flashes and is gone. "Anyway, we should move closer, because if these guys get busted, you might be able to send in that tracer thing while they're distracted."

"Sure." I stand, and soon we're soundlessly moving down the hall to the stairs. The tracer is keyed to David's DNA, and if he's anywhere in the storage facility, it should find him.

We go single file down the stairs, Trajan first because he doesn't need help to see in the dark. Except for the occasional piles of trash, the hall and stairs are bare, lacking even the slightest residual aural energy. I've got one hand on his shoulder, the other holding my Glock at the ready. The stairwell smells like urine and mildew, and despite my best effort to stay focused on the threat in front of us, part of me is conscious of the dense muscles shifting under my hand.

The idea that we are witnesses to a robbery is pinging something in the back of my mind. I'd spent the last two years in Germany searching for someone who seemed to be assembling the tools for a major magical bomb, and while this is the wrong city and the wrong personnel, I have too much invested not to react to an obvious theft.

Near the bottom, he slows us. I don't ask why. I just drop a round into the chamber and aim at the floor.

Trajan glances over his shoulder once. The flash of recognition passing between us settles me, and when he takes the final few steps, I follow.

We land in a small room with doors in two of the walls. One must lead into the building's lobby and the other to the outside. I ease over to one door, and Trajan takes the other. The space is desperately quiet except for the whisper of my breathing.

Gently turning the knob, I open the door a crack and peer into darkness. Even with my goggles, there's nothing to see. It must be the lobby because the outdoor dark has more life to it. This is the absence of any light.

I close the door. To my right, Trajan gently opens his door an inch. I shift to one side to give him better coverage if something's waiting for us.

He opens it a few more inches. "Hmm?"

The door flies open, and a fist bigger than Trajan's head smashes him to the ground. I start firing. The doorway is filled with a single large body. A troll. My bullets bounce off whatever he has strapped across his chest. I go for the head instead, but he takes another swing and knocks the gun from my hand.

The creature is huge, easily eight feet tall and much wider than any human. They're not smart, but when you're that much bigger and that much stronger, you don't need a PhD. It either found us by dumb luck or we'd done something to give ourselves away. I abandon my handgun and make a run for the lobby, hoping to lead the thing away from Trajan.

I can't run very fast in the pitch black, afraid of putting a foot wrong and ending up on my ass. The troll follows, but when he reaches the door, he gives a little rage squeal. I stop in time to see the vampire's white hands wrap around its throat. The creature claws and thrashes, bellowing loud enough to make my ears ring, but somehow, Trajan hangs on.

No one seems to be disturbed by the commotion we're causing. I pull my backup pistol from the holster on my hip and take aim again. Trajan must have been having some success, for the noise from the troll drops to a raspy holler.

"I have a shot." Or I will if they stand still for another few seconds.

"No," a strange voice says, cool and feminine, so close to my ear, I can feel her breath. "Put the gun down."

I freeze. No one should have been able to sneak up on me like that. Inhaling, I try to identify who's behind me. I don't get much of a physical sense, no scent, no body heat, no aura, nothing brushing against my skin. Just the voice, and the breath, and another cool command. "Drop it and put your hands on top of your head."

Still I resist. "What are the consequences?"

"I don't think you'll like them." The edge of a blade skims my throat.

"Yeah. Persuasive." I slowly lower my arms. Something about this situation sets off more than the obvious alarm bells. This isn't simply a gang of losers looking to make some petty cash.

The troll crashes to his knees. Trajan keeps his grip, though his hands spasm when he realizes my predicament. After the briefest flash of surprise, his expression—and his grip—locks down.

The person behind me shoves hard enough to drive me to my knees, grasps a handful of my hair, and jerks my head up to make more room for the blade.

Anger stabs sharper than the knife at my throat. I haven't even sent the tracer out. Instead I'd wasted time fawning over Trajan, too distracted to keep us safe from this foolishness.

"What do you want?" I grind the words out. I have an even chance of getting an answer, but that's better than no chance at all.

Whoever's behind me jerks harder on my hair, making my eyes water. "I want your friend to let my associate go."

My captor's shivery lisp makes my skin crawl. Trajan's expression is flat, lacking any emotion, his eyes hollow. The troll's face turns purple and his bellow drops to a wheeze.

The blade presses more firmly against my skin. "I'm really not kidding."

If I drop my elbows straight down, I can likely shove the knife away from my skin. Then I'll need to duck and roll in order to avoid being stabbed in the back. The troll starts to slump, and without giving Trajan any warning, I make a move, my elbows slamming into muscular arms. With another lurch, I throw my body out of the way.

Trajan pushes the troll in my direction as if anticipating my move. I avoid it, but the big lump gets stabbed.

I'm on my feet and running as fast as I can, and Trajan's right behind me. I shoot a glance over my shoulder. The knife is dripping blood so dark, I can't even tell if it's red. I'd never much bothered with what color blood trolls have.

More startling, the person holding the knife is invisible.

Doubling my speed, I careen around the end of the building. I don't want to lead any of the black hats to our rental car, so we need to buy some time. The were's storage site is across the street, and as near as I can tell, we're not being followed. But if the being who'd threatened to slit my throat drops the knife, I'll never see her coming.

We run past an alley. Trajan ducks in. "Hey."

One gasped word grabs my attention, so I pivot and — hoping he has a plan — follow. Thirty feet in, we come to an old fire escape clinging like a rusty appendage to the side of a brick building. The bottom rung is well above my head. Trajan leaps, catching hold with one hand. The other he holds out.

For me.

I take hold, and he pulls me up, grunting with the strain. I still have no idea of we're being followed, and the uncertainty tightens every muscle. I cling to Trajan till he hoists us high enough that I can catch hold of the corroded metal ladder.

The thing groans beneath our weight, shifting the pegs holding it against the wall. The air is foul with refuse and urine, but none of it smells fresh. Trajan brackets me, and together we take one rung at a time. The top of the building is in sight when the ladder jumps as if someone has grabbed the bottom rung.

"Keep going," Trajan says, his voice still tight with effort.

I follow his direction, reaching for another rung. The rough bars abrade my skin. I keep going, helped by Trajan's strong, solid presence. We're about four feet from the top, maybe one or two more rungs.

"Fuck."

The expletive catches me off guard. His whole body shudders. I stop moving entirely.

"Go. The bitch has silver. I'll catch up."

I'm afraid to leave him, afraid of what I'll see if I look back. The moon's hanging low over the horizon, and darkness surrounds us.

He gasps again. "Go."

I go, crawling up the final rungs of the ladder and shimmying onto the roof. Trajan's dropped several rungs. He's awkwardly kicking thin air. There's a knife hilt sticking out of his calf.

There's not a lot I can do for him.

I sight down the barrel of my pistol. Damn it. I can't see who he's fighting. After a minute or two, I stand down. I pull the package of tracers from my pocket and activate one. They're small, half the size of a hummingbird, and they carry a charge that'll keep them flying for at least an hour. Tossing the thing off the side of the building, I should say a prayer for luck, but I don't actually know any. Finding David soon is good, but if we find him here — with random robbers, crazy Invisible Woman, and her troll sidekick — he'll have had a rough time of it.

Trajan howls and drops another few feet down the ladder. The whole thing grinds as if the century-old screws are pulling away from the brick. The leg with the blade sticking out of it doesn't look like it's holding any weight. He's got both arms wrapped around the ladder, and he kicks with the good leg. From the way his foot stops dead, I can tell he hit something.

That must give him a break, because he reaches down and pulls out the knife. Maybe he meant to toss it away or maybe he could see a target, but the old fire escape's ladder gives it up. With Trajan still holding on, the thing crashes to the ground.

CHAPTER TWENTY-ONE

'm oh for two.

I'd brought the Alpha's son to see his father and had him snatched right from in front of me, and I'd tried to help my ex find his new boyfriend and dropped him into an alley with an invisible opponent.

The moral of this story is, don't trust the Elite to get you out of trouble.

The building where I'm standing is only about four stories tall, but it's hard to make out the figure of a vampire in the general darkness covering the old pavement. The fire escape is barely a shadowy lump, and as far as I can tell, Trajan is underneath it. Distant traffic hums along in the background, but the alley is silent. If the crew who were packing boxes out of the storage facility heard the crash, they're long gone.

Before I leave the rooftop, I do one more thing. I send a message to Dante, asking him to send me some backup. Communicating by text will minimize the amount of scorn he can rain down on me. *Yeah, I fucked up. Get over it and send help.*

Gun drawn, and with my phone out for light, I find a door that leads inside and run downstairs.

This building hasn't been deserted all that long. Flashes of color mark the phone's white light, the residue left whenever a human has passed. I wind down the stairs, stopping at every landing to listen for company. Nothing. *Shite.*

The main floor must still be a functioning office space. I choose a hallway that should take me to the back door. Along the way, I pass open office doors with the occasional pinpoint red light from a desktop in sleep mode. My gut's knotted with fear and anger. One of the primary rules for the Elite was not to get attached to anyone. The difficulty of our work, along with the secrecy it requires, made all but the most ephemeral relationships impossible.

But no. Connor Joseph MacPherson had to have it all and fuck the consequences. I'd half expected Trajan to snap my neck for kicks. So many nights I'd spent hunkered down, watching a target, imagining how our reunion would go.

For every tacky Hallmark moment, I saw two or three ways I'd end up dead.

I come to a small lobby with a large double door. The top half of each door is glass, and while

I can see the crumpled fire escape, there's no sign of Trajan and whoever he was fighting.

I dim my phone's light, in case there is anyone out there, and debate my next steps. If I open the door and set off an alarm, I'll bring the street cops running. If there's a lock and chain on the outside of the door, I won't be able to open it. If Trajan's duking it out with the Invisible Woman, I won't be much help to him anyway.

All those options suggest it would be smartest for me to wait until Dante's backup crew arrives. Waiting? *No.* That might be my best option, but no way.

I head back the way I came to see if there's something I missed. Two doors down the hall, I find an office with a window. Piles of paper cover the desk. I shine my light on it and scan the few closest to me. Bill of sale. Invoice for services rendered. Draft of Spring catalog. I give that one a closer look.

Crystals. Amethyst. Lavender. Rue. Huh. The business's name is Frank's Magic Warehouse. For a warehouse, the place sure has a lot of offices. The were's storage space would be better suited. The were's storage space, which someone appears to be robbing.

Chills crawl up the back of my neck. A theft of magical materials might not be related to the case

I'd been working on, but my inner resonance tells me I need to pay attention. The missing fae princess shouldn't be linked to a theft of this kind, unless…

I snap a photo of one of the invoices so I'll have the business's contact information, then turn my attention to the window.

Goddess knows what shape Trajan's in, while I've been faffing about with invoices. The desk butts up to the window, and I crawl across the top, holding my breath that I don't leave things too obviously awry.

The window latch is easy to open. There's a screen, but with a sharp smack in each of the corners, I pop it out. I scoot through, close the window, and take off running for the fire escape.

Deciding everyone must have gone off without me, I scan the area with light from my cell phone. Traces of Trajan's aura, along with some spindly silver streaks, presumably left behind by Invisible Woman. I stoop to look closer when a loud crack jerks my attention back to the alley. The troll hops out of a drunkenly swinging door, and before I can respond, he's on me.

He slams me back against the building, knocking my head hard against the brick. I've got my gun out, but he's too close and moving too fast. He winds his big fist up for a punch. I duck at the last second, taking most of it with my left shoulder. I manage to get a shot off, or at least the gun's report is echoed by a monstrous bellow. I get one step away, then a second, but my foot

lands awkwardly in a patch of broken cement. He grabs me by the hips and pulls, wrenching my knee. I go down, firing blindly over my shoulder.

Ádh mór balbh. He lands on me, but in a stroke of dumb luck, instead of a wrestling move designed to take me out, he pins me with deadweight. Blood trickles from a wound above his right eye. His heft has forced my knee into an angle it wasn't meant to assume, and the pain is increasing with every beat of my heart.

I wriggle around until I can get my good knee underneath me, then hoist the big body off. The troll flops onto the road, and I'm faced with a new problem. My phone squirted out of my grip when I went down, but there's a pile of debris against the wall that's glowing with a familiar white light. I crawl across the alley to retrieve it, and text Dante again.

Also send a cleanup crew.

Because Goddess only knows what the local authorities would make of the body of a troll. The local cops probably saw a picture once while they were at the academy, but the real thing is hard to prepare for.

I need to find Trajan, but walking is hard. My bad knee won't take any weight, so I hop toward the street, grabbing the wall or the remains of the fire escape as I go.

Fortunately, I don't find the Invisible Woman, but unfortunately, I don't find Trajan either. Also in the fortunately column, the tracer returns. The thing is designed to drop a sensor the size of a pea when it reaches its target. That sensor will give me a limited visual of the location, along with a microphone, so if nothing else, I can tell David we're coming.

The tracer is still carrying the sensor, so David is still MIA.

The street is dark and silent. From my position in the shadows, I have a decent look at the storage facility. The side door is shut, and both the truck and the Mini are gone. I'm debating whether I can hop all the way to our rental car when something crashes behind me. I pivot, biting back a cry when I land on my bad leg.

A figure moves down the alley. If it's Invisible Woman made visible, I'm probably going to die. I manage to prop myself up and get a hand on my gun. I should be afraid, but it's as if mortality has stiffened my spine. I raise my arm, sighting down the barrel. "Stop."

The figure slows but does not stop. The only thing between us is the body of the troll.

"I mean it. Stop." *One step closer and I'll shoot.*

"Connor."

Relief sends me sagging against the wall of the building. "Traj?"

"It's me." He continues, moving deliberately as if he's in pain. When he's close enough, I try to read his expression. He's not giving anything away.

"Dig this, man." With a flip of his hand, the onyx handle of a dagger appears between his fingers. "Small but mighty."

"Dig this?" I crack a grin.

"Shut up." He shakes his head, dark hair flopping into his face, but the ghost of a smile flits over his lips. "That piece-of-junk fire escape dumped me almost on top of her." He glances over his shoulder at the troll. "Had to chase her down, but…"

His words peter off. "What was she?" I prompt.

"Oh, a vampire." The dagger disappears into a pocket. "Some of us have *invisibilia*. It's not all that common, and it's a huge energy drain, so even those with the gift don't use it very often."

"I called for a cleanup crew for the troll."

"Yeah, nice work."

I holster my pistol. "I also called for some backup. It's gotta be midnight by now, and if whoever has David is hiring trolls and superpowered vampires, we need the help."

"Agreed."

He mutters something, but when I ask what he's said, he shrugs. "Let's just find David, okay?"

"Okay." Standing this close to him, the soft curve of his lower lip draws my attention. As much as I want to kiss him, I've just agreed to help him find his lover. Tamping down my own desire, I start sorting through our priorities for the search.

The car's engine clicks, little sparks of tension in the silence. Trajan's behind the wheel, and there aren't many things quieter than a vampire. We're staking out the weres' training center from a darkened corner of the parking lot across the street. To our left is an auto repair place, though the generally seedy air suggests they spend more time parting out vehicles than repairing them.

The building under surveillance is at the end of the road in the gray zone between suburban and rural, surrounded by the kind of straggling understory that grows whenever there's no one to maintain the landscape. At night, the trees aren't much more than a shadowy smudge.

"That shrubbery's conveniently located, don't you think?" I shift in my seat, trying to find a position that doesn't put pressure on my knee. "For a bunch of weres, I mean."

Trajan huffs a laugh. "Wolves tend to stand out on a city street."

I smile, deliberately keeping my gaze on the building. We're at the last of the likeliest sites. I'd set the tracer off as soon as we parked, so now it's just a matter of patience till it comes back around. I shift again, left hip to right. I want an ice pack and a couple of Percocets. Or a hot bath and a shot of scotch. Something.

"I think he's close."

Trajan just answered my unspoken question and distracted me in one move. He'd tasted David's blood, and while sharing blood creates a bond, it's less specific than an actual DNA trace. "Good." I drag my protesting brain to the problem of David without looking at Trajan. His vampire super-vision will show him all the secrets in my face.

I'm too aware of him, the way he holds himself so still, the sloppy spill of hair across his brow. So many things to say, so many explanations I'd rehearsed and discarded and picked up again. In all my lifetimes—and there have been several—he's the first who made me want to stay.

The soft chime of my phone drags me out of my meandering thoughts. I answer, surprised to see Randolph Collins's name displayed on the screen.

"I got a call." The force of the alpha's personality vibrates through the phone. "They said if I don't step down as alpha within four hours, they'll kill him."

Damn it. "Did you recognize who called you?"

His first response is a muffled curse. "Not…well…they used some kind of voice distortion, so no, I didn't." He pauses, and I give him time to think. "I can guess who it might be."

"The person who benefits if you step aside?"

He gives a frustrated snort. "Yeah."

"I think we're close to David, and if I'm right, we'll have him out well before the deadline." I can't really promise more than that. "And by the way, when we checked out one of your storage facilities, there was some activity. Four weres on two legs, one on four, loading a pickup with boxes."

"Shit."

"It didn't look like an official operation. Any guesses what they might have been after?"

"Best I can do is tell you what's missing."

I'm not surprised. The senior Collins tells me he'll be back in touch, and I hang up knowing he'll be running the list of his real friends and loyalists.

"Dear Dad." I toss the phone into the center console.

"I heard."

Vampire. "We've got four hours, maybe less."

"And then what? You planning to disappear again?"

Trajan always was too blunt for his own good. "I guess that's up to you."

His bitter laugh is no more than I deserve.

"I always thought the wolves were the strongest, you know? So organized, always standing behind their alpha."

For now, I roll with his subject change. "I guess I did, too."

"But they're going to end up with a vampire war on their hands if they're not careful."

"How do you figure?" My knee throbs, but at least he's given me something to think about.

"If I get killed going after the alpha's kidnapped son, you don't think Jacques will start something?"

Glad I'm looking out the window, because I'm pretty sure Jacques won't do anything unless he can make money off it. "You can't get killed. We still need to…" Whoa, do I really want to say this? "I hope we can—"

"Later. I want to hear everything. I want to know exactly what went down." His low voice brooks no discussion. "Let's get this done and—"

"We'll talk." I try to match his candor, and it takes every ounce of my will to keep my eyes on the scene in front of us. If I meet his gaze, even for a moment, I will not stop. A glance will be followed by words, which'll be followed by touch. My palms itch with need for his cool skin.

Unlikely I'll get the chance to move past words, but a stubborn little corner of my mind remains convinced that as long as he hasn't killed me, I have room to hope.

Another chime, this one higher pitched and more insistent. The tracer has dropped its sensor. *Good.*

I open the app on my phone. It takes a moment to sort out up from down with the limited visual the little chip provides me. Trajan leans in, and I hold the phone where we can both see.

"What the hell?"

I shush him because I've got the audio activated, and until we know who's in the room, I don't want to give anything away.

At the bottom of the app's image there's a directional widget. I tap it to shift our view from side to side, then up. The chip is on the floor in a puddle of blood-streaked water. I shift the directional indicator around again, and we both swear out loud. David's in a chair, and while the angle's wrong for us to get a complete view of his face, what we can see looks pretty beat up.

Easier to see are the silver bands holding his feet to the chair. We can't see them, but the way his shoulders are cocked, I'm pretty sure his arms are pinned behind his back with silver, too.

I make another circuit, right and left, up and down. He's surrounded by weres, wolves, all of them on two legs. One douses him with a bucket of water and ice. David's head rocks back, muscles and sinews taut. Another of the weres hits him with a prod of some kind, and he arches as if he's been shocked.

His scream is shredded, a weak echo of itself, as if he has nothing left after hours of abuse. At my side, Trajan's so still, he might have turned to stone.

"David Collins."

The speaker stands in the center of their circle. I touch the image, focusing the sensor around on him. He bears a striking resemblance to Randolph Collins.

"Brendan," Trajan growls.

The speaker moves toward David. David twitches, as if he'd kick his uncle if his feet weren't tied down.

"We've wasted enough time here," Brendan says, and another voice agrees. I scan the circle again.

Trajan stops me at a young wolf. "His cousin Marcus. Supposedly his best friend."

If I was angry before, now I'm enraged. My knee is a mess, but I could still shift and go in when the team arrives.

And make a difficult situation exponentially more challenging.

Leaving aside the secret I'm not ready to share, I turn my attention back to the screen. One of the weres grabs David's right hand, pulling at his fingers. His hands are fisted so tight, the were has to work to pry them apart. "Here, you stupid fucker," he mutters, and presses a pen against the side of David's hand, forcing his thumb to hold it in place.

Trajan's got the car door open. "We need to get in there."

I lock my grip around his upper arm. "Only if you want David dead. If we wait for backup, we'll be able to take them all down."

"Now bring in the form," the first voice says, dragging our attention back to the screen.

"Fuck. They're going to cut him out of the pack." Trajan braces himself as if he's ready to run in there and make it stop.

I recall enough werewolf lore to know that cutting someone out of the pack only takes a brief ceremony with a quorum. David jerks his legs against the brackets holding them in place, trying and failing to thrash his arms. If they say the words and force him to sign, he'll be a lone wolf.

"No." He cries out, terror strengthening the sound.

His uncle starts up again. "And so we are bound by a force stronger than death. Who here answers my call?"

From around the room there's a chorus of "I hear."

David groans. I focus on him. He's making a pitiful effort to open his swollen eyes, as if even now, he's trying to see his enemies.

"Our mother the moon sees all and knows all, and with her as witness, I move to set this child apart from her light. If any object, this is your last opportunity to speak."

Silence, except for the rustling and breathing of excited men, and the "no, no, no, no, no," David can't suppress. One were slides a mundane office clipboard under David's hand, and the other forces him to clutch the pen, forces his hand to move.

A sharp snap, as if someone had cracked a whip in the center of the room.

"That'll do."

David is not moving. At all.

"You don't look so good, Davey. I hear that getting cut out of the pack hurts like hell."

This is a new voice, familiar and mocking. I scroll over to focus on the speaker. "He's dead," Trajan whispers. "I'm going to kill that son of a bitch and enjoy doing it."

"It's all right, though," the same were continues. "If Daddy doesn't step down as Alpha in the next four hours, you're gonna be so dead it won't even matter."

"Step down as…" Rocking his head from side to side, David giggles, then outright laughs. "You're a dead man walking."

The were backhands David, hard, knuckles and a fat ring cutting his lip. "Dead," Trajan says again.

"You're in no place to start spouting threats, son." Uncle Brendan waves a quelling hand at the were with the ring.

David spits a wad of blood and saliva in the direction of his voice. "It's not a threat, babe. One of us is going to kill you."

They hit him with the prod one more time, punishing his defiance, and then they file out. I wait until I'm sure he's alone and bring the phone close to my mouth. Again, I avoid Trajan's gaze, but this time, it's because I'm afraid of what I'll see in his face.

"David?" I have the chip directed as close as I can get to David's face. His eyes are closed, and he doesn't respond, so I turn up the volume. "David?"

He jerks, gives a cough, but doesn't open his eyes. Maybe he can't. They're pretty swollen.

"David."

He rocks his head from side to side.

"David, it's me. It's Connor. I'm with Trajan." I find I'm leaning forward, speaking directly into the phone.

"Yeah."

I'm not completely sure he's formed an actual word. "Hang in there, David. We're coming in."

He's breathing harder. Watching his struggle is painful.

"Too late." He sounds lost.

"We're outside, David, and we're coming in. Is there anything else you can tell us? Any particular thing we should know?"

David's not a trained professional, so he might not know what to watch for, but he's smart and he's the son of the Alpha.

"Come on, Davey," Trajan mutters. He's leaning forward too, just as invested as I am.

"We're coming in, David. What do we need to worry about?"

He squirms in his seat. "Cold." The word is hard to hear. "So damned cold."

"We'll bring blankets," Trajan says, and I nod in agreement.

"And we'll hurry."

I check the time. We've got about two and a half hours before the midnight deadline. My phone chirps, telling me Dante's team has arrived. I spend a few minutes dealing with logistics, then turn to the vampire.

"Trajan Gall. Stop, man. Just stop."

Trajan's got his head in his hands, all but grinding his teeth against the self-flagellation.

"If we'd arrived half an hour ago and the team was with us, we might have been able to stop it."

"We failed him." The pain in his words tears at me, hitting me deep.

I smack the dashboard. Dante's team is spreading out around the building, so if anyone tries to escape in wolf form, we'll have the chance to stop them. I can barely walk, so there's no way I'm going out on a wolf hunt.

But you could shift…

I swallow down that unwelcome thought and focus on the situation at hand. The team's leader messages me back. "They're good to go," I say.

Trajan opens the door and gets one foot on the ground before he stops, looking at me over his shoulder. "You'll be okay out here?"

I wave him on. "I've already texted the team leader to let him know you're coming. Just…" I catch my lower lip between my teeth, a bad habit I'm trying hard to break. "Just…be safe, okay?"

He climbs out of the car, pauses like he's going to say something important, then eases his way to the street. He moves vampire-quick, and my breath gets caught in my throat.

In a very real sense, he's carrying my heart.

I shift in my seat, the dull throbbing pain in my knee competing with the stabbing pain in my chest. *If* we get through this, and *if* we bring David through this, and *if* Trajan will have me back, it may be time for me to leave the Elites — and all my secrets — behind.

PART FOUR: SILVER MOON

CHAPTER TWENTY-TWO

TRAJAN

I want to be angry. I really, really do. I want to hate Connor for leaving, hate him for nearly two years of pain and loneliness and rejection. Instead, I'm torn between searching for David and staying behind to protect the man who left me.

Yep. That's right. I want to protect the man who not only left me, but made me believe he was dead, and who is apparently a part of our super-secret police force.

Maybe I should be more of an asshole.

Meanwhile, I manage to find the Elite team leader without looking back at the car. He's over on the far corner of the property, standing so still, he must be a vampire. He is. I get about ten paces away, and I catch his scent. Vampires tend to repel each other, like magnets of opposite polarity, and I have to force myself to keep walking.

Six feet away, he holds up his hand. "Gall?"

"Yeah." *You were expecting Frank Sinatra?*

"Okay." He scanned the area. "I've got men around the perimeter. You and two others will make the first approach. Your goal will be to locate the target and flush out any of the weres holding him. You armed?"

I nod, opening my jacket to show Connor's holster. It says something about the Elite that they'll plug any random vampire into their crew.

"Good." His voice is smoky, soft, and his dark clothing molds to his muscular form. "Try not to get into a gunfight if you can help it."

I shrug. Gunfights make for complications, and I avoid those whenever possible. The leader sends a text, and in moments, a pair of figures comes jogging across the parking lot. They take turns offering to shake my hand, mumbling their names like they don't really want me to know. Tall, and lanky, their energy marks them as at least half elf, which means they can fight like the devil. They're also both wearing hoods, but one has tatts covering his neck. I call him Mutt and his partner is Jeff.

"Joss said you've fed from the target, so you should be able to track him once we get inside."

Mutt's got an accent, and from the flatness of his vowels, I'd say he's from Australia. I just need one *g'day, mate* to be sure.

"Yeah, I've been picking up his vibe from here."

"Good." Mutt pulls out an actual paper diagram and waves me and Jeff closer. "It looks like the front doors open into a small lobby with two offices on each side. There's a bank of elevators here" — he points to the middle of the page — "and three big rooms run across the back. Upstairs, there's the same basic configuration, with offices in the front, but only two big rooms in the back. The rest of the space is a locker area, and the big rooms are for training."

He pauses, and Jeff clears his throat like he's going to say something, but nothing comes out.

"Is that it? Because if it is, I'd like to get going." The clock is ticking.

"There's a basement, too." He turns the diagram over. "Accessed by either the elevator or one of two stairwells. One stair is next to the elevator, and the other's in the back." As he tucks the paper away, his glare says he's daring me to walk away. "From the look of it, there's an infirmary down there, along with a bank of cages and two big rooms that are likely used for the wolves who need to learn to shift."

Cages? I'm not real excited about the basement, and from his deep scowl, Mutt isn't either. "Why do I think that's likely where he is?"

"We're going in the front door, but unless we run into anyone, I think we should start at the bottom."

I shrug. I don't want to do this, don't want to walk into a building at night where there are an uncertain number of armed wolves.

But I really don't want David to get hurt any more than he already has been.

And I really, really want to smash some heads together. *Payback, you jackasses.*

Mutt pulls an AK-47 from behind his back. "I lead, you come second, and he'll follow." He nods at his partner. "And try to let us do the shooting."

Jeff doesn't say anything, but his frown and his gun are the mirror images of Mutt.

I hold up a hand. "Let me check with Connor before we go in." They shoot me a pair of matching impatient glances, but I pull out my phone anyway. I give him a quick call, asking what's going on in David's room. He says something about David having company, but it's the things he doesn't say that make me nervous. If they've killed him, the elves won't need their fancy weapons. They'll have to stand out of my way while I take down the lot of them.

When the call is done, I pull out Connor's backup pistol, and the three of us head across the narrow lawn to the front door. The elder Collins gave us the code for the burglar alarm, but surprise, surprise, it hasn't been armed. There's no warning beep or flashing light when we come through the door.

I catch Mutt's eye. He doesn't like it either.

Jeff closes the door, and for a moment, we all stop in the entry. The place is dark except for the red glow given off by the exit sign over our heads. There's no sign of anyone, no sound of any activity. Mutt takes a step toward the back of the building, but before I can follow, a wolf's howl, long and mournful, freezes us in place.

The sound trails off, then swells, a second voice joining the first. The ceiling is covered with white acoustical tile, so the howling shouldn't echo, but it does, and it's impossible to tell where it's coming from.

I give Mutt a look, basically letting him know he better move or I'll take over. His brows arch—elves are nothing if not haughty—but my challenge prompts him toward a closed office door. I'm pretty sure all the offices are empty, because except for the howling, it's quiet. Torturing a guy makes noise.

And it was torture. The acknowledgment burns on the way down. David's a handful, a flaming, raucous, beautiful handful, but he doesn't deserve this kind of betrayal. My incisors stretch and sharpen, something that only happens when I'm about to lose it. Yeah, I better catch at least one of these assholes alive.

The first office is empty, but before we go door-to-door, I close my eyes and reach out with all my senses. David's essence tugs on me, drawing me toward the basement, but nothing else grabs me. I mouth the word *empty*, but Mutt's haughty expression doesn't change. He moves to the next room, and my gut clenches, every instinct screaming that something bad will happen if he opens it. Without thinking, I make a running leap and tackle him.

"Fucking lay off," he squawks, smacking at me until I get his hands pinned.

I catch his eye and calm him with my will. I'm about to ease up when the snub nose of a gun tags me in the back of the head.

"We don't have time for this," Jeff says, his accent less pronounced.

"Don't open the door." I keep my gaze on Mutt, who's lying quietly underneath me. "There's something in there."

Muttering, Jeff reaches past us and opens the door. Nothing. He crosses to the other two, opens the closest. Nothing. Opens the next—

Boom.

Jeff gets lifted off his feet. He lands on his ass, close enough to kick me in the thigh. Mutt and I scramble up, weapons out.

"I'd say we rang the doorbell." Neither of them laughs at my joke. "Look, I'm pretty sure David's downstairs, and since I don't want them to kill him now that they know we're here, I'm going down."

Jeff's standing, not quite steady, but I don't see any blood.

"You two cover me." Or not. So much for the pride of the Elite and notorious elvish fighting mojo and blah blah blah. Without waiting, I take off, moving for the rear stairs as fast as I can.

The stairwell is dim, lit only by ankle-high lights in the upright of about every third stair. After my eyes adjust, it's as bright as noon. I jet down the stairs, spine tingling from the sense that I'm being followed. Maybe it's just my new elf friends. I'm moving too fast to check it out. Then I hit the bottom and slow myself.

Here, it's truly dark. Even my vision only picks up hints and weak shadows. The only light, in fact the only thing I can make out clearly, is a bare bulb hanging over a four-sided cage that seems to be set in the middle of a much bigger space.

And David's sitting in the middle of the cage.

A wolf howls, the sound bouncing off the cement floor and echoing in space.

"We see you, Trajan Gall. Drop your weapon."

Aw hell no. The voice comes from somewhere in the darkness. I don't answer, because what's the point.

Then a pinpoint of red appears on David's forehead. Some kind of laser.

"I told you to drop your weapons." Laughter punctuates his command. I don't think he's funny.

I do a little reverse geometry and scan the shadows, following the line of the laser to its origin.

"Five….four…."

"Jesus, that's a cliché even by my standards." I can't find the source, but I can see the trajectory, dust motes sparkling in the tiny beam of light.

"Three… Two…" I coil, ready to spring.

"One" — I leap into the beam, hollering the whole way.

"No."

David bleats, a weak sound that breaks my heart. Did he get hit? I lunge for the cage. Can't see any blood. Claws scrabbling behind me. Wolves. I reach for the bars, but a burning pain in my shoulder stops me.

Dammit. I got shot again. Metal, not silver. Guess I'll be thankful for small favors.

A pair of wolves comes out of the darkness. I shoot one mid-leap. The other stops, crouches, growls. The red laser sight swings across the floor, traveling up my body. I can't see it, but I imagine it stops at my head.

This'd be a humdinger of a time for those elves to show up.

"I figured the big bad vampire would be harder to kill."

I wish I could see the guy, to know who I need to exact revenge upon. "Not dead yet."

Another explosion, this one closer to the stairs. The wolf in front of me flinches. The laser light drops to the ground.

A third explosion rocks the whole building, followed by heavy footsteps on the stairs.

"Shit." With a muffled thump, the weapon fires.

I duck, swinging wildly with both arms to try to redirect the bullet. It doesn't hit me, and when I spare him a glance, it hasn't hit David either.

Voices, speaking Elvish. The beam of red light sweeps across the floor and gets lost in a hail of gunfire. The wolf attacks too, leaping at the Elite squad. I hold my position, determined to protect

David, who's the most vulnerable of all of us. In my quick glances, I've been able to determine his lips are pink, so he's breathing, but not much more than that.

The fighting dies down, the elves and their vampire leader coming into the circle of light cast by the bulb over the cage. Other members of the team are hog-tying the wolf, and another has handcuffed the pleasant chap who greeted me.

I figure it's safe enough to let David out. The cage door is locked — of course — but it doesn't take much effort to bend the bars enough for me to open the door.

I step in. David's head is tipped back, his eyes swollen shut. I'm about to speak when, with a growl, something hits me from behind. Another wolf, the biggest one yet, uses my body as a springboard to get to David's throat.

And with a solid thud, a bullet takes it out.

Connor's standing on one leg just inside the circle of light, pistol in his hand. He's unsteady, but before he tips over, the vampire leader offers him help. Someone finds the overhead lights, and I'm still blinking away the glare when another agent finds him a chair.

"When things started exploding, I couldn't just sit in the car." Connor's speaking to me, even though there's activity all around us. I nod, silently promising I'll tend to him in a moment. Behind me, David groans.

"Anybody got metal cutters?" I ask the group at large and drop to my knees. One of the elves comes over with a small snipper, and I get rid of David's bindings. Moving carefully, I lift him from the chair.

"It doesn't matter," shouts the guy who'd been too stupid to kill me when he had the chance. "He'll die anyway. He's not pack anymore."

I step out of the cage with David in my arms, coming to a stop beside Connor. "Too bad his father's not going to let you live long enough to find out how wrong you are, you twit."

CHAPTER TWENTY-THREE

e move to a different hotel. Randolph Collins insists on sending a physician to examine David, and I agree only on the condition that the doc meets me somewhere and I drive him in blindfolded. Him, not me. I don't want Randolph, or anyone else from the pack, to know where we're staying.

Besides, I figure someone should look at Connor's knee too, though he'll argue me to death if I try to make him the center of attention.

Our hotel room has two king-size beds. Connor's in one with an ice pack on his knee and a glass of bourbon on his nightstand. David's in the other, and he's still out.

I'm still not sure how I feel about Connor. I mean, I know how I used to feel about him, before I thought he was dead. But if getting back with Connor means leaving David, I'm not sure I can do it. One's my past, the other's my present, and hell only knows what the future holds.

Despite the blankets and pillows I've packed around David, he's shivering. I brush my fingertips across his forehead. Hot. Really hot. Without giving in to an internal debate, I shed my shirt and climb into bed with him, spooning him against my chest. It's like holding on to a fiery coal, but maybe I can cool him off some.

"I'm glad…" Connor stops and clears his throat. "I'm glad you have him."

He sounds so lost. I gulp down the urge to comfort him. He made his choices, and now he has to live with them. He had promised to explain, though, and this is as good a time as any.

"So why did you leave?"

I shut my eyes, my nose buried in David's hair. He needs a bath, some expensive hair product, and knowing him, he'll want some manscaping, but his earthy scent is comforting. There's a pause, as if Connor's taking a sip from his bourbon. We could have asked for separate rooms, but I like having us all together.

And not just in case there are more rogue wolves coming for David.

"I've been part of the Securitas for ten years, a member of the Elite for most of that time." His voice is scratchy, and he pauses for another sip. "I was based in LA, which is big enough and busy enough that there was little talk of assigning me anywhere else." He lets the silence echo. "Until there was."

"Until there was."

He shifts in the bed, and I hope the doctor brings him some real drugs for his knee.

"I worked a variety of cases, tracking raging incubi, cleaning out an infestation of zombies. That kind of thing." He sighs. "When you and I met, telling you I worked in security gave me enough of a cover. I could explain the hours and the occasional blood."

"Blood," I scoff.

"I am sorry, *mo shiorghrá*." He clears his throat and continues. "Then about three years ago, a fae princess went missing. I made a poor choice, and my identity became known to certain unsavory characters. My handlers decided I should disappear completely, and that as an extra precaution, you needed to believe I was dead."

David squirms, and I realize I'm holding him so tight, he probably can't breathe. I relax, pressing a kiss against his head. "So you faked your own death—and kudos for that, man. You're a helluva good actor—and disappeared." My words are sarcastic, bitter, but it's like he's lanced a boil and now all the shit's coming out.

"Yes. I've been in Europe on loan to the French government for most of the last two years." His grimaced as if his knee had just sent off a spasm of pain. "There were rumors of an alliance, a group who wanted to destabilize the supernatural community. When Jacques offered you as David's bodyguard, that pinged for some people. I got tagged to come to LA to keep an eye on things since I knew the players." He rakes a hand through his hair. "Honestly, I insisted on taking the case, but I had no idea how hard it would be to see you again."

I cradle David closer. Seems even the Elites thought David and I had been set up. "That makes…some sense."

Connor exhales hard, as if he's been holding his breath until he heard my response. "I think we need to stay out of sight until Randolph Collins gets his house in order."

"And we should probably get out of here as soon as David can travel."

"His aura's pretty shredded. It's going to take a while."

"Okay, wait." I close my eyes again, not sure I'm ready for any more surprises. "You can see auras?"

He squirms a bit at that. "Yeah."

"Handy trick. You sure you're just a garden-variety human?"

"Yes." He says it quickly, and while he meets my eyes, it's only for a moment. *Okay.* Still keeping secrets. One of the reasons I'd been attracted to Connor in the first place was that I couldn't influence his thinking the way I could a normal human. Until now, I'd never asked the question.

Until now, he'd never had cause to lie.

Damn it. Time to lighten the mood. I don't have the energy for more drama. "Why the hell did you shoot me in the parking garage?"

"Come on, Traj, I didn't use silver bullets."

"Seriously?" I tip my head back, letting the overstuffed hotel pillow cradle it. "You're so full of shit."

He grins. I don't, but my anger fades.

"The pack was making noise about searching your place and I was pretty sure Jacques gave them your address. I wanted you to clear out before they showed up."

"And a bullet was the most efficient way of doing that?"

"More or less." After a long stare into his drink, he gives me a warmer smile. "Now, I don't want to get in the way of…" He waves in my general direction, including David in the gesture.

I don't know how to respond. Maybe this is his backhanded way of scoping my level of interest. Am I interested? David's weight is warm and heavy in my arms. I don't want to have to choose, and in a moment of uncharacteristic clarity, I imagine what it would be like if I didn't have to.

"Come over here. Maybe if he has one of us on either side of him, it'd help."

The glass of bourbon hits the coffee table with a sharp clink, and with a string of muttered curses, Connor shifts closer to our bed. He tosses a pillow over for his knee, followed by the bag of ice. It takes him a minute to navigate the narrow space between the beds and to settle himself on David's other side, but at last he makes it. Tentatively, he rests one hand on the pillow next to my head and the other on David's arm, making an arc around both of us.

"That beard, though…" I don't realize I've said the words until Connor starts to laugh. The Connor I knew was clean-shaven. "This will take some getting used to."

Dawn is coming, and the three of us are going to have to find our way forward. For now, I follow the rhythm of their breathing and let myself drift off to sleep.

The strangeness doesn't truly settle over me until I wake. The room is brighter than any vampire room, though heavy drapes keep out direct sunlight. Both David and Connor have shifted in their sleep. They're also both awake.

"Good morning, sleeping beauty."

David's voice is weak but chipper, and I want to hold him down and kiss him till he squeaks. But Connor's right there, his auburn curls flat on one side. His heavy-lidded gaze a reminder of so many things I'd packed away, refused to think about. The combination of David's warmth and Connor's presence turns my dick into an iron bar.

On cue, David squirms, rubbing his ass on the hardness. "Well, hey there, Vamp Man, is that an armadillo in your pocket, or are you just happy to see me?"

"A little of both, I guess." I nuzzle his ear as I speak, but my gaze is locked on Connor.

I'm still watching him when David wiggles again. When I glance down, our lips meet, and the kiss I've been denying us comes together in the sweet press of lips and tongues and swallowed sighs.

Even more surprising, when I finally break the kiss, Connor has moved closer. He's got a hand on David's shoulder, and his look of concentration turns my mouth dry.

"His aura is still…" Connor's voice trails away.

David blinks once, slow, and when I meet his gaze again, he's somber. "I feel like the top layer of my skin's been rubbed off."

I cuddle him closer. "This help?"

He burrows in, and I do something that might be more selfish than anything else. I reach out for Connor. "You too."

Connor rolls up on his side, shifting the pillows around to support his knee. He and I are both shirtless. David is naked.

And in not very much time, David is aroused.

His lips are pressed to my skin, right near the notch at the base of my throat. His fingertips find one of my nipples and start flicking and pinching. I was already hard, and now my cock is ready to slice right through my jeans.

Leaving off my nipple, David reaches back for one of Connor's hands, tugging it in between us. He's licking my skin while he flattens Connor's hand against his belly. Connor and I lock gazes. His expression is reserved, tentative, but ever since that night at the club, I've known David has a threesome kink. "Come here," I whisper, and Connor scoots even closer.

"Yeah," David sighs. "It helps."

Cupping my face, David steers me in for a kiss. His lips are soft, but the kiss has taken on an edge of urgency. He demands access, pushing in with his tongue as soon as I part my lips. His taste is salty and familiar, and even better, Connor's warm whiskey scent underlays David's. I could keep kissing him forever, but I don't. I break the kiss, tilting my head so I can whisper in his ear. "Don't forget Connor."

Something flashes across David's face, some combination of lust and gratitude, and he rocks against Connor's chest. "Come here," he murmurs, getting a hand around Connor's neck.

Uncertain of my own response, I try to withhold judgment. Their lips meet, and Connor gives a little gasp. He reaches around David, and his knuckles brush against me.

This. Having Connor close enough to touch almost drives me wild. The passion and care he's showing David is beautiful, and when they end the kiss, David's soft chuckle gives me another layer of assurance.

Bending down, I give David's neck a lick, then latch on and suckle. My incisors are sheathed; he can't afford to lose any blood and neither can Connor. I'm hungry, but not so starved that I can't control myself.

I'm working on giving David a hickey, and he and Connor kiss again, longer and deeper than before. They end with a gasp, and Connor puts his hand on my arm. "Look." His voice is gratifyingly strained. "I think I know the answer, but I won't be able to relax until I ask. Are you okay with the three of us being together?"

David nips his chin. "You guys are healing me. Without you two"—his eyes widen, like he's standing at the edge of a precipice—"it would be bad."

Bad enough he might not survive. Somewhere along the way I'd learned lone wolves, even those who cut themselves off voluntarily, often commit suicide, unable to withstand the unnatural loneliness. David was slight enough that I could reach over him and take Connor around the waist, holding David even tighter.

"What do you want, puppy?"

"Mmm." He shifts so he's lying on his back between us. "I said I wanted a man in every orifice, right?"

Connor's eyebrows rise. "Every orifice?"

"Yes." He reaches for Connor's cock. "Feels like you're hung like a phouka, too."

Rubbing the side of his head, Connor gives David a rueful look. "You keep saying that, but it still isn't true."

But David wouldn't have made something like that up out of whole cloth. Later I'll have to remember whether phoukas can see auras, but right now, my hands are—literally—full. It's more entertaining to figure out how three men can fit together when two of them are injured.

And I really want to kiss Connor.

"Here." I sit up, pulling David with me. "Let's get his jeans off."

The two of us go to work on Connor, who helps as much as he's able. His right knee is swollen all to hell, ringed with purple and green bruises. I take charge of pulling his jeans off, leaving David to distract him with another blazing kiss. Then, while I slide out of my jeans, David crawls down between Connor's legs.

"I'm guessing this is where you want me."

I'm not sure if he's asking me or Connor, but it doesn't matter. "Yeah."

The two of them take my breath away. David's pale hair and tan skin is gorgeous against Connor's auburn and cream. After giving me a wink, David bends forward, laving Connor's belly with kisses, making his slow, deliberate way to Connor's cock.

On his knees and bent forward, David's giving me a beautiful view of his ass, round and proud. With light fingers, I stroke his hips, his flanks, every so often running down his crack and brushing a fingertip over his hole.

He groans, or maybe it's Connor. I glance up, and my ex's gaze is locked on me. He's flushed, his curls going wild. The tip of his tongue runs along his upper lip, almost hidden by his mustache. I could easily lean over David for a kiss, and I want to, but…

I don't. Not yet.

Leaving them to it, I crawl across the bed. I've got lube in my bag—I hope—and from the happy noises behind me, I have a minute to find it.

I'm fishing for the tube when David nudges my ass with his toe. "Get back over here, Traj."

He sounds plaintive, needy, and as much as I want Connor to enjoy himself, I'm pleased that David wants me, too. Armed with lube, I clamber back over to them.

I end up on my knees beside them. David swallows almost all of Connor, whose hips flex in response. Mindlessly, I stroke my own dick, aching for more contact. David's slurping and Connor's groaning and I want a piece of both of them so bad, I might lose my mind.

I'm obsessed with Connor's lips, the memory of his taste. I could kiss him, but I can tell from his grimace that he's talking himself off the ledge.

There'll be time for that later.

Instead, I scoot behind David. I pop the top on the lube and squirt a palmful. With slick fingers, I resume my game, tracing the contours of David's ass, his crack. I dab his hole with lube, mostly teasing, and in between slurps, he whines, high-pitched and greedy.

"You like that, puppy? You want me inside you?"

I'm watching David bob up and down on Connor, when a soft "Hey" distracts me.

"What?"

Connor's dark gaze is fixed on me, his grimace telling me he's close. It's like I've been kicked in the gut; his expression is so familiar, the context so different. I mean, I've had threesomes before, but never when I couldn't name my feelings for the other two men.

Who the hell am I kidding? I've had 175 years to learn the names of all kinds of feelings. I know what this is. I just don't want to admit it.

"Get in here."

I can't break the stare-down. By touch, I lube myself, find David's hole, and tease a finger in. He pops off Connor's dick. "More."

I give him more. Two fingers. In and out, scissoring, stretching. We've done it enough that I know it doesn't take long to get David ready. After a minute or two, I pat him on the hip. "Now?"

He nods, his cheeks caving in from the suction. I line up with his hole, and push in.

He's so damned hot, so tight. I work in slowly because I have to. I give him time to relax and give myself time to stay in control. I move too quick and it'll be over before I start.

The whole time, Connor's watching, the strain in his face as big a turn-on as the tight squeeze of David's ass.

Finally, I'm in, and I stretch out over David's back, skin to skin, clasping his wrists. I'm too low to see Connor without craning my neck, but David needs the contact. I thrust, shallow and steady. The tension is building in the small of my back, making its way over my ass to my balls. No matter how hard I try, I'm not going to last long. This is just too good.

Connor goes first. He shouts, his body going rigid, and I ease off, allowing David to swallow him down. The sound Connor makes, again so familiar, does me in. I thrust harder, faster, crashing into David four times, five, and then I shoot, losing myself in wave after wave of pleasure.

We pause, all of us breathing hard. The smell of sweat and sex is intoxicating. I want to run. I want to fly. I really want to kiss Connor.

The moment passes, and I slide out of David's body. He's the only one who hasn't spent. I lie next to Connor and pull David between us. This all feels familiar, as if we've been together for a long time. David interrupts my musing with a sharp nip to my shoulder.

"All right, all right, it's your turn now."

I take hold of David's rigid cock, a squirt of lube in my palm. Glancing at Connor, I nod encouragement, and he wraps his hand around mine. Together, we stroke until David's growling with every thrust. He grabs my arm so hard, his nails break the skin, and he's clawing at Connor's chest with his other hand.

Finally, David bucks, hard, and jets of jizz paint his belly.

"Trajan."

Connor calls my name, and before I can answer, his mouth crashes into mine.

It's like he's set free a part of me that's been locked down for years. Our tongues tangle, his taste so familiar and well-loved.

David's cock softens. I release him, and, without breaking contact with Connor, I get an arm around David's shoulder. He sighs against me, his trust a generous bonus to Connor's kiss.

We're all three wrapped together. The kiss ends, and Connor and I stay forehead to forehead, both of us breathing hard.

"You know, I'm thinking we should stay right here tonight," David says. Connor and I laugh, but neither of us complains.

"Whatever you say, puppy." I follow up my words with a kiss, then catch Connor's eye. "And I'm glad you're alive, *amore mio*. I'm glad you're alive."

PART FIVE: TEMPERED GOLD

CHAPTER TWENTY-FOUR

DAVID

Some days, things kinda suck. Others, you're fucked from stem to stern. That's me today, only I'm feeling it stem and stern.

I've got a gaping hole where my pack used to be. Let that sink in for a minute. A HOLE. A missing chunk. The foundation—hell, the walls and ceiling and insulation that protected my sense of self. And the only replacement I've got is a well-meaning vampire and his mysterious sidekick. Or ex. Whatever.

We're hiding out in some soulless hotel near Dulles Airport. Maybe it's National Airport. No one has really told me and I can't be bothered to ask. I'm not even sure of what we're waiting for. If I had my druthers, I'd shift and take off running.

But I can't shift without the pack there to hold me steady, and if I take off running, I won't know where to go.

I'm curled in bed with Connor wrapped around me like a big phouka blanket. I've taken to calling him pookie, but he swears he's just human. He still smells like whisky and horses, so he's lying, but whatever.

"Hey pookie, is it time to get up yet?" I swivel my ass, rubbing against his thigh.

"Quit it." He slides away.

I let him go, because really, we don't know each other. Trajan and I had the beginnings of…something, before my world exploded. Now I'm not sure what's real emotion and what's just naked relief at having someone, anyone, willing to stand by me.

"We probably should get dressed," Connor says, shifting farther toward the edge of the bed. It's king-size, the only luxury element in the whole place. There are two king-size beds in the room, and if I felt better, I'd want to practice trampolining from one to the other. But I feel like ass, so no tramping for me.

I've always been a tramp, but this is new territory.

"Jesus."

"What?"

Connor's question surprises me because I don't realize I've spoken out loud. "I'm not even making sense in my own head."

His hand, warm and strong, clasps my shoulder. "Come on. Let's get pretty for when Trajan gets back."

He doesn't let go, and I don't try to get away. "Tell me again what happens next?" Because my thoughts are friable, unmoored. The only thing I cling to is my name, David Jeremiah Collins, and the two men who sandwich me in bed every day.

"Come on," he whispers, sliding his arm around me and lifting me off the bed. We drag the blanket off on our way to standing. He props me up, keeping a hand on me while he tosses the bedding out of our way.

"He's bringing your father." He doesn't stop touching, brushing the hair away from my face, his fingertips warm, caressing. "We could both stand a shower."

I wonder idly if he means to shower with me. I mean, I don't really care one way or the other. Couple of months ago, I'd have been all over him. He's tall and butch, with the kind of straight-ahead stare that wraps around me almost as palpable as his arms. He sees me in a way I can no longer see myself.

At his prompting, I stumble to the bathroom. His knee is still bunged up, so I try to cooperate. I brush at the waistband of my shorts, and the fabric slides off. They might have fit a week ago, but I can't keep food down, as if without the pack to hold it, my body is determined to fade away. I've been in bed for two days, too unmotivated to speak, let alone argue, getting worse as time goes on.

The two of them have taken turns changing my clothes and cleaning me up. Now they tell me we're going back to LA.

Whatever. DC? LA? I don't give a shit.

Connor turns the water on, spraying me with cool mist. I stay where he puts me, close enough that I can reach out and touch if I need to. I don't. Not right now. But that could change.

"Hold on." He sticks a hand under the stream. "Yeah, it's warm enough. Get in."

He takes hold of my elbow and guides me into the shower, stopping to remind me to step up over the edge of the tub. I manage one foot, then clank my shin against porcelain on my way to getting the other foot in. Maybe it hurts. I can't tell.

I stand there breathing. The water is hot. The heat'll slough off the extra stuff. Except, there's barely any of me left, nothing extra. Lifting my hands, I clear some of the water out of my face. Time to pull it together. "Need some shampoo." I hold out my hand, and wordlessly, he squirts some gel in my palm.

"Smells cheap."

"I'll be sure and lodge a complaint."

Ignoring his chuckle, I shut my eyes and rub my head full of suds. The scent of strident roses replaces the old leather Connor gives off.

"So tell me again" — soap leaks down into my eye and I blink fast — "what's the deal with LA?"

He reaches in, strong fingers helping me rinse the bubbles from my hair. His silence makes me nervous.

"Do you remember what I told you about my work?"

I pivot so the stream of water washes down my back. "Maybe." Liar. My brain has the retention power of a bowl full of Jell-O.

He scrubs my back with a soapy cloth. I shut my eyes, allowing the water — and the attention — to soothe me. The warmth helps me focus. What did he say about thefts? For a moment, I take advantage of my relative sentience and prod my laggard memory. "You work for the Elite, and were assigned to investigate…something."

"Thefts, a missing princess, an illegal alliance," he prompts.

"Yeah, those things." The fog in my head shifts, leaving everything a mottled gray. "So we're going back so you can keep working. Is there any conditioner?" I stick my hand in his direction.

He squirts cream into my palm, and I rub it into my hair. The smell is as brash as the shampoo. "So, when do we leave?"

"Red-eye tonight."

The sudden gravity in his tone prompts me to open my eyes. His expression is blank.

"We made arrangements to see your father before we go."

The words shake me. "No." I can't. The pain would be…

"He said if we don't agree to a meeting, he'll send in a squad to bring you to him."

I hunch my shoulders, the steady drum of water almost too much to tolerate. "May as well get it over with, then." Because it's never going to get any better. At first, they were talking about driving back to LA, but my zombified state made that impossible. If I can manage a flight, I can manage a brief conversation with my father.

If I can manage a flight, I can manage a brief conversation with my father.

If I can manage a flight… I tip my head back, filling my mouth with water, then spit into the corner of the tub. "Okay."

I can't imagine anything worse.

"Sheena'll pick us up at the airport."

He says it like I should be reassured by that. I guess I am. I like Sheena well enough. If I was flying to Seattle, my sister wouldn't bother. She'd tell me to catch an Uber, and then we'd text the whole way.

Eventually, I'll need to go back to Seattle, to clean out my apartment if nothing else. But not yet. The idea that I could land at SeaTac airport without letting Abby know I'm coming washes over me like a shower of nettles. Not yet. Maybe never.

There's a bar of soap sitting on the ledge under the showerhead. I grab for it, forcing my mind away from anything more critical than the rough stubble around my balls. Damn I need a good wax job. I run a hand across my chest. Stubble there, too.

"Quit playing with yourself and get outa there." Connor's voice has a rough edge. I shoot him a glance, but he's staring at the floor. He's in shorts too, with a bulky wrap around one knee. For a minute, I'm distracted by the cut of the muscles in his thighs, drawing my eye to the V hiding under his sweatshirt.

Okay, so maybe I am coming back to life.

"You could join me."

My voice is breathier than I'd like, but when he lifts his gaze, I hold steady. The heat slams into me. "I would but"—his fists clench—"I'm not sure your Dad would want to walk in on anything."

I nod, nerves squashing my incipient hard-on. "Your turn, then."

He offers his hand, and I give him another good long stare. I step out from under the spray, shake some of the water out of my hair, inhale hard to grab ahold of my emotions. Our hands touch. Clasp. I step out and he doesn't back away, my wet skin brushing his cotton.

"You need help getting dressed?"

My mouth is watering, I want to kiss him so bad. The realization makes me laugh. One minute I'm dwindling away, the next my dick catches fire and I find a reason to go on living.

At least until my next orgasm.

"I can manage." I've waited so long to answer his question, he blinks like he's trying to retrace our steps.

"Yeah."

I slip past him, but he grabs my arm. "Whatever this is, you and me and Trajan, we'll have to…"

His voice fades, dragging my mood down with it. Yeah, we'll have to…something. It hasn't all been rolling around in bed, but we've done enough that I can tell the difference in vampire cum and phouka just by the taste. Right now, I'm too wasted to deal with anyone's emotions but my own.

Somehow, Connor has added to my suitcase a pair of jeans that make my butt look sick and a hoodie from Stussy that manages to be relaxed without being sloppy. There's an iron in the hotel room closet, but I ignore it. Dad's lucky I'm dressed at all.

I'm sitting at the room's small table, staring at my laptop, when the shower knob squeaks and the patter of falling water dies away. I've turned on one lamp, leaving most of the room in shadows. Connor's dried off, dressed, and his hair is combed before I gather the nerve to open the laptop.

Then the door's lock jiggles, and every muscle in my body stiffens. Trajan's here.

With Dad.

I'm clutching the tabletop with one hand, knuckles turning white. Trajan comes in, tall and dark, his presence soothing despite the circumstances. Dad is right behind him, and for a moment, everything stops.

Beat.

Beat.

My heart forces blood through my veins.

Beat.

The sound overwhelms everything. It's his heart, beating in time with mine. This thing, this connection, should have been severed.

Beat.

He comes toward me. Terrified, I push away from the table and stand. He keeps coming, and I try to get out of his way, stopping only when I'm plastered against the wall.

Beat.

Trajan and Connor block my view. They've put themselves between me and Dad, and for a moment, the pounding lessens. I shouldn't be able to feel him this strongly. The war between relief and fear threatens to drag me down.

"David." My father's voice grounds me in a way it really, really shouldn't.

"I'll make him leave whenever you want me to, puppy."

Puppy. I can't help but smile. Weak, but there it is. "It's okay. Just" — I drag in a breath and let it go — "give me a minute."

I put one hand on Trajan's back and the other on Connor's. Between the two of them, I feel steadier. My father's presence fades some more. Another breath and I'm ready to talk.

"Thanks, you guys." I step between them. "Not sure what to say, Dad."

He's blinking too fast and grimacing in a way I've never seen before. "Let me fix this. Please, son."

The blanket of energy created by the vampire and the phouka surrounds me, driving the last of my father out of my head. "I'm not sure I know what you mean."

Pinching the bridge of his nose, he pulls his command face into place. "Yes, you do." Another blink, his gaze reaching for the ceiling. "You're part of my pack and always will be, and when I'm gone…"

"When you're gone, it won't matter."

My father's gaze hardens, and for another long moment, we stare each other down. "I want you to know I will do everything in my power to bring you justice."

"Good. You've got some work to do."

"Wasn't it the pack's delta that contacted you in LA?" Trajan asks.

"What?" Dad jerks like he's been punched. "My brother?"

I grimace at Trajan. "He and my cousins met with me and tried to get me to sign the contract. I refused." Dad looks so crushed, I can't help but feel bad for him. Life sucks when people don't play by the rules. "Then somehow, they figured out I'd be here and were more" — it takes me a minute to get the words our — "forceful this time."

He rakes a hand through his hair. "Brendan said you'd gotten mixed up in something in LA, that you were trying to sabotage me." His voice drops to a whisper.

Well, at least he knows his brother isn't his friend. "Sorry, Dad, but you can see how I can't spend the next however many years watching my back." *Though I might be busy with a little revenge of my own.* "I just" — I shrug — "I like dick and lipstick, and I don't see that changing anytime soon." I'd never said anything like that to him before, and part of me feels like I've just stepped off the edge of a cliff.

But there's a vampire and a...whatever he is ready to catch me. They can't possibly realize what they're offering. For now, I'll hang on, and we can work out the details later.

"There may be one or two bad apples, but—"

"No, Dad. I love you and Mom and I love Abby, but Marcus was with the group who...who..." I have to stop or the screaming will start. *Breathe. Just breathe.* I choke down the pain and clear my throat. "You've got a house to clean, and the best way I can help you is by staying out of it."

His lips are tight as a seam.

"But…" I grip Trajan and Connor more tightly. "You have my loyalty. I won't rejoin you now, but when you need me, I'll be there."

My father's face flushes, but he still doesn't speak. After a long moment, he holds out his hand. I ignore it. Touching him is a bridge too far.

One of those rickety rope bridges slung across a crevasse with no discernable bottom.

Slowly, as if the weight of the world has come to rest on his shoulders, he turns and walks out of the room.

CHAPTER TWENTY-FIVE

W ell, this has been a fun trip." Trajan's fiddling with a straw, bending it in half, then letting go so it snaps straight.

"Sure has." Connor runs a hand through his copper curls. His beard is getting real close to peak hipster. I'm tucked between the two of them in a row of lobby seats, facing the big window so we can watch the approaching flights. We're booked on United Flight 4765, a red-eye from Dulles to LAX. It's a five-hour flight, so it should still be dark when we land. All three of us have pretty much flipped to vampire time, but I'm sipping a Coke to keep myself going.

Maybe I'm going too fast. Connor's hand lands on my knee, which has been pumping like a piston. "Sorry."

"Thanks." His shy smile turns my crank, which is good because right now, my crank is the only thing keeping me alive. I'm not quite the zombie I was two days ago, but it's been rough.

"Sheena's going to disembowel me." Connor keeps a hand on me, but he's looking over my head at Trajan. "When we land, I mean. She'll know."

Trajan's fondling the back of my neck where my hair is growing long, a cool sort of comfort. "She'll do what, now?"

"I just want it out there, before she sees…this." Connor's weight has shifted, allowing us to drift apart. Not far. Maybe half an inch.

Or maybe a mile.

Trajan doesn't say anything, but they're still staring at each other over my head. The lobby is filling up with passengers. Soon, the ticket agent will announce the start of boarding, and by some miracle, Trajan has scored us some first-class seats. I'm not sure I'm ready for the conversation Connor wants to have, so I zone out. I like Trajan, and I like Connor, and I don't want either of them to leave me, and that's enough for now.

"I'm not sure what you're worried about." Trajan's emphatic comment penetrates my fugue state. Connor barks a laugh, though this is anything but funny.

"Passengers waiting for Flight 4765, your flight will begin boarding in ten minutes." At the ticket desk, a young woman wearing more makeup than I ever would — which gives her a lot of leeway — speaks into the microphone, provoking a burst of activity as the passengers around us start to gather their things.

The three of us sit silently, waiting for the agent to announce it's time for first class to board. Connor's pensive, his injured knee wrapped with a thick bandage, his cane leaning against his outstretched leg. They've reached some kind of impasse, and it's my fault. I've put all of us in an impossible situation.

When the agent calls for first class, Trajan goes first, shouldering his way through the crowd with Connor and me following. We end up sitting all in a row with me at the window, because I don't want people brushing against me when they walk up the aisle, afraid they'll take little pieces of me when they go. Trajan sits on my right, and Connor is across the aisle. The little luggage we have is tucked into the overhead compartment, and a flight attendant makes the rounds, offering cocktails and soda.

Trajan asks her about vampire accommodations, in case something goes wrong, and then we settle back into silence.

Another flight attendant sashays over. He's skinny and blond, and when he leans over to ask if I want a cocktail, I'm pretty sure he aims his booty right at Connor. My wolf rumbles, and I have to stifle a smirk. I'm a possessive bastard, all right, and while jealousy is an awkward emotion, getting anything from my wolf is a relief.

The other two are quiet, and I try to not to wonder what Abby is doing right now. She must feel my absence almost as much as I feel hers. My eyes slide closed and my breathing slows, until Connor speaks up again. "I mean, it was one thing to drag me in like some roadkill you found on the street. This is different, a lot different, and I'm pretty sure Sheena'll have her own version of exsanguination ready when she sees us together."

I raise one eyelid, equal parts relieved by the distraction and scared by what they might say next.

"No she won't. She works at a damned sex club. We're not her first threesome."

I'm not sure Connor and Trajan are talking about the same thing, but Trajan's tone clearly communicates that it's time to drop the subject already.

Still, Connor waves him away. "Don't be obtuse, *mo shiorghrá*. You're her closest friend, and she's an Amazon. You think she'll give me another chance to hurt you?"

This time, I laugh, quick and bitter, because *damn*, way to cut to the chase.

Trajan shifts in his seat. "I'll explain how things are."

"How are they?" Connor leans into the aisle in our direction. I can guess why he's pushing. I mean, if Sheena had a hate-on for me, I'd be scared shitless.

At the same time, I don't know what to say. If I'm subtracted from the picture, they're just two guys who used to have a thing and who now have a second chance. It might take time, but Sheena would get used to the idea.

But subtract me from this picture, and I'll curl up in a ball and die. *Literally.* It's not enough that we all sorta liked each other to begin with. I need to give them something, some reason we should stay together that doesn't amount to emotional blackmail. I mean, we don't need to sleep in the same bed. It just feels really good when we do.

Vowing that as soon as I figure out where pack ends and relationship begins, or vice versa, I'll share. For now, I curl up against the window and shut my eyes, hoping sleep will blot out the shame I feel for dragging Tray and Connor into something so damned complicated. I must do more than pretend to sleep, vampire-time be damned, because when the pilot asks us to put our seatbacks in the upright position, I'm ready to go. *In more ways than one.*

Somewhere between Kansas City and Colorado, me and my wolf started to figure things out. Yes,

I'm lost without my pack and who knows if I can shift and *blah blah blah*, but I'm still alive. The fuckers stopped short of killing me.

Critical error.

And I might not have the pack around me, but I'm not without allies. Trajan's literally sitting at my right hand, cool and still and strong, and across the aisle I have a representative of the freakin' Securitas. I don't know what it's going to look like or how much it's going to cost, but my uncle Brendan and his crew of chickenshit backstabbers will regret what they've done. Gripping that thought with both hands, I play through various scenarios as the plane begins its descent.

I've never been what you would call religious — from what I hear, God doesn't love queers — but I did utter a grateful *thank Christ* when the plane touched down at LAX and we were still a couple of hours before dawn.

We had enough to get jacked up over without frying our vampire.

We end up at Trajan's condo high over Santa Monica. It's a bird's nest of stone and glass, as unlike a vampire's lair as I could imagine. Funny thing...we walk in and he finds a note on the countertop. His cleaning person is charging Trajan extra because the place was such a mess.

Connor leans close to Trajan, reading over his shoulder. "I told you Brendan Collins sent some idiots up here."

Brendan Collins. Uncle Brendan. I hover right outside their circle. "How much do you owe him? I can reimburse you." Although, since I'm no longer pack, will my bank card still work? *Jesus. Add that to the list of things I'm pissed about.*

"Whatever it is, we can deal with it later." Trajan pivots and heads into the living room, stopping in front of an incongruous old computer printer that's tucked on a shelf in the corner. He squats and lifts the thing's top. "Damn."

"What is it?" Connor asks.

Trajan fiddles with something and comes up smiling broadly. "They didn't find it." Waving his left hand, he shows off that gargantuan ring he'd worn when we first met.

"You got your pimp ring." I laugh because he's so damned pleased with himself.

"More than that." He pulls out a packet of papers. "A penny saved will buy a damned big house one day."

"A house?" Connor's expression is hard to read.

Trajan drops onto his oversized sofa, still holding his bank notes or whatever they are. "I mean, we can stay here for a while, but..."

How cute. They want to play house. I sink down in the chair across from him. The windows behind Trajan show the sun is almost ready to climb out from behind the San Gabriel mountains. "So here's what I think."

Connor takes a seat on the other end of the sofa, his posture relaxed but his gaze guarded. I feel like I'm taking some kind of oral exam with my professors watching my every word.

"You two are kind and generous and sexy as hell, and I'll be forever grateful to you for stepping up and standing with me the way you have." I catch my bottom lip in my teeth, not quite sure how to get across what I mean. "But I want to reassure you both that you won't be stuck with me forever."

There's a pause where I think we're all unsure of what to say next.

"Stuck?" Connor glances at Trajan, who gives a slight shake of his head. "I don't think anyone here is stuck unless it's you."

"Well, I mean, you two are a thing, and I don't want to interfere with that."

"Aw, puppy ..." They share another glance. "Way I see it," Trajan says, "is that we three are a thing, unless that's not what you want."

I spring up, my guts roiling. "See? There you go again being all cool and noble and all." I end up standing at the window, gazing over the city where lights prick the morning gloom and the eastern sky is lightening. "I can't tell what I'm really feeling and what's just noise, you know?"

Connor comes up behind me, warm and strong. Trajan's shy of the light so he stops a few steps away.

"Okay," Connor says, "I hear what you're saying. Let's just take things day by day and see where we end up."

I nod, afraid to open my mouth in case bullshit comes out.

"What do you want, David?"

Trajan's voice grounds me and his question helps me focus. "I want to take Uncle Brendan down, and my stupid-ass cousins with him."

"How do we do that?"

We? I can feel Connor's nod behind me, and I smile. "Not sure, Traj, but I promise you I'll think of something."

"I know you will," he says, and Connor chuckles.

"Let's get some rest, and then you can plan your world domination," Connor says, and shifts his weight toward Trajan. I follow them into the bedroom, marveling at my good luck.

The room is large, the king-size bed covered with a deep brown velvet comforter. The curtains are drawn and a single lamp sends out a pool of soft amber light. As soon as he closes the door, Trajan wraps a hand around my wrist. "C'mere, pup."

Connor pauses in undoing the buttons of his shirt, his eyes lighting up. "You thinking what I'm thinking?"

Trajan shakes my wrist. "If you're thinking we need to convince this young man that he's more than a problem to be solved, then we are."

"What?" I try to jerk my arm away from him. "That's not what I meant."

"Hush," Trajan says. He bumps my knee with his, making my leg buckle. His grin makes it clear that the time for serious talk is over.

Taking the hint, I slide down to my knees. He moves behind me, catching hold of my other wrist and raising my hands over my head. His grip is firm, but I could break free if I chose to. He's close enough that the bulge in his jeans is bumping against my head, and he murmurs, "Want to play, puppy?"

Connor's shifted from unbuttoning his shirt to loosening his jeans, and I moan my response. *Hell yes, I want to play.* I want them to use me, to ground me, to make me feel whole.

Stroking his cock, Connor closes the distance between us. He lines up with my mouth, and I open for him. He slides in far enough for me to wrap my tongue around his beautiful cut head.

Trajan draws my arms up higher. "Go ahead," he says. "Show him how you feel."

Connor takes hold of my head, holding me steady while he thrusts, letting me take him deep. My own dick is so hard, it almost hurts, but the energy from Trajan and Connor has caught me as securely as their hands.

Trajan murmurs something I don't catch. Connor speeds up and I lose myself in the sensation, his hard cock, the scent and flavor of musky man. When I suck hard, he whimpers, so I suck again and again. His thrusts get harder, and a burst of salty-bitter cum hits my tongue. Before he loses it completely, Trajan reaches down and grasps Connor's cock right at the base.

"Hold off, *amore mio.* I want to show you something."

Connor's lips are drawn in a grimace, but he nods and takes a step back.

"Now come on." Trajan pulls me up to standing. "Let's get him undressed."

The two of them go to work, all hands and mouths and heavy breathing. They're still dressed when they lead me to the bed and stretch out on either side of me. Trajan pulls a bottle of fancy lube from some nook or cranny and squeezes some in Connor's palm.

They go to work, an exquisite choreography designed to drive me crazy. In turn, they kiss me, suckle my neck, and tease my nipples. One of them strokes my cock, and the other has a finger sliding in and out of my hole.

I honestly don't know whose hand belongs to who.

I'll admit it takes a minute for me to get past *my hair's a mess and I haven't manscaped or even fucking showered and I must look gross.* Having two men intent on proving a point chases away my insecurities quickly enough, and I relax. They take me to the edge and hold me there until I'm all but sobbing. Then Trajan growls a command, and Connor slides between my thighs, my legs resting on his shoulders.

Somehow, they're both undressed, and Trajan is behind Connor and bending him forward which folds me tighter and then they're both thrusting and I'm clawing at the sheets. My body is an instrument of pleasure, tuned to the phouka's thrust, the vampire's drive. I'm barely holding off my climax when Trajan cries out, buried deep in Connor's body.

We all pause until Trajan climbs up the bed and stretches out next to me. Connor begins thrusting again, wrapping his hand around mine so we're stroking my cock together. He smiles down at me, sweat on his brow. Trajan traces a line on my neck with his fingertip, from my ear to my notch at the base of my throat. First his finger, and then his tongue, following the track of my pulse. For a flash I'm distracted. *What is he…?* Connor begins thrusting wildly, no rhythm, all animal need, and I lose what's left of my control.

My climax breaks over me like a cresting wave and in that moment, Trajan bites.

I scream.

Pleasure takes me to a place beyond anything in my experience. All I can do is ride it out.

Ride it out, stripped bare and held close by the vampire and his phouka mate.

Ride it out and catch a glimpse of home.

CHAPTER TWENTY-SIX

e've been home a week. To clarify, we've spent the last six days at Trajan's condo in LA, having us a big-time sausage fest. I mean, Trajan has survived without any of that nasty plastic-bag blood. Connor and I are taking turns feeding him, and they're taking turns fucking me, and none of us are asking any questions. We've crossed a line or charted a new course or something. I still have to tiptoe around the crevasse where my pack used to be, but I can speak in complete sentences and haven't burst into tears in over seventy-two hours.

Small favors, man. Small favors.

When Jacques calls, Connor is trying to walk without his cane. Trajan won the argument; Connor took a nip of vampire blood during a ferocious exchange of bodily fluids—with me in the middle of their supernatural sandwich. His knee is improving, and so, somehow, am I.

"It'll take me at least an hour to get there," Trajan says. He sounds apologetic, as if he's so used to being subservient to whoever this Jacques person is, he must take responsibility for things outside of his control. Like LA traffic. Because nobody controls that shit.

Connor's near the shoulder-high fireplace partition that separates the dining area from the living room, so he has something to grab if his knee gives way. I'm in lotus pose near the window, pretending to meditate. Trajan hangs up, and Connor and I both look at him like a couple of kids waiting to see what Pops is going to say.

He scrapes back that random clump of hair that's always hanging in his face and gives us a grim smile. "He wants to meet me at El Caballeros, over on Melrose."

"What's up?" Connor poses the question that's on the tip of my tongue.

"I never know, really. The last time he summoned me like this, it was to tell me I'd be watching a certain werewolf while he was on spring break."

"So this is all Jacques's fault." I stretch my legs out in front of me, shaking my knees out to get the blood flowing.

Trajan shrugged. "Your dad contacted him with the request."

"Your uncle suggested it." Connor takes a few steps away from the fireplace. "That was weird enough to bring in the Securitas."

I remember hearing about the Jacques-to-Brendan link somewhere along the way. Sitting still for a moment, I assess my two closest allies. I have the skeleton of a plan, and this phone call might just be the trigger I need. "I'm coming with you."

"What? No." Trajan goes full Italian bodyguard, biceps bulging more fiercely than his frown.

Connor gives a shrug of his own. "If he's coming, I'm coming."

"No."

I glance at Connor. "We're both totally going." Ignoring Trajan's bluster, I stand and stretch to my full five-foot-whatever-inch height. "I haven't dressed up in way too long."

Trajan tries to argue, but Connor and I stand united. "Besides," Connor says, "I haven't seen Jacques in quite a while. It'll be good to catch up."

He gives the impression he wants more than a friendly visit, but things were going my way, so I zip the ol' lip and switch gears from Zen yoga dude to what-the-hell-will-I-wear?

Which is a hard question, because my luggage seems to have been spread all over the damned place. I'd come to LA with two suitcases and enough makeup and product to last the millennium. Some had gone up in flames in a cabin in the woods, and some ended up at Sheena's storage locker somewhere. We don't have time to make a side trip south of the Ten, and whatever is in the small bag I took to DC is so not the image I want to project.

I'm nothing if not resourceful, though. I put on the tightest jeans in the DC bag and then dig through Trajan's closet, figuring anyone who's been a vampire since the 1870s has to own something a little outrageous.

Apparently, he had a bohemian phase in the '60s.

It's larger than my usual size, but the ivory blouse with a high collar and a spill of ruffles and lace down the front is effing perfect, and when I put on the coolest fur vest EVAH, the look is made. Trajan's bathroom tastes run cheap, but he does have product, so what I lack in heels, I make up for in hair. *Tall…taller…tallest.* In the time it takes Trajan and Connor to make themselves presentable, I am transformed.

They're in the living room when I stalk out. "My kingdom for a decent lipstick."

Trajan murmurs something that sounds suspiciously like "That's my boy," and I glare at him. Connor doesn't say anything, but the heat in his gaze brings more color to my cheeks than any blush ever would.

Trajan's dressed as an LA hit man, and the subtle brocade on the lapels of Connor's deep burgundy jacket finds a middle ground between threatening and flamboyant. We pile into the Prius and head out into traffic. The commute gives me time to finalize my ideas. Yeah, I'm going to work this little dinner date for all I'm worth.

A lone wolf can't call out another pack's Enforcer, but a vampire can, especially one as old and powerful as Jacques.

"One thing," I say, deciding it'd be better not to broadside Trajan and Connor with my plan in front of Jacques. "I'm going to ask for a favor."

I'm in the backseat, and Connor looks over his shoulder at me. Trajan's got his eyes on the road, but there's a watchfulness to his silence.

"I'm going to challenge Uncle Brendan, make him face my wolf, but I'll need your help." Except for the hum of the tires on the road, the silence in the car is complete. "I'll need Jacques's help, too."

Connor's gone from watching me to staring at Trajan. After a moment, he clears his throat. "That's a high-risk roll of the dice."

"You've never seen my wolf, pookie. I can use *beurteilung* against Brendan."

Trajan hits the turn single, making a right at the corner of Jack in the Box and CVS. *At least they haven't said no.*

"Seems like Jacques has some kind of relationship with Brendan already. Are you sure he's the one you want to ask for help?"

Trajan sounds thoughtful, and I appreciate that he's evaluating my idea rather than dismissing me out of hand.

"I think we can work this to our advantage," Connor says. Trajan scoffs, but I hold out for what Connor says next.

"We need to see how deep the connection between Jacques and Brendan goes. If they really want to destabilize the supernatural world order, it's unlikely Jacques will play along."

"So if he says no, then we can assume he and my uncle have some nefarious goal in mind."

"And if he says yes," Connor says, "then either there's no deep, hidden scheme, or—"

"Or your maker is a conniving asshole with beef jerky where his heart used to be."

"Well, he is a vampire," Trajan says through laughter, though his next comment sets me back a step.

"Your plan makes sense, David, but I gotta say I'm not crazy about this. Who'll be your second? I mean, Connor and I will help, but neither of us can shift."

Technically Connor can, but I let that go because I'm not sure how a horse would fare against a wolf. As relieved as I am that they're onboard, Trajan's raised a sticky point. I'm still parsing responses when he pulls into the restaurant's parking lot. Once the Prius stops, he catches my eye in the rearview. "Would your sister do it?"

"Abby?" I open the car door, still caught in his gaze. "She would, but I'm not sure she should. The consequences to her if I lose would be more than I can ask of her." *Like death.*

"But you're not going to lose, right?" Connor's got his shy smile on, the one that melts my heart every time I see it.

"No, I won't lose."

"Good, because I like you, and Trajan likes you, and I think the three of us are good together."

Trajan glances at me. "What he said. I didn't know I wanted this, but I do. I choose us."

Blinking fast, I scuttle my butt out of the car. Connor used that smile to break down my defenses and went in for the kill, leaving the final blow for Trajan. I'm still sputtering when Connor takes hold of my arm. Together, we follow Trajan into the restaurant.

The place is old-school LA Mexican, with red clay tiles on the floor, pumpkin-colored walls covered with prints of the Virgin Mary and La Calavera Catrina, and those colorful cut-out fiesta banners encircling the ceiling. We follow a young woman whose personal brand is somewhere between punk and goth to a table near the back, where an older man sits by himself.

There's a small bottle of tequila on the table and two snifters. He's got one and the other is in front of an empty chair. Fortunately, the table is big enough for all of use, although there's a pause before he invites us to take a seat.

Trajan introduces us, and still, Jacques doesn't respond. His eyes are a shade of blue that makes me think of the center of an iceberg, deep and layered and horribly cold. His suit, though. The purplish color of the sky at dusk, and man, if being a vamp means you can afford bespoke suiting, sign me up.

"Good to see you again, Connor." Jacques scoots his chair away from the table and stands, offering Connor his hand. If he's at all nonplussed to see someone who used to be dead, it doesn't show. They shake, and then he turns to me.

Suddenly, my clever idea about asking him to issue the challenge for me seems like the work of a grade school kid. He offers me his hand, and boy howdy do I want to run the other way.

Instead, I man up and shake. His touch makes Trajan feel like a heat wave and he's using his gaze to dig around in my soul. He must have touched something tender, because I give an instinctive growl and jerk my hand away.

He coughs gently, smiling around the hand he uses to cover his mouth. "Nice to meet you, young alpha. Please, let us all sit."

We do as we're told. Trajan starts off by asking why Jacques wanted to meet him, but his maker waves him off. "Later, Trajan Gall. I want to hear from our young guest." He gives me another one of those soul-searching stares, one I'm unable to dodge.

"I understand your vacation ended rather badly, wolf. No thanks to your erstwhile bodyguard."

His tone makes Trajan blanch, and I have to clench my teeth to keep from growling. "It is what it is, sir." I give him a slow blink, breaking the connection he'd established, and when he tries to crawl back into my head, I'm ready for him. Third time's the charm and all. I block his prying gaze, earning a scowl that makes me shrug. "Things could be worse."

Because yeah, they totally could be. I've got Trajan to my right and Connor to my left, and if Jacques tries anything really rude, they'll back me up. They've been walking the walk ever since I was cut out of the pack. The four-seater table is small enough that I can rest my hands on their thighs, connecting our energy.

A waiter stops by. He's more Goth-glam than our hostess, and without looking at the menu, I order a beef burrito and a beer. Connor orders too, and Jacques waves a wad of bills at the waiter so he'll bring another bottle of tequila and two more glasses.

When the waiter's gone, Trajan breaks the silence. "Randolph Collins told us it was Brendan Collins who suggested he hire a vampire to look out for David while he was in LA."

Jacques gives a laugh that dissolves into a spurt of coughing. He's one of the most frightening supernatural creatures I've ever met, but this cough is a definite sign of weakness.

"It was Uncle Brendan who led the charge against me. He forced me to break my ties to the pack." *God, but the words burn on the way out.*

"Seems like you must know Brendan fairly well." Connor's cool observation gets at the heart of the matter, but Jacques waves him off.

"Never met the man, actually. I don't know why he told his brother to contact me."

Trajan's snort perfectly captures my own sense of disbelief. A werewolf wouldn't randomly suggest asking a strange vampire for help. Still, his denial works for me. "I'm wondering, then, if you'd mind calling *beurteilung* against him on my behalf."

Jacques's smile slips for a single heartbeat. "What? Bertiloo? What's that?"

"I'm going to challenge him to the ring, to face the consequences of acting against me, but I can't do that on my own. I need someone older, more powerful, with more clout." *And did I mention powerful?* I might be laying it on a little thick, but he needs persuading.

"My understanding is that *beurteilung* is the wolves' equivalent of the vampire counsel, a place where behavior is judged and punishment called for." Connor's explanation earns him a sneer from Jacques. His rational observations make him the good cop to Trajan's irritable bad cop.

"That's close." I interrupt their budding stare-down. "We're less about testimonials and evidence and more about throwing two wolves in the ring. The one who walks out alive is judged to be innocent."

Jacques gives me a narrow look. "I thought lone wolves couldn't shift."

Squaring my shoulders, I give him every ounce of confidence I can muster. "When the time comes, I will."

He smirks. "No pack, no shift."

"You call him out, and I'll take care of the rest."

"Prove it."

Trajan smacks his palm on the table. "That's enough, Jacques. If David isn't worried about shifting, you shouldn't be either."

My need to cover my right hand in fur and claws is about a milligram less than my fear of doing so. The thing is, I know I can do it. I just can't force myself to try.

Jacques takes a sip of tequila, appraising each of us in turn. "You two support this farce?"

"You mean, do we respect David enough to help him make things right?" Connor asks, his remote expression belonging on a member of the Elite. Which, duh.

"I agree." Trajan rubs his knee against mine. "If you set things up, Jacques, David will be ready."

"Fifty thousand." Jacques twirls his snifter, sounding bored. "Twenty-five up front and another twenty-five thousand dollars afterward, whether or not you win."

I'm still trying to un-bug my eyes when Trajan starts to laugh. "That's all this is about, isn't it? How much did Randolph Collins pay you for my services?"

"None of your business."

Trajan leans toward Jacques, bracing himself on his elbows, his eyes shooting sparks. "Then we're even. That's the last favor I'm doing for you."

My knowledge of vampire lore isn't nearly as complete as it should be, but I have a vague notion that the scion owes his sire some level of service indefinitely.

Still, the way that Jacques rolls his eyes and tries to laugh hints that either I'm wrong or they have a different arrangement. "Oh, all right. I'll do it. Trajan, I'll call you tomorrow with the date."

Trajan stands, hands still on the table. "See that you do."

Connor and I follow his lead. Connor's "Thanks for the dinner" is a lot more polite than anything I'll come up with, so I keep my mouth shut. Since the waiter hasn't actually served our food yet, I catch him on our way out so we can take it to-go.

I tell him to give the bill to the guy in the fierce suit.

CHAPTER TWENTY-SEVEN

We have a date, and bless Jacques's frozen, undead soul, he's making them come to me. My best guess is the LA location was just something he tossed in there because he wanted to be an asshole, but whatever the reason, I'm glad.

On May first, we're going to meet at a place in the desert that's known for quasi-legal pit fighting, and we're going to have it out. That gives me time to work out the two big flaws in my plan:

I need to find a second, and I need to shift.

I'm back in the lotus position, staring through the window at the ocean's ebb and flow and pondering my two capital-P Problems. Most of the drapes are closed—because vampire and sunlight—but I've got a three-foot strip open for the view.

I'm not stressed about things—or at least I'm telling myself I'm not stressed—but solutions need to present themselves. Soon. Like, ten minutes ago soon. My wolf is strong enough to shift multiple times in a day. Surely he's strong enough to appear with a vampire and a phouka keeping the rest of me intact. There's only one way to find out, but I can't bring myself to try.

It's too early for Trajan to rise, and Connor and his laptop have taken over the dining room table. I'm distantly aware that a phone is ringing, but manage to ignore it.

It's harder to ignore the doorbell.

Connor answers the door, which gives me a heart attack because *who the hell is here?* Then Abby walks in. Mom is right behind her.

Mom and I don't talk much. It's nothing personal. Mom doesn't talk much to anyone. She's a poet and something of a mystic. She lives alone in a small house with a view of the ocean, surrounded by trees. For her to travel to Seattle is a big flaming hoo-haw.

For her to travel to LA means Armageddon is on the horizon.

I unravel my legs and stand facing them. My internal crevasse where the pack used to be has apparently swallowed my vocal cords, because words won't come.

Abby approaches, the set of her shoulders radiating caution. She's about my height, her hair a lighter shade of brown, and she takes my hand

and brushes a kiss over my cheek. I swallow hard. The best I can do is to give her fingers a squeeze.

Mom stays halfway across the room. She's shorter than me and slight, with long curls she pulls back from her face in a loose knot. I can't imagine how Abby got her here. They must have come by car. Once, Mom told me she has to stay in one place long enough to catch the words that come out of the air.

Flying would be moving her too fast.

She meets my gaze, though, and her smile is a balm for my hurt. "There is a cancer," she says, her voice rippling over the words the way water tumbles over rocks. "You need to find the cure."

I still can't find my voice. *Damn, but this is hard.* Everything I lost, every damned thing, stands represented by these two. Abby, my sister and my closest friend, and my mother, who…*damn.*

When it becomes clear that I can't respond, Abby clears her throat. "What she means is, you're not alone. The pack is divided, and by challenging Uncle Brendan, you have the chance to bring us back together." She makes *the face*, the wrinkled-nose-pursed-lips face that I've seen so many times, the one that means she's about to say something unpleasant. "At least you've shown us who needs to be culled."

"You must win." Mom says it like the outcome has been foretold, which, hey. Maybe her talking air spirits have given her some info that the rest of us don't have.

Connor comes around the fireplace and although my voice is shaky, I manage to get through introductions. Abby's cheeks flush pink when he shakes her hand. She always did have a thing for guys with beards. He takes a step towards Mom, but her corresponding step back clues him in, and he stops.

"Can I get you something to drink?" he asks, putting my manners to shame.

"I'll take a pop if you have it," Abby says, still somewhat starry-eyed.

Mom's attention has been drawn to the view of the ocean. "Tea please."

What are the odds the vampire has a packet of teabags? I'm going to say slim to none, but Connor will think of something. Abby volunteers to help with beverages, leaving me and Mom alone. She comes closer to the window, though not necessarily to me. "What he did hurt every one of us, and for that alone, I would see him punished."

"That's my plan."

She moves closer to the window and pulls the drape out of the way, exposing the strip of flickering gold the sun has cast across the water.

"A mother grizzly will kill a man if she feels her cub is threatened."

I don't respond. I shut my eyes instead, trying to focus on how good it feels to be in her presence, instead of how bad it hurts. We stand together in silence. I figure that being here is her way of defending her cub. I don't know how long she plans to stay, and it occurs to me she might have an answer to one of my Problems.

"I'm not worried about beating Uncle Brendan. I've seen his wolf and I've seen him fight, and I can take him." Saying the words out loud gives me the confidence to keep going. "Is it possible for me to shift with—"

Connor and Abby return, and damned if he doesn't have a small steaming teapot and a mug. He and Abby have bottles of seltzer, and he brought me some water. Connor and I take the big chairs and give Mom and Abby the couch. Sitting near them makes me ache in a new way, so I start babbling to cover up the pain.

I ask Abby about school and some of our mutual friends and what band is playing where. Mom sips her tea like it's a meditation, and Connor bolsters me by his presence alone.

Abby's going on about a new club that's opening in June when Mom interrupts her. "I've never met one of the Old Ones before."

Abby and I glance at each other, a nonverbal convo that says we're both confused. I look away, blinking at the flash of grief that ordinary moment gives me. It's like a dead person has come back to life. I want to act like things are normal, but she'll leave, and it'll be like she's died again.

I'm far enough up in my own head that at first I don't catch Connor's reaction. I blink into the sudden silence and realize he's gone rigid. Mom is sipping her tea, her attention inward, while Abby's glancing between the two of them.

Who'd said what, now? I play back the last thing I remember. Something about the Old Ones. *Aw shit.* Maybe he's not just a phouka. Either way, "We are not here for that."

"What?" Abby's eyes grow wider.

"Do you hear me, Mom? New subject."

She raises her chin. "As you wish."

"Thank you."

Connor doesn't say anything, but he gets up and walks into the kitchen. Abby's got her lips pressed together as if it's the only way she can keep from asking what's going on. Mom's in la-la land and I decide a major topic change is in order. "How long are you two staying?"

Abby grins, going along with it. "Till after you and Uncle Brendan…"

Wow. "That's amazing, but can you leave your house for so long, Mom?"

They both smile. "She's got most of it with her. We rented a motor home to get down here, and we'll stay for the duration."

Now I really don't know what to say. I never expected anything like this.

"Well, you need someone to be your second, don't you?" Abby asks.

"I didn't want to ask…"

She shrugs like she hasn't just offered to face death on my behalf. "My wolf isn't as badass as yours, Davey-cakes, but she's no slouch either."

Mom murmurs something, and we both turn to her. She sets the mug on the end table, moving deliberately as if she's about to make some kind of pronouncement. "You must win," is all she says, but with a fierceness that brings home exactly what's at stake.

My life, my sister's life, and the future of the Collins pack.

That's a tall order for a short guy. Better get me a shmancy new pair of heels.

Because defiance is better than the alternative.

In order to go shopping, I have to ask Mom for some money. Seems getting cut out of the pack froze my bank account, a common safety feature that prevents an angry lone wolf from emptying the pack's accounts. I might be plenty angry, and while I fit the technical definition of a lone wolf, my circumstances were…unusual.

At any rate, Sheena and I make a begging trip to the RV park. Mom's idea of how much I might need for such a trip doesn't exactly match mine, so Sheena decides we'll go to Santee Alley rather than, say, Rodeo Drive.

Now it turns out Santee Alley is an open-air market in the fashion district, a three-block stretch of small shops and kiosks with just about every nation represented in one way or another. They have everything there.

Every-damn-thing.

And stuff is cheap, so even though I've only got, like, $50, I'm going to be just fine. Takes me about five minutes to start working out my budget. Flash shoes, statement coat, and maybe a big silk scarf that I can wrap around my chest as a halter top. It takes Sheena a minute or so longer than that to start ticking things off her agenda.

"Tell me about this *beurteilung* thing."

She's not asking. We're standing on either side of a rack of high (high!) heeled boots in every color of the rainbow. I pick up a pair of sparkly blue lace-up booties, lips pursed because I don't want to mix business with pleasure. She's watching me, not the shoes, and her arms are crossed like she wants to prove that her biceps are thicker than mine.

I lift the shoes so the overhead lights will make them sparkle, but her frown is harshing my vibe. "It's a mechanism for redressing wrongs." I use the fancy words so it'll seem less like raw violence.

It's pretty damned violent, though.

"Trajan told me that the winner is the one who walks out of the ring."

I move onto a blue-black patent leather pair. "These are sweet." Ignoring her, I scan the little shop for someone who could bring me a pair in my size.

"Is that how it works?"

Her tone suggests she's losing patience with me, but damn. I've hashed this out with Connor and Trajan, and then again with Mom and Abby. "We have a plan. It's going to be fine."

She shuts up. Temporarily, I'm sure. I find a salesclerk and ask him to find a pair of size nines and while we wait for him, I look everywhere but at Sheena. I literally have my back to her when she starts to talk.

"How old do you think I am?"

I glance over my shoulder. She doesn't seriously think I'm going to answer that, does she?

She chuckles and continues her monologue. "Smarter than you look. At any rate, I'm pushing one hundred years old. That's a long time, and while I'm not immortal, it explains why Trajan is so important to me."

I ease around. Her arms are still crossed and her expression is the opposite of happy. "He's been the constant. Lovers come and go, coworkers, friends, they're all temporary. Trajan's the only one who'll see me through till the end."

It's the ripples I hadn't counted on. I still think calling *beurteilung* on Uncle Brendan was the right thing to do, but man...

"If you lose, Trajan's going to be torn up emotionally, if he's not actually murdered by your pack of rabid dogs."

I don't really have an answer for her, so for once, I keep my damned mouth shut.

"Look, I get it. You got screwed over in the worst possible way, and you're man enough to try to make things right. I can respect that, but if you lose, your uncle better kill you, because if Trajan gets hurt and you're still alive... I will."

On that happy note, I cough up $12.99 for a pair of killer, knee-high, patent leather boots that'll boost me to just over the average man's height. Now I just need to find the right coat.

And I need to reassure the Amazon that I'm not going to get her bosom buddy killed.

We meander through the throngs of people. She gets distracted by a shop selling bondage gear, but not in a good way. Mostly she stalks around muttering about wannabes and noobs. I'm keeping an eye out for the perfect coat, while also wondering if I'm making a huge-ass mistake.

The way I see it, I can't rejoin the pack as long as I've got a target on my back. Speaking of backs, I spy the most gorgeous blue velvet duster. It's hanging in front of the shop on the left, almost like it's been waiting for me. I hustle over and claim it.

I slip it on, and while it hangs nearly to the ground, it'll be perfect with my new heels. It'll eat up most of the rest of my cash, but it's worth it. While I'm waiting for the clerk to ring it up, I have a moment to stare into my own navel. I knew that calling out Uncle Brendan would have a risk attached, but I hadn't anticipated all the possible consequences.

This is why I'm not truly suited to be the pack's alpha. I'm a good fighter, I'm loyal, and I'm smart, but I'm impetuous. Dad must have had a stroke when he heard what I'd done.

What if something happens to Trajan, to Connor? Pretty sure Abby would have to be dead before she'd let anyone get to them. *Jesus.* I stumble, nearly dropping my bags. *What the hell have I done?*

I stop and shut my eyes. *Breathe.* Inhale through the nose, exhale through the mouth. Again. Deeper. Exhale slower. People move past me the way a stream would flow around a branch pinned by rocks. There is only one right answer.

I have to win.

Which means I have to shift.

That settled, I look for Sheena. Time to go home. I find her talking to a familiar black-leather-clad biker dyke. Sheena's friend isn't alone. There are at least three more biker-types in the vicinity, not counting a possible lipstick lesbian to my left.

"I remember you," I say. Sheena and the biker chick stop talking and stare at me. Sheena's somewhere between amused and annoyed. Her friend is fully annoyed. I extend my hand, because shaking hands is polite. I think. "We met at that bar when Trajan and I were looking for Sheena. Your name is"—come on, memory, cough it up— "Linda? Lydia? It's Lydia, right?"

She's looking at me like I'm something she stepped in on her way here, and she doesn't take me up on my offer to shake.

Sheena picks up the slack. "Yeah, David, this is Lydia. He's the one you were just asking about."

"Not so fancy now, are you, little wolf?" The biker chick looks like she'd be happy to skin me alive.

I mean, I wasn't that big an asshole when we met before, was I? "It's good to see you again too, and all your friends." I gesture at the crowd around us, because suddenly, there are biker chicks on every side of us.

The pack leader gives me an appraising stare. "You got balls, at least. I hope Brendan don't cut them off and make you eat them."

Hang on a minute. I don't know what I'd done to piss her off, but no one gets to speak to me like that. I might be a lone wolf, but damn, I'm still a Collins. I reach for my wolf, not to shift, but just to let himself be known. He won't play. Stubborn fuck. "Only one way to find out."

"Be nice if you could be there," Sheena says. She's giving me a look too, like *play along for once.* It's a good idea, though.

I straighten, pretending for a moment that I'm not wearing trendy distressed jeans in a crowd of shoppers. "I'd be honored if you would attend as a witness."

The outcome does affect her, in that if I win, the Collins pack is secure and things go back to normal. If I lose, Brendan will likely try even harder to take Dad out, and if that happens, the whole hierarchy comes undone.

She doesn't look like she quite believes me, but she nods. "We'll come."

But I can't tell whether she means to cheer me on or to dance on my bones.

Trajan agrees with me. "Of course you're going to win, puppy."

We're in his big bed, curtains open so the city lights sprawl underneath us with the dark band of the ocean just beyond. Trajan's lying beside me, one of his legs pinning mine to the mattress. Connor is on the other side, laptop open, hands poised over the keys.

"I've been poking around," he says. "Your Uncle Brendan has been in this situation before."

If he's still here, he must have won. "There's a reason Dad made him the pack's enforcer."

Connor nods, scratching a thumb through the thick copper beard on his chin. "There are some differences, though." He clicks from one page to another. "He's always been the one to call *beurteilung*, and he's never fought a true alpha."

My stomach twists in a weird figure eight. "Am I, though?" I whisper.

Connor and Trajan, each so powerful in their own right, stare at me as if I'd said something blasphemous.

"Yes," Trajan says. "You are."

Connor takes my hand. "Yes." He tugs on me, pulling me closer. "And another thing I found. The more blood we share, the tighter our bond will be. I'm not sure it'll completely replicate what the pack can do, but it's the best we have."

I'm only wearing shorts, so it won't take much to get me naked, but first I want to know the parameters. "When you say share blood, does that mean I need to drink from both of you?"

"I'll start." Trajan reaches across me for Connor's arm. "Once I bite, you'll have a turn."

This shouldn't excite me. I mean, we're sharing blood in hopes it'll help keep me from getting killed. Still, when Trajan draws Connor's wrist to his mouth, my dick starts to swell. By the time it's my turn to taste Connor's blood, I'm practically rocking my hips.

Connor's eyes darken as Trajan feeds. Then he moves his wrist to me, blood welling up from two perfect puncture wounds in the thin, pale skin. I lick away those beads of red, and he whimpers.

His blood is unlike anything I've tasted before. It's light, effervescent. If they said it was spun from starlight, I would believe it. Trajan had to have tasted the difference. I close my lips around the wound and suckle for a moment, sealing the exchange by kissing his palm.

Connor pulls me in for a real kiss, and I can't help but notice how the essence of his taste matches the sensation his blood left on my tongue. I believe Connor has reasons for keeping his true nature a secret, but dude is not simply human.

While Connor and I are kissing, Trajan takes hold of my arm and draws it close. He bites a spot near the crook of my elbow, and the combination of Connor's taste on my tongue and Trajan's lips on my skin have me writhing between them. Too soon, Trajan pulls off with a kiss. Connor and I ease off, and he props himself on his elbow so he can reach the spot Trajan bit.

Trajan's feed went right to my dick, but Connor's is different. He gives as much as he takes, wrapping my spirit in warmth. When he's done, I'm no longer afraid. I can take my uncle in a fair fight. Dad will be able to clean out his enemies, and everyone I care about will be safe.

The sensation lasts until I wake the next afternoon. In the darkness of a vampire's sleeping chamber, I realize that in addition to Trajan and

Connor, I'm sleeping with guilt and fear and self-doubt.

I get up because the bed is way too crowded.

CHAPTER TWENTY-EIGHT

I dress carefully. Black leggings borrowed from Abby. A silk scarf of Mom's tied around my waist like a wide belt that comes to my nipples. No shirt. My fearsome new boots, and finally, the midnight-blue duster.

I keep the makeup simple. Liquid eyeliner from Urban Decay, mascara from Maybelline, and a MAC lipstick named Ruby Woo. I'm done with dressing to look the part. If this is my last day on earth, I'm going down in style.

For the last week or so, Trajan and Connor have taken turns pulling me aside and offering to help me shift. I've declined. I figure it's either going to work or it won't, and if I turn into a pile of goo before we even get to the pit, things could go bad for the family even faster. Instead, I study what Connor's learned about Uncle Brendan's fighting style and I compare that with memories of my previous fights.

Every wolf fights when they're kids. Mock fights. Play. It's part of the game. We might draw blood, but we don't fight to the death.

Something about the process of dressing and applying makeup calms me. The time for doubt has passed. My thoughts take on a new clarity. When the time comes, I'll shift, and then I'll fight, and then I'll win.

I stalk out of the bedroom. Trajan and Connor are waiting for me, sitting side by side on the couch. My men. My pack. I approach them, and they both stand. They look magnificent. Connor, with his bright auburn hair and hipster beard, is wearing a classic black suit, a corporate devil to Trajan's gangster black.

We're quiet for an awkward moment. Maybe they're trying to come up with just the right words, some balance of affection and encouragement and other things we have trouble naming. "I don't deserve you," I murmur, knowing it's the truth.

Trajan waves me off. "Let's get this done so we can come back here and celebrate properly."

He takes my hand, and for once, our skin temperature is nearly the same. My mind might be clear, but nerves are having their way with my body. Connor's got my other hand, though, reminding me what warmth feels like. If he has any reservations about a member of the Securitas attending an illegal wolf fight, he hasn't voiced them. He closes the moment we didn't quite have with a quiet *"Mo mhuirnin,"* and while I don't speak Gaelic, his tone makes his feeling clear.

We take the Prius, stopping to meet Sheena. She's taking her own car, as is Trajan's friend Stone, but we'll caravan so we all arrive together.

The drive takes forever and we're there so fast I can barely catch my breath. The place is a compound, with three low stucco buildings arranged around a central ring. The ring is sunk maybe ten feet in the earth, and a bank of risers surround it. Four fifteen-foot light poles mark the points on a compass, flooding the ring with a white light that'll only get harsher as the night goes on.

There are a few other wolves present, but no sign of Brendan or any of my cousins. Abby is there, with Mom, who sits by herself in a seat on the top row of the bleachers. Mom is holding a string of beads, and her lips are moving continuously, spinning threads of a prayer I can almost see.

We enter the ring as a group, Trajan on my right and Connor on my left, with Sheena and Stone behind us. Abby comes over, the only one of us not in black. She's wearing an old pair of sweatpants and a hoodie. "Figured I'd be shifting so it wouldn't matter what I wore," she says with a shrug.

"I'm just grateful you're here."

She takes my elbow, and for a moment, we lean against each other. Maybe we should be talking strategy. I don't know. The only thing she needs to do is keep Uncle Brendan's second from interfering if the fight doesn't go his way.

When the fight doesn't go his way.

The bleachers are filling with weres and other supernaturals. Jacques arrives, flanked by a lovely young woman on one side and a lovelier young man on the other. He's clearly here for the show and has no intention of fighting. One of the possibilities I'd imagined—and dreaded—had Trajan jumping in if things went badly for me, a move that would turn this pack issue into a larger war between supes. Not a good look for any of us.

The crowd is somber, but there's an undercurrent of tension, as if they're uncertain who to root for. Lydia walks in with her crew of were-bikers. They don't look my way but choose seats in the front row close to our group. There's a subtle show of support there, and I'm grateful.

We're waiting in a group when Brendan arrives. Abby has already shifted, and she's at my knee. Brendan and seven of my cousins enter the ring in two lines, including Marcus, who may have been my best friend next to Abby. The sight of him at Brendan's elbow is a new betrayal.

We haven't progressed much beyond staring at each other when a line of black SUVs comes out of the desert. Everyone strains to see who is in them. Everyone but me. I'm in my own head, frantically coming up with a plan to shift. I know how to reach for my wolf. The question is whether the bonds Trajan, Connor and I have made will hold while I do.

I'm shocked out of my panic when my father and three other officers with the American Were Authority stride through the entrance. Immediately, all eyes are on Dad, because except for me and Brendan, he has the most to lose here.

He walks directly to the center of the ring, an older were at his side. I recognize Peter Gilbert, Dad's Beta, the vice-president of the Were Authority. Dad holds up his hand, silencing the crowd. As soon as the air is still, he begins to speak.

"Contests of this nature and gravity fall under the jurisdiction of the Were Authority, and it is on that authority that I am here. However" — he looks out over the crowd — "tonight I have asked Peter Gilbert to oversee this event, for reasons that should be obvious."

With that, Dad steps aside. Rather than take a seat in the stands, though, he walks directly to where we stand. "David, Abby, I have a favor to ask."

"Of course," Abby answers him.

"Abby, would you be willing to watch the thing from the stands with your mother? She needs the help, to be honest, and David, I'd like to be your second."

Abby's wolf bows, showing him respect, and heads for the stands. I can't speak, but I manage a nod. Dad is not going to fight my battle—I know him too well to ever think that—but he's here, and he'll have my back.

As long as I can shift.

For one long moment, doubt tries to undermine my self-confidence, but I force it back. I *have* to do this. I've shifted back and forth multiple times in a day. Surely I can manage one shift here.

A flash of light from across the ring tells me Brendan and his second have found their wolves. Dad looks at me, expectant, while I make a production of removing the duster and then my boots. I unwrap the scarf and lay it over the duster.

This is it. The moment. Now or never.

Trajan comes up behind me and puts a hand on my shoulder. Connor does the same. The feel of them, the vampire's cool touch and Connor's warmer one, ground me. I shut my eyes and call to my wolf.

I don't care how scared you are. We're doing this.

I open myself to the wolf, at the same time reaching for the bonds of pack to hold myself secure. The bonds are there, thinner, less profuse than they'd once been, but they are there. I grab my metaphysical 'nads and let go so the wolf can take over.

I shift.

It's not as fast or as fluid as I used to be, and it hurts like holy hell, but for the first time in over a month, my wolf is free.

My first move is to show my father respect, and then…and then…I look right at Uncle Brendan. His wolf isn't as big as mine, but he's husky, with a notch in one ear from an old fight. He's ready, and it's too late for me to be scared.

Let's go.

CONNOR

David's wolf surpasses anything in my imagination. Huge, dark, and powerful, he struts around the ring, giving everyone a show. His uncle watches, evidently waiting for David to come to him. David may well make the opening salvo. It would be like him to try a killing blow on his first thrust.

Randolph Collins sits quietly, as watchful as his brother, but bleeding power. He has a lot at stake here, and I can't help but wonder if he'll jump in if things go badly for David. Not that I think they will.

Across the ring, Brendan's second is having trouble keeping his nerves in check. When David gives a short, sharp bark, the younger wolf jerks like he's been shot. I'm reassured by that. When David gets his uncle in trouble, this youngster won't join in.

For extra insurance, there are members of the Elites stationed at intervals in the crowd. No one knows this but me; not Trajan nor David nor anyone else who's involved. I'm on damned thin ice with the organization, and getting them here meant I cashed in the rest of my chips. The Elites don't get involved in pack politics, but between pulling David out of the fire in DC and the potential for an inter-supe war, they have a stake.

Over the last few days, David and I spent quite a bit of time talking about how wolves hunt, how they fight, and how they kill. It was all I could offer; he'll fight this battle alone.

So we talked wolf. They say that older wolves are better fighters because of their experience.

Tonight, it's clear David hasn't been listening. There's no hint of submission in his posture; if anything, he's calling his uncle out, mocking him, daring him to make a move.

Trajan's standing next to me, arms crossed, stiff with tension. I trace the road that brought us to this point, losing Traj, reconnecting, finding David. I've made mistakes—*mo shiorghrá* forgive me— and despite them, I've found something more valuable than I'd ever imagined. On our own, Trajan and I were two halves of a whole. Adding David has made us all richer. We didn't set out to find a third, but now that we have him, we're keeping him.

We just need David to win this thing.

I swear David's wolf is laughing at his uncle, who still hasn't moved. In the wild, wolves hunt in packs to drive intruding wolves from their territory or to chase down game. Weres are different. Like wild wolves, they don't have the anatomic ability to rotate their paws and use their claws to fight, but weres have more in their repertoire than snapping an opponent's tendons so they can't run.

I'm not sure what Brendan is playing at. He might intend to draw David in, then take a swing at him. David's dancing just outside his uncle's reach. Teasing him. Darting in. Leaping away.

Brendan's lack of response is making David look like a youngster who's teasing their elder.

That must be his strategy. Make David look bad so the rest of the weres blame David for calling his uncle out. David's expression shifts, as if he's realized the same thing. The next time he swoops in, he goes for the throat.

Brendan jerks aside, and David snaps his jaws on his uncle's snout. It's not a killing blow, though if his uncle had slower reflexes, it might have been. David's drawn blood, and it brings Brendan to his feet.

The older wolf shakes his head, sending up a spray of red. David is waiting in the center of the ring, poised to leap in either direction. With no preamble, Brendan lunges, striking as fast as a snake. David's wolf whirls, somehow managing to evade Brendan and tag his uncle's haunch at the same time.

They pace each other, circling the ring. David's upright tail and the angle of his head show that nothing his uncle has done has shaken his confidence. Brendan snaps and snarls in a way that might be threatening if his opponent moved with less assurance.

David leaps at his uncle, and the two engage. Teeth flash, and more blood sprays. One of them yelps.

Brendan breaks free.

He circles the ring, circles David, who doesn't move. Only his eyes track his uncle. Brendan is bleeding from more than one wound, and if David is no longer as jaunty, he's no less poised.

David gathers himself. This is what we talked about. Give Brendan some room, and then take it back. David launches himself, and Brendan runs away, which is its own kind of defeat.

The ring is only forty or so yards in diameter, and in a burst of speed, David is on his uncle. They clash, and this time, David comes away with fresh blood streaming from one ear.

The blood spurs Brendan on, and he becomes the aggressor. He attacks, hitting David in a blur of claws and teeth. The onslaught is designed to demoralize an opponent, to give them no room for escape. David yields one step, a second, and my heart seizes in my chest, refusing to beat.

His uncle has David pinned against the wall, except he doesn't. David slips to one side as if he's made of smoke. He ducks and thrusts, his own chest heaving with effort. Before Brendan can respond, David plows into his uncle's ribs headfirst.

Brendan goes down, and in the scramble, David lands on him, his jaws locking on the back of

Brendan's neck. Brendan thrashes, lurching and flailing to shake David off.

David does not yield.

Breathing hard, muscles straining, David pins his uncle to the dirt. His jaws tighten, and Brendan's motions grow weaker. In a matter of seconds, it's clear who the winner will be.

A sharp bark draws David's attention. Randolph's wolf stands in front of them. The three have some unspoken communication, and David loosens his hold.

Brendan faces his brother, his alpha. He struggles to stand, and when he fails, he lifts his muzzle, baring his neck. In a single strike, Randolph Collins tears out his brother's throat.

The crowd falls silent.

Brendan Collins's dying body shifts, and it's as a man he bleeds out in the dirt. I've got my arms around Trajan, holding him still, although I don't remember when I caught hold of him or what he meant to do. Behind us, Sheena begins to clap, slow and steady. Others in the crowd join in, and it is to the sound of applause that the American Alpha shifts to his human form.

Randolph is built like some kind of earth spirit come to life, perfectly proportioned, utterly male. He raises a hand and the clapping stills. "My son," he says, gesturing to David, "has had his revenge, and so have I. The Collins Pack is mine, and I am your Alpha. Anyone"—he looks around at the stands—"any one of you who would raise a hand against what is mine will meet the same fate."

The first wolf to bow is Brendan Collins's second. Most of the crowd bows as well, and even David lowers his head, but only briefly.

"We have work to do," Randolph continues, "and amends to make, but for now, let us bury our dead with honor."

David leaves the ring, heading for us. I'm no longer restraining Trajan. Now we're hanging on to each other, though neither of us would admit it. David's progress is interrupted by a group of women, all of them wolves. They're sporting biker leathers and death-metal tats, and the leader drops to her knees in front of David. He nudges her, not rejecting her fealty outright, but more comfortable as her equal. She grins at him and rises. "You little bitch," she says, and her friends laugh.

He goes to each of them and nuzzles them, spending long enough that I begin to suspect our pack will soon be growing. I don't know what the three of us have done, binding ourselves with spirit and blood, but these ties won't be easily broken.

CHAPTER TWENTY-NINE

Randolph Collins chose the restaurant, A steakhouse in the Financial District with dark-blue walls and caramel-leather booths. The recessed spotlights and candles on every table give just enough illumination to show off the food.

And candlelight flickering through a snifter of tequila is kind of pretty.

David sits between me and Connor. We finally had time to retrieve his belongings from Sheena's storage place, and he's dressed in a mouthwatering combination of black leather and bare skin. Across the table, Randolph is preoccupied with ordering the correct wine for dinner, while Abby and David's mother watch David with sad eyes.

Setting the wine steward free, Randolph folds his hands. "Abby tells me you've withdrawn from the U this quarter." His tone is deliberately affable, and his attention is squarely on David.

"Seriously Dad, you aren't even going to wait till we get our appetizers?" There's an edge to David's grin. "Hang on, my guys"—he points at me and then at Connor—"let me show you how it goes. Yes, I withdrew, no I don't have plans to return, and no, I don't know what I'm going to do next, but if I never again put on a suit, that'll be just fine. Did I cover everything?"

The question is addressed to his father. Connor and I exchange glances. He's having as much trouble keeping a straight face as I am. *That's our guy.*

The waiter arrives with a platter of oysters and a second one with grilled shrimp. Both are liberally garnished with shredded leafy vegetables. The wolves ignore the cabbage or scallions or whatever and make short work of the shellfish. Connor tries some of the greens decorating the shrimp platter and declares they are excellent. None of the rest of us answers his implied challenge.

Slurping three or four of the oysters gives David even more mojo. He raises his cocktail glass—a gin martini just like his father's—and loudly clears his throat. "I'd like to drink a toast to fresh starts and new beginnings."

Everyone raises their glasses and David reaches for my hand under the table. Our fingers intertwine, and he continues, "Because that's what this is. Dad's going back to DC, Abby and Mom are heading back to Seattle, and I'm staying here."

Another glance from Connor tells me he's as relieved as I am. Not that I really thought David would take off right away, but his dad has a point. Dude is young, not yet twenty-three. I don't want to lose him, but I also don't want to stunt his growth.

Glasses clink, and we all drink. Abby has a soda because she's under twenty-one, and Mom is drinking tea because to do otherwise would upset her aging hippie persona. Randolph downs a healthy swallow of his martini and sets the glass down. "I hear what you're saying, son," he says, clearly determined to yield in order to win.

My money's on the pup.

"You've had a bad time, but once you're back in Seattle, we'll work on bringing you back into the pack. You've only got two quarters left for your business degree."

Connor actually laughs. He looks at David, brows raised. "You're majoring in business?"

David tipped his glass. "Damn skippy. Finance, even. If you need someone to help balance your portfolio, I'm your guy."

Randolph sits back, arms crossed. "You joke, but you'll put that knowledge to good use when you're alpha—"

"Come on, Dad."

"What?"

David tightens his grip on my hand. "I'm not part of your pack anymore, and"—he pulls my hand into his lap and my knuckles bump Conner's—"I can't see going back right now. Maybe never."

"But—"

Randolph starts to sputter, but Mom cuts him off. "But nothing, dear. David is old enough to make up his own mind."

"He's a kid."

"No, he's not." Mom's gaze is sharper than daggers.

"I was old enough to call out Uncle Brendan and take him down." David sounds cool, as if he's stepped up and taken control, and that remoteness makes him more effective.

"He's his own man, Randolph." Mom sets down her teacup and puts an arm around Abby, who's watching the discussion with wide eyes. "And furthermore, you remember how well it worked to shove me into the role of alpha wife?"

Randolph and Mom are locked in a stare down. "Do you remember?" Her tone demands a response.

He blinks first and rakes a hand through his hair. "You left."

"I did, and a smart man would let experience be his teacher."

For the first time since I met him, the American Alpha's posture signals concession.

"So…" Abby steps into the breach. "Can I come visit once school's out for the summer?"

"Absolutely!" David launches into a detailed, off-the-cuff itinerary, while Randolph Collins swirls the remaining gin in his martini glass and Mom gives us all a vague and lovely smile.

Conner and I hold on to David's hands until dinner is served, and later that night, we show him just how much he means to both of us.

"So this is home? *Damn*." David pirouettes in the center of the huge living room, stopping in front of the floor-to-ceiling windows overlooking the Pacific.

"It is." I can't help but smile. Like most of Jacques's houses, this one is over the top, but he suddenly feels he owes me a favor, so.

Connor comes up beside me. He's wearing cut-off sweatpants and an old tee and he smells like sweaty man. He and David spent the afternoon moving stuff from our various locations to here, which was a nice surprise to wake up to. My dick swells, and I wonder how fast I can get both of my men undressed.

Both of my men. The words still amaze me. My past, my present, and my future, right here in Jacques's overwrought mansion in the hills over the Sunset Strip. Concealed lights shine up from the ground, highlighting the landscaping. A thin band of city lights prick the darkness between us and the ocean.

I wrap an arm around Connor and pull him close.

"Look at you two, all snuggly-like." David laughs, and when I hold out my other arm, he joins us. "Tell me again how long we get to stay here?"

"Well…" I reel him in with an arm around his waist, "…Jacques is feeling guilty right now." I shrug. "I figure we're good for a couple of years at least."

"Good thing, since I'm suddenly in need of a job," Connor says. After ten years, he's left the Elites. He says he never wants to fake his own death again.

"So does this mean he and Brendan weren't up to anything evil?" David asks.

Connor scratches at his unshaven cheek. "I think it means that I'll be keeping an eye on him and doing what I can to help your father figure out who's behind the thefts."

"Connor MacPherson, Private Eye." Connor and I both grin at my proclamation.

"Part-time phouka and possibly one of the Old Ones," David adds.

I laugh at David's wild ideas, but Connor rocks his head back, staring up into the cathedral ceiling. "Half," he finally says.

"Half what?" I'm sorta chuckling, but sorta not because I don't want anything to harsh our vibe.

"Half Tuatha dé Danann."

My jaw drops so low, it's a wonder I can talk. "You're fucking kidding me… Why?… How?"

"Jesus, Mom was right. You are one of the Old Ones." David's looking from one of us to the other like his head's on a swivel, his eyes as big around as his mouth.

"Half," Connor repeats. "Only half." He's got his jaw clenched, and it occurs to me that if he's kept this secret since I've known him, I can wait a little while to find out more.

"Look, you know what?" I raise both hands, showing Connor my palms instead of a white flag.

"I'm not in the mood for this right now. We were having a good ol' time here, and I'm just going to forget you said anything."

"Until later," David says, pointing at Connor with an obvious look of *like hell we're done here.*

Connor crosses the floor toward me. "Yes, later." Meanwhile, David gets busy tugging my shirt from where it's tucked into my trousers. Because he's twenty-two and always thinking with his dick. "We need to christen the place in style," he says

I'm way ahead of you, pup. Doesn't take much effort to relieve Connor of his shorts—and *good God* he's commando. Takes David even less time to wriggle out of his crop-top-and-baggy-jeans-with-suspenders combo.

In a couple of heartbeats, our clothing is strewn everywhere and we're in the big window. David's on his knees, sucking us off in turn. He hums, his lips smiling around my cock, one hand working into my crack. I'm sucking on the soft skin between Connor's ear and his beard, fangs sheathed…for now.

Tuatha dé Danann? Oh ffs.

David moves from me to Connor, which causes *amore mio* to tip his face toward the ceiling. I lick down the side of his throat, nipping at his neck. "Wait," he gasps. With one hand on David's head and the other on my waist, Connor takes a step back. "I need to say something, and then we can…get back to it."

Snickering, David starts stroking each of us, though the distraction has softened things. "This better be good, pookie."

Connor reaches for David's elbow and draws him to his feet. "I hope it's good. I just need you both to know" — he presses his lips together and gazes out over the ocean for a moment — "this isn't just sex to me, and it's not just about being David's pack."

I pull Connor closer. *You always were my beating heart.* David sighs and presses a kiss to Connor's shoulder.

Connor laughs softly and continues, "I care about both of you, and this is going to take work, you know? But I'm willing to go there. No secrets. Not anymore."

You'd think after 175 years, I'd more adept at handling emotion. You'd be wrong. I'm kind of a doofus. Clearing my throat, all I can come up with is, "I'm in."

"You two saved me," David says, his face still pressed against Connor's chest.

I shrug. "Seems like you saved yourself. You're the youngest here, puppy. I don't want me and Connor to turn into your ball and chain."

"Am I the ball or the chain?" Connor says, because humor is easier than truth.

I laugh. "Fine, I'll be the ball."

David gives us a sly smile. "Did somebody say *ball*?"

A couple of firm strokes later, Connor and I are both ready to burn rubber. Yeah, we have work to do, but my guess is we'll take it as it comes. Meanwhile, David drops to his knees and Connor's got his tongue in my mouth and for the first time in decades, I have a reason for hope.

About the Author

Liv Rancourt is a multi-published author of m/m romance. Because love is love, even with fangs.

Liv likes to write stories about vampires, either contemporary or historical. Sometimes she branches out into other paranormal realms, but there's always magic, and there's always romance. She also co-authors two m/m paranormal romance series with Irene Preston. Their partnership works because Liv is good at blowing things up and Irene is good at explaining why.

When Liv isn't writing she takes care of tiny premature babies in the NICU. Her husband is a soul of patience, her kids are her pride and joy, and her cat Praline (pronounced PRAH-leen) is endlessly entertaining. Happy reading!